The Road to Eden's Ridge

The Road to Eden's Ridge

M. L. ROSE

Rutledge Hill Press™
Nashville, Tennessee

A Division of Thomas Nelson, Inc.

www.ThomasNelson.com

Published by Rutledge Hill Press, a division of Thomas Nelson, Inc., P.O. Box 141000, Nashville, Tennessee 37214.

The following copyrighted lyrics are used with permission:

"This Old Song" (pages 1, 121, 217), words and music by Mark Dix, copyright © 2001 by Mark Dix BMI. As heard on the CD *This Old Song* by Mark Dix (available through author's website: www. markdix.com).

"Ol' Boys in Memphis" (pages 9, 36), words by Taylor Kitchings and Ike LaRue, music by Taylor Kitchings, copyright © 1999 by Taylor Kitchings.

"Slipping Out the Back Door" (pages 33–34), words by Brady Peterson, music by Bruce Peterson, copyright © 2001 by Brady Peterson and Bruce Peterson.

"Today," "I Don't Do Memories," "You Should'a Told Me It Was Love," and "It Was Just Love" (all on page 46), words by David Kelly and music by Nancy Kelly, copyright © by David Kelly BMI.

"Country Boy Wannabe" (page 97), copyright © 2000 by Taylor Kitchings.

"Blue Eyes Crying in the Rain" (pages 213–214), written by Fred Rose. Copyright © 1945. Renewed 1973 Milene Music, Inc. International Rights Secured. All Rights Reserved. Used by Permission.

"If I Ever Write a Song" (pages 262–263), words by Myra McLarey, music by Bruce Peterson, copyright © 1990 by Myra McLarey.

"Until I Couldn't Have You" (pages 265–266), copyright © 1995 by Heather Myles/Calhoun Street Music BMI.

"No One Is Gonna Love You Better" (page 275), copyright © 1998 by Heather Myles & Myles O. Melody/Happy Valley Music BMI. Recorded as a duet with Merle Haggard on the CD *Highways and Honky Tonks* (available at www.rounder.com or 1-800-ROUNDER).

All other lyrics contained in this book were written by the authors and are included in the general copyright of this book.

Library of Congress Cataloging-in-Publication Data is available

Rose, M. L.
    The road to Eden's Ridge / M. L. Rose.
      p. cm.
    ISBN 1-55853-993-X
    1. Country musicians—Fiction 2. Women singers—Fiction. 3. Nashville (Tenn.)—Fiction.
4. Maine—Fiction. I. Title.
    PS3618.O785 R63 2002
    813'.6—dc21   2002002039

Printed in the United States of America

02 03 04 05 06 — 5 4 3 2 1

For Bob and Steve,

and all of you who know that

Elvis gets it right when he sings

"True Love Travels on a Gravel Road"

Foreword

A teacher once told me, if you're going to tell a story, then tell it true. And I have tried to tell it true. But for the sake of privacy, I have altered certain details. And I have changed names—including those of Ben McBride . . . and Hadley's Curve . . . and Eden's Ridge.

There are those of you, though, who will recognize them all.

—M. L. Rose

Part One

I may be crazy,
I've got it all wrong,
But I think there's
Time for one more song.

—MARK DIX, "THIS OLD SONG"

One

August 15, 1998

Later on, no one would agree as to when this story began, but for Lindsey Briggs it would always begin with a voice calling from the closet, "There's nothing blue in here, Lindsey. How could we have forgotten something blue for you to wear?"

Wearing something blue was the least of Lindsey's concerns as she—Pepsi in hand and still wearing cutoffs and a tank top, even though her wedding was less than an hour away—stood in the middle of her bedroom in the old Maine farmhouse and looked around—a look of puzzlement on her face. The three attendants' dresses, each a different shade of blue, hung from the closet door. Her dress with its many yards of satin hung over the dressing screen. Jeans and T-shirts lay tossed on the rocking chair and draped over the end of the antique sleigh bed, with one T-shirt hanging precariously on a vintage phonograph cabinet in the corner of the room. Socks, sneakers, shoeboxes, and clothes hangers cluttered the planked chestnut floor, along with empty Pepsi cans, discarded potato chip bags, and tiny balls of foil that had once held Hershey's kisses.

How did it get to be in such a mess?

Her bridesmaids, both college roommates and both named Jennifer, were already in their long slips, their make-up perfectly done, their sun-streaked hair pinned up in soft curls. One sat on the bed waiting for her toenail polish to dry. The other ransacked the room, looking for the mate to her white-strapped sandal. Lindsey looked at herself in the full-length mirror that stood in one corner of the room. Her own brown hair resisted curling. She would pull it back in a sleek knot once she got dressed. *I really must get dressed.*

At that very moment, the mellow chime of the grandfather clock in the downstairs hallway announced the time. *Like a countdown.* In exactly one hour Lindsey would walk down the aisle. She couldn't believe her grandmother had not been upstairs checking on them every few minutes to make sure they were getting dressed and would be ready on time—the way she had done on Sunday mornings of Lindsey's childhood.

Seconds later, Katy Mills, Lindsey's best friend since first grade and her matron of honor—and obviously in the late stages of pregnancy—backed out of the closet on hands and knees, dragging an old wooden apple box with black letters stamped on the side:

Frost Orchards
Eden's Ridge Road
Hadley's Curve, Maine

"Look what I did find," she said with obvious glee, carefully balancing herself as she rose from her all-fours and beaming at Lindsey the way she had done when she once showed Lindsey a kitten she had found by the side of the road.

Lindsey's heart jumped when she realized what Katy had dragged out. "How did you find this without a flashlight?" she asked incredulously as she put down her Pepsi, hurried to the box she hadn't looked through in years, and knelt down beside it. "There's no light in that part of the closet."

"It wasn't in the eaves. It was right inside the door. I practically stumbled over it," Katy said, leaning over Lindsey in anticipation.

"California and Ohio," Katy said, turning to the bridesmaids, "you need to see this. Lindsey's life is stashed away in this box." Katy had christened the roommates after their home states, having decided her other option was to call them Jennifer #1 and Jennifer #2.

Lindsey pulled back the heavy plastic tucked over the top of the box. Nestled inside were record albums, homemade cassette tapes, ribbons and trophies she and Fiddle, her horse, had won, other memorabilia—and an Indian Head tablet. Lindsey lifted the tablet carefully and opened it, knowing what it contained: The many songs that Lindsey had written from the time she was eight years old. She turned the brittle pages. Lord, she had thought these were so good at the time. Then she came to the one with the words, "written by Margaret Lindsey Briggs, age 10" penned in a child's scrawl. And below that,

> I've got friends around me and loving family too,
> But I still spend lots of time missing you.
> I don't miss the sunshine on cloudy days,
> But I miss you in every way.

She had written that for her parents who had been killed in a car wreck when Lindsey was two—on the edge of remembering.

She closed the tablet. *Too much to think about now.* She would go through it later, when she had peace and quiet. When she got back from her honeymoon in Italy. When she and Herschel were settled into their new condo in Boston. When. Whenever.

Lindsey pulled a record from the box. The faded cover showed a rugged-faced cowboy, his brown hat at a cocky angle on his head, and a smile that must have melted hearts.

"Oh my God, a Ben McBride album," Katy said, reaching for it. *"Ol' Boys in Memphis.* Let's play it." She started toward the old phonograph in the corner.

"No. Not now. Besides, it's worn out and scratched from the thousand times I played it," Lindsey said, suddenly awash in memories.

"Who's Ben McBride?" California asked.

"The country music legend," Katy answered, looking at California in disbelief at such a question.

"Even I know that," Ohio said. "He was my grandmother's favorite singer."

"And he was Lindsey's grandfather's best friend," Katy said.

"You may have noticed my maid of honor has a tendency to exaggerate," Lindsey said to her bridesmaids. "He was just an army buddy who came here once before he was famous," she added, and a nostalgic smile swept across her face as she gazed at the faded cover. It was the voice of Ben McBride on this same old phonograph—which used to sit downstairs in the parlor—that had lured her like the Pied Piper to country music. That and the jukebox at the Corner Store, which to this day still had the old country songs on it—and would as long as Madge Butters lived. Madge, at ninety, was still proprietor at the combination general store, service station, and café that had once been the gathering place of the young. It was now a gathering place of the old.

"Hey, you were the one that used to brag that your grandfather and Ben McBride were best friends," Katy said, rejoining Lindsey in rummaging through the apple box. "And there the two of them are together." She pointed over her shoulder to the mantle where family pictures were jammed into each other—as if that picture were unquestionable proof.

Lindsey looked away from the box to the picture of Tad Frost and Ben McBride she had treasured since her first star-struck days: two lanky young men standing in front of a small truck, arms flung around each other, both smiling dashingly. Tad, who would become her grandfather, in his barn boots. Cowboy boots on Ben McBride—and in his hand a cowboy hat like the one on the cover of the old album. Grandma Sarah had taken that picture with her new Kodak during that one time the yet-to-be-famous singer visited the farm several years after the end of World War II. Lindsey had, indeed, boasted as a young girl that Ben McBride had come to see her grandfather one summer afternoon and stayed for supper—and of course she had exaggerated their friendship, as kids are wont to do. But every time she looked at that picture, she knew it did not lie.

"Ta-da," Katy said, holding up another record as if she'd just found treasure. It was an LP album, *Best of Country*, with selections by all the greats— Ben McBride, Johnny Cash, Loretta Lynn, Tammy Wynette, Willie Nelson. Even Gene Autry. "We've got to play this one," Katy said, pushing herself back to her feet and heading for the old phonograph.

The two roommates perched on the bed to listen as Katy slipped the album from its dust jacket, balancing it carefully between thumb and fore-finger. Lindsey continued her digging through the box. "Remember our bus duets that drove Mr. Wheelock batty?" Katy asked Lindsey with a grin. A conspiratorial exchange of glances, and Lindsey was on her feet. She and Katy put their arms around each other—Lindsey, as usual, towering over her five-foot-tall friend—and the years disappeared as the two of them began singing "Stand by Your Man," with Katy slightly off-key. By the time they got to the last chorus, the two roommates—who had, many times, heard Lindsey sing that song full-throated in their shower—joined them, and the four of them finished with a dramatic flourish.

"I still say that's what you should have for a processional instead of that tired old wedding march," Katy said as she, *Best of Country* still in hand, tossed the T-shirt from the phonograph onto the floor and lifted the lid.

Lindsey looked at the mantel clock. "Grandma Sarah will have a fit if she comes and finds us in this state of dress."

"Or undress, as the case may be," California said as she made her way to their dresses, handed Ohio's to her, and then took her own off the hanger.

But instead of reaching for her own dress, Lindsey knelt down again and found her way to the bottom of the apple box. Like a kid at Christmas, Katy would say later.

"How's this for something blue?" Lindsey asked, her voice full of mischief as she lifted out a squashed blue-felt cowboy hat, pushed it into some semblance of shape, and set it jauntily on her head.

"Oh, my goodness. Is that what I think it is?" Katy said.

"The winning hat," Lindsey said, tipping the too-small hat to her bridesmaids. Ohio and California, dresses in hand, sat down on the bed with a we'll-be-the-audience-while-you-let-us-in-on-this look.

"It all began with that hat—and *that* record," Katy said, gesturing to the Ben McBride record propped against the box. "We were in fifth grade . . ." She put the *Best of Country* album on the spindle but held the record-changer arm suspended, obviously delaying while she took on the role of storyteller.

"Fourth," Lindsey corrected, falling into the repartee they had long ago become accustomed to.

"Whatever," Katy said, not missing a beat. "Lindsey was one of at least twenty acts in the talent show. Anyway, Lindsey's Aunt Lily was the piano teacher—she taught me too, taught all of us. But Lindsey was really good on the piano even then, and she was signed up to play something by Beethoven . . ."

"Brahms," Lindsey inserted, still digging through the box, still wearing her blue hat.

"Whatever. Anyway, when it comes Lindsey's turn, instead of playing Beethoven, she marches out on stage wearing her purple organdy dress, *that* cowboy hat, and a pair of red cowboy boots, and lugging this cheap guitar she had bought with the money she got from her 4-H rabbit project." Katy gestured to Lindsey as if to say, now the floor is yours.

Lindsey, still kneeling, began to mime playing a guitar. (Her beloved Martin was already packed away. Somewhere.) She pushed the hat back even farther on her head and belted out,

I see the water in the evenin' light,
Think of the old town in the night,
Where the air is gray and the wind is cool
And those ol' boys in Memphis are playin' pool.

Lindsey and Katy broke into laughter.

"What's so funny?" California asked. She had stepped into her powder-blue dress and now stood waiting for Ohio to zip it.

"What's so funny," Katy said, "is that Lindsey's Aunt Lily, who was really her great-aunt, was not what you would call a country music fan. And she was sitting so proud on the front row expecting Lindsey to play Beethoven."

"Brahms!" Lindsey said, laughing even more now—at Katy's insistence on Beethoven, and at the memory they both shared as well.

"And," Katy said, trying to contain herself enough to tell the story, "instead, her great-niece—the girl she helped raise—is up on stage singing a song about drinking. And Miss Lily, I assure you," Katy said, "never had a drink stronger than sherry in her life." Katy, laughing uproariously, motioned to Lindsey to get control of herself enough to continue the song—trying to sound like a ten-year-old stage performer,

I can see them yet, ol' boys in Memphis, they are placin' bets,
And the taste of bourbon is in my mouth
As I watch that river flowin' south.

By now, Lindsey could no longer sing; she and Katy were laughing so hard they had to hold their sides. "I guess you had to be there," Katy said when the two of them finally were laughed out.

"Was your aunt upset?" Ohio asked, turning her back for California to zip the dress she called cerulean. Katy called it sky blue.

"She couldn't be upset," Lindsey explained as California handed Lindsey a tissue to wipe the tears of laughter from her eyes. "First prize was a trophy—

plus tickets to see the Boston Red Sox, and Aunt Lily loved the Red Sox. Listened to them on the radio every chance she got." She stood up, took her hat off, threw it on the bed, and began looking around for her hairbrush.

There it was on the mantle next to a silver-framed picture of Lily, who had died three years earlier. An aneurysm. In this picture—made a few years after the war—Lily is twenty-five, standing beside the grand piano at the Hadley's Curve Opera House. There are those who still remember Lily's piano concerts at the old opera house. Who still pass down the story of how Lilian Frost went to Juilliard, then came back home to pass down her love and knowledge of music to the young at Hadley's Curve. Who tell how her parents—middle-aged when she and Tad were born—died during the war, and how Lily looked after the Frost place until her brother came back to help her. And then when Tad was killed in a logging accident in 1950, how the task of holding onto the farm and providing for Sarah and her two small children fell to Lily—who proved more than equal to the task.

"She sure was a piece of work," one of the regular old-timers at Butters' store had told Lindsey recently, probably not knowing he had borrowed that phrase from Shakespeare.

In the picture, Lily looks regal in a dark dress with a scalloped neckline and fitted skirt. That flyaway hair tied back in an effort to tame it. Those square shoulders. The strong chin. Like a young Katharine Hepburn. Everyone said so.

"Earth to Lindsey," Katy said. Then she said to the bridesmaids, "The next day—after the talent show—Lindsey announced to everyone at Butters' that when she 'got grown,' as she put it, she was going to go to Nashville, Tennessee, and be as famous as Kitty Wells, Patsy Cline, and Dolly Parton."

"Who is Kitty Wells?" the roommates asked in unison.

"You see why I didn't share that much of my previous life with them?" Lindsey said to Katy, putting down the brush she'd just found and holding out her hands in mock dismay.

"I'll have you know I love Patsy Cline," California said in good-natured defense.

"I dare you to go down the aisle in that hat, Lindsey Briggs," Katy said, gesturing to the blue hat—as she finally secured the *Best of Country* album with the changer arm, switched the record player on, and watched the album drop to the turntable. The needle arm obviously wasn't going to automatically find its way to the album—so Katy gently placed it there on the first groove. The voice of Hank Williams filled the room with "If You've Got the Money."

"Boy, did we have our lives mapped out back in junior high," Katy said, her voice edged with whimsy. She handed Lindsey the brush, noticing that she still had not fixed her hair. "Lindsey was headed for Nashville. And I was headed for New York to become editor of *Cosmo.*" Katy looked in the mirror and sighed dramatically. "But here I am with a husband in the navy, and one and three-quarters kids, and headed for Japan as soon as this one's old enough," she said, patting her belly.

"Eight-ninths," Lindsey inserted as she absently put down the brush and looked around the room for something. She didn't know what. Maybe it was her shoes.

"Whatever," Katy was saying, running her hand in circles around her protruding stomach. "Anyway, instead of heading for Nashville, here you're off to live in Boston—and on Beacon Hill at that. So much for childhood dreams. Yep, 'Herschel's got the money, honey,'" Katy sang, adjusting her words to Hank's song.

"I still can't believe you didn't take him up on his offer to pay for an extravagant Boston wedding," Ohio said.

"Well, you didn't know Lindsey's Aunt Lily." And as if on cue, Lindsey and Katy, trying to imitate Lily Frost, said emphatically and in perfect unison, "The Frosts don't take handouts."

"Still," Katy said, picking up the brush again and handing it back to Lindsey, "I just hope you know you deprived all of Hadley's Curve from

11

ever in their lives attending a reception at the Ritz—or as Madge calls it, 'the rich Carlton.'"

"Does she know better?" Ohio asked.

Lindsey and Katy once again caught each other's eyes as they answered in true Mainer fashion. "Maybe she does, and maybe she don't."

"Ayuh," Katy said, still imitating the Maine old-timers, "sure woulda liked to have seen if that lobstah we catch up here tastes any better at the Ritz."

"Well, anyway," Katy added, pointing to the record player to call attention to Hank Williams's song and getting back to her point, "apparently Herschel has the time. But instead of taking you honky-tonking like Hank, he's taking you to Italy for three weeks."

"You poor thing," Ohio said in mock sympathy as she resumed looking for her left shoe.

"And speaking of *time*," Katy said to Lindsey, who had just found a third sandal and absent-mindedly handed the extra shoe to California, who handed it to Ohio, "you and I had better get dressed or you'll be late to your own wedding. And your grandmother won't be able to show her face at the Corner Store."

"Lindsey is never late for anything," Ohio said, putting on her left shoe. "She's the one that's always pushing us to be on time. What is it with you today—those last-minute jitters?" she said to Lindsey.

The hallway clock chimed the quarter hour. "There's still . . . time," Lindsey said. "The church is only a mile and a half down the road . . ." She let the words trail off. She had no idea why she was delaying putting on her dress—or why her mind kept running off in unpredictable directions.

Katy walked over to her midnight-navy dress, took it down, and tried to step into it, but it wouldn't go past her swollen belly. She sighed a huge, long sigh and then hoisted it over her head.

Soon Lindsey and her bridesmaids were laughing hilariously at their attempts at pulling Katy's dress over her head without breaking the zipper. They had just succeeded when they heard a pecking on the door. It opened and Sarah Frost, a short, slightly plump woman, walked into the room, obviously ready for this most important day in her granddaughter's life— her gray hair, closer to blue today, was in tight but soft curls, and she wore a pink dress, white pumps, and a white hat with a band of pink flowers. Lindsey had polished her grandmother's fingernails the night before. Pink, of course. Sarah Frost *was* the color pink.

Seeing the general degree of unreadiness—and seeing that the wedding dress was on the dressing screen instead of on Lindsey—Sarah patted her hands together twice, the way she had once scurried chickens into the barn. "Girls, your car is waiting. They need you at the church five minutes ago." She turned to Lindsey. "Your Uncle Max will drive us—as soon as you are ready."

In a flurry, Sarah Frost helped fasten hook and eyes, find Katy's shoes amid the clutter on the floor, and tuck straps and loose hair into place. Sarah took the blue felt cowboy hat from the bed—her back was turned, but Lindsey felt sure her grandmother smiled as she said, "Honestly, girls." Then Sarah hung the hat on the corner of the mirror stand and said, "I think today calls for a veil."

Sarah Frost shooed the girls out of the room with a reminder that their flowers were in the downstairs hallway. Ohio and California gave Lindsey a hug—and kisses on her cheek—then told her they would see her at the church.

Katy waited to be last. After having Lindsey pat her belly for good luck, she gave Lindsey a long, long hug and then pointed furtively to a pair of beat-up cowboy boots just inside the closet door. With an impish smile on her face, she whispered, "I double-dog dare you to wear them." Then she gave Lindsey a thumbs-up and went out the door as Johnny Cash began singing "Folsom Prison Blues."

Sarah Frost walked over and turned off the record player, placed something beside Lindsey's boom box on the dresser, and began picking up the clutter while Lindsey took off her shorts and top and put on her slip and hose. Her grandmother then held the dress, and Lindsey stepped gingerly over and into the mound of satin.

Sarah Frost made small talk as she fastened the tiny buttons, then she turned Lindsey to face the oval mirror. "The day your mother wore this dress was the happiest day of her life. And now you . . . you are truly a vision," Sarah said, a gentle smile on an already gentle face. "I wish . . ." There was no need to finish the sentence—they knew the various endings. One of them: *I wish your mother could see you in that dress.*

Lindsey had long ago memorized every bead, every tiny pearl button, every gather in the voluminous skirt of her mother's dress, from the wedding picture on the mantel. Memorized it in such detail because she had no memory of the woman who had worn it.

Sarah Frost watched as Lindsey finally pulled her hair back into a soft twist, and then she helped her pin on a simple veil. "We'll wait for you downstairs—and don't forget that shiny penny for your shoe, there by your tape player," her grandmother said, stretching on tiptoe to kiss Lindsey softly on the cheek. Then Sarah Frost left the room and closed the door behind her.

For the first time in days, weeks, or months it seemed, Lindsey Briggs found herself alone, her only company the slow ticking of the old mantel clock. And suddenly she knew she needed this time. Time in this big, old farmhouse where she had been raised. Time in this room. Time to herself.

They're waiting. Herschel's waiting. The rest of my life is waiting. It's time to go. It's time.

Today, at the church she had attended since she was a child, it would be her grandmother Sarah sitting where Lindsey's mom should have been. It would be her Uncle Max, her mother's brother, walking her down the aisle and giving her away. And there would be an empty space on the pew where her Aunt Lily would have sat. Just the other night, Lindsey had thought of writing a song about who should be sitting on those pews on her wedding day. But she hadn't written a song for years. Lindsey turned and looked at herself in the mirror. What had happened to the eight-year-old in a brown suede cowgirl skirt and vest who learned all ten verses of "Red River Valley" to sing at the country fair? What had happened to that ten-year-old in those red cowboy boots and that purple organdy dress, who knew exactly what she wanted to do—and be? The same girl who announced on her thirteenth birthday that she and Fiddle were switching from English to Western. She looked over to the old apple box, to the ribbons she and Fiddle had won after that. And then there was the girl who in her high school valedictory address quoted Thoreau and then sang a song she had written just for her class. What had happened to that girl?

That girl had won a scholarship and gone to Harvard like she knew she *should*. Like everyone expected—*the chance of a lifetime*. So she had packed away her dreams the way she had packed away the things in the old apple box.

Not intentionally. And not at first. In fact, during her freshman year, she and a fiddler from Texas and two guys from Colorado *had* jammed together when their schedules allowed it and played for a few student functions. They were even featured on the *Hillbilly at Harvard* radio show. But two of the band members graduated that year. Besides, the study load at Harvard was enormous, and she had a work-study job that supplemented her generous scholarship.

It all got to be too much.

The summer after Lily died during Lindsey's junior year, Lindsey brought her guitar home and left it there. Never time to play anyway, she told a concerned Sarah. But when she was home, she always turned to the guitar as if it were an old friend. And of course she always remained a country music fan. Even during her busy senior year, she dropped everything to hop the Red Line to Johnny D's—two stops from Harvard—to hear Iris Dement, Guy Clark, Sleepy LaBeef, and Heather Myles. And once she dragged Herschel to Great Woods to hear Loretta Lynn.

Herschel. Early in her senior year, she went to Kinko's at two o'clock in the morning to make copies of a project due the next morning. And of course, the machine jammed. "Here, let me help," said a voice just as she was getting ready to kick it. And that's how she met Herschel—who was in his last year of law school. Herschel liked to joke that he first picked her up at two o'clock in the morning and took her for a drink. And then she'd explain that the drink was coffee at Store-24. Herschel proposed at the end of her senior year. Both Jennifers proclaimed him the catch of a lifetime—handsome, ambitious, nice, and from a Boston family of considerable means, including their own law firm. But Lindsey turned him down, said she just wasn't ready to settle down.

Herschel proposed again six months later when she was working in the development office at the Harvard Business School—and feeling there had to be something more. She turned him down again and left the business school to work for a nonprofit, knowing what she did there was good and worthwhile—even if she still felt directionless.

The Friday after Thanksgiving, Hershel took her out to dinner and had the ring put in a glass of champagne. He really was a great guy, she told herself. She didn't understand why she kept telling him no. So she said yes. Then she went out and bought a ten-year-old Chrysler LeBaron convertible whose odometer was on its second go round and whose top often would not go up on rainy days or down on sunny ones. It was the only rash thing she had ever done in her life.

She brought Herschel home that Christmas. He gamely tried to fit in, but his discomfort with all things about the farm was obvious. The animal smell of the barn. Sarah's laying hens. Aunt Lily's rusted green truck, a true antique, that Lindsey had always liked to tool around in. Herschel was even leery of the old claw-foot bathtub with a rubber hose for those who wanted a shower.

Lindsey found his city-boy uneasiness amusing. But she didn't find it amusing when they drove to see Loretta Lynn and Herschel spent the whole drive back criticizing Loretta's songs, Loretta's clothes, and Loretta's corniness. It was the only real fight they'd ever had. Well, that and the battle over where the wedding and reception would be. Herschel and his family quickly found out, as someone at the Corner Store had put it, that Lindsey could stick to her guns when she made up her mind. Herschel's family, of course, vowed to have a reception later for their friends in Boston.

Lindsey reached for her can of Pepsi and walked over to get the penny for her shoe. It was sitting on top of a cassette tape. A tape of her own songs she had made at the local radio station when she was in junior high school. A tape she had forgotten she had. What was it doing out on the dresser?

Just one song. She slipped it into the boom box, took a swallow of her Pepsi, wishing she had a sip of her grandmother's sherry instead, and punched the power button. And soon, the amateur but promising sounds of a guitar, her guitar, playing what her grandmother had called a country-blues beat. Then Lindsey's twelve-year-old voice:

> I'm on my way to where I'm going,
> Going to a place I've never been.

Oh, Jesus. Lindsey, giving in to the weight of the dress, the weight of the day, sank slowly to the floor and sat cross-legged, almost disappearing into the snowdrift of satin.

> But it's the place that I've been heading
> All my life, all my life.
> I want to find a place of blue skies,
> As blue as my Aunt Lily's eyes.

Lindsey closed her eyes, brown eyes like her mother's. As a child, she had prayed for eyes like her Aunt Lily's—eyes so blue folks still remarked about them when they talked of her. What was it her physics teacher had said about blue?

Blue light is most likely to bounce and scatter. Sixteen times more likely than red, scatters more than indigo and violet even. The only color that, because it scatters, is more likely to come to your eye. Here she was—minutes before her wedding—remembering a physics lecture at Harvard. *Speaking of scattered . . .*

She shook her head to clear it. She turned and looked at herself in the mirror.

"Do you, Lindsey Briggs," she said aloud, "take Herschel Philip Bosley the Third? . . ." Suddenly she couldn't remember what color his eyes were. *Do you, Lindsey Briggs, take Hershel Philip Bosley the Third, even if you can't remember what color his eyes are?*

A long shaft of afternoon sunlight streamed through the bedroom window and was captured by the prisms on the bedside lamp. They bent the white light into long, thin rainbows that flitted across the walls and danced on Lindsey's wedding dress. She blinked back tears and traced a faint rainbow with her index finger as her twelve-year-old voice continued on the tape.

> I've got so many songs inside me,
> So many songs I have to sing. . . .

Do you, Lindsey Briggs, take? . . . She couldn't remember his name. But she could remember her seventh-grade teacher's name, Mr. Neal. The one who first taught her the mnemonic to remember the order of colors in refracted light: ROY G. BIV—red, orange, yellow, green, blue, indigo, and violet. *Do you, Lindsey, take Roy G. Biv? Do you, Margaret Lindsey Briggs, take anyone?*

Rainbows moved across her dress again. *A body will continue to move in a straight line if not acted upon by an outside force.*

She closed her eyes one more time. Took a deep breath and let it out slowly. She felt the weight lifting.

She stretched as far as she could to set down the can of Pepsi—so she wouldn't knock it over. She hiked up the armloads of satin and stood up. She walked to the closet, reached inside, and picked up the worn cowboy boots that Katy had pointed to. She stood there doing a balancing act as she worked her stocking feet into the boots. Then she dropped her skirt and faced herself one last time in the mirror.

Do you, Lindsey Briggs, know what you are about to do?

––––––––––

The wedding that did not happen was the talk of Hadley's Curve late that summer. Folks divided into camps as to the exact reason Lindsey left her fiancé standing at the altar. Or, to be more exact, standing in one of the Sunday school rooms in the basement of the little Congregational church as the last guests were being seated.

Freda Tarker, the church pianist, had just walked past the groom's makeshift dressing room on her way to the inside stairs that led up into the foyer. She reported later that the groom, who had on a beautiful blue cummerbund, had just handed the best man the ring and was about to slip into his tuxedo jacket when someone came clumping down the back outside stairs. Freda turned to see who had made such a noise, and all she saw was a cloud of white entering the groom's dressing room.

The next thing Freda heard was the groom's startled voice saying, "Lindsey!" Freda was sure there was more surprise than displeasure in his voice. But maybe there was a bit of fear, too. Then the groom said something about it being bad luck to see her before the wedding, and Lindsey said, "That's just it." That's when she told him there wasn't going to be any wedding. Freda said it was apparent by the "kind but firm tone" in Lindsey's voice that this was not a case of the bride's getting mad at the groom for something that happened at his bachelor's party. She didn't sound mad at him about anything.

Anyway, it was at that point that the groomsmen slipped sheepishly past

Freda and joined the three attendants huddled in the hallway; they all began talking in hushed whispers. Freda waved them all back into the fellowship hall, since it wasn't anybody's business, and she herself was following behind when she dropped her sheet music, which is why she couldn't help but hear bits and pieces of the conversation on the other side of the door.

The groom, trying to calm Lindsey, said it was just last-minute anxiety. And Lindsey said no, it was coming to her senses about what she really wanted in life. And then something about his not taking it personally, that she just did not want to be married. Period. Then there was a long silence—Freda could swear at least a full minute—before finally the groom said, "Your timing is terrific."

And Lindsey said something about finding something in the back of her closet and something about finding herself—which is what young folks are always saying, of course. Then something about her speech at her high school graduation—how she had told her class to remember the words of Thoreau about stepping to the music of a different drummer but had not heeded those words herself. And now she was going to do that. It was when Lindsay said something about country music that the jilted young man started laughing. But it wasn't a ha-ha laugh at all.

The door opened, and Lindsey walked out of the room. Then she stopped, turned back to the groom, and said quietly, right in front of Freda, "I am so sorry to hurt you this way. It's an unfair thing to do, but it would have been even more unfair to marry you." Freda was pretty sure there were tears in Lindsey's eyes, and she looked like she was going to go give him a hug, but he stormed past her, rushed up the stairs, and caught his parents as they were going to be ushered in.

Lindsey stood there in the basement hallway until Herschel and his parents had driven away. Then she took a deep breath and went into the fellowship hall to deliver the news to the wedding party, who probably had heard most of it anyway.

Lindsey gathered her skirt up once again—Freda couldn't be sure, but she thought she noticed a pair of worn, brown leather cowboy boots underneath the gown. But surely not. Then, Lindsey walked up the steps and down the aisle—but there was no music, and she walked alone.

She turned to face the puzzled guests to say that there would be no wedding, but there would still be a reception and dance at the Country Way Restaurant. "After all, we can't let that roast beef go to waste," she said, and smiled bravely.

At the coffee gathering at the Butters' Corner Store on Monday, someone said it was a shame because Lindsey and that young man made a nice-looking couple. And someone else nodded and said, "All that money she would have married into."

And several, both men and women, cradling coffee cups in work-and-weather-worn hands, said, "Ayuh."

And someone added, "I always did say Lily and Sarah spoiled that girl rotten. Then they sacrificed what little they had to send her to Harvard."

Madge Butters, who even at ninety still came daily to the store she and her husband, Forrest, had started—came to have breakfast or lunch or just to sit, and came especially to tell her grandson and his wife when they weren't running things right—said, "I'd hardly say a girl who lost her parents before her second birthday never had to go without. And she lost Lily before she was truly grown-up." She added, "That girl worked her head off in 4-H, gave guitar lessons and riding lessons and worked here in our store summers, and got a scholarship that took care of much of her education."

Others agreed by their "ayuhs" or by their nods or by their silence.

"Well, it seems to me," someone said, "the Frost women lived without men so long they come to think they don't need 'em around a'tall." And they reminded each other that this wasn't the only time Lindsey Briggs had left a boy out in the cold. She had, after all, given Bobby Cummings his class ring back the night of their high school graduation, just when Bobby had finally saved up money for a diamond. And someone said, "It's too late for her to get Bobby back, since he's married off. Ayuh, if Lindsey don't watch it, she'll end up a spinster like Lily."

Albert Tikander, one of the old men who had frequented the Corner Store since he was a towheaded boy, lifted his cup with his broad hand and said, "Well it warn't by choice that Lily didn't marry . . . since Jackie Tate was the one she was gonna marry."

Even after all those years, there was always a short space of silence among the Butters' Corner regulars at the mention of any of the young men who had marched off to that war of their youth more than fifty years ago. Young men who, had they come back, would have married local girls and raised their children in Hadley's Curve. Young men who had come to Butters' Corner Store to put gas in their cars before picking up their dates, and then after the movie, had brought their dates back for a hamburger and a coke and sometimes danced to the jukebox even though it wasn't really a dancing place.

After all that time, the old men paused for a second, reminding them-selves that had those young men not been killed in that war, they would be sitting at this very counter as old men. Jackie Tate had been one of those young men—killed on a Sunday morning in December on a ship called the *Arizona*.

And since small Maine towns do not forget their war dead, they passed on the story of how Jack Tate was the only man Lily could ever love. Even young folks in Hadley's Curve knew that was why Lily Frost—as beautiful as folks claimed she had been as a young woman—had lived her life as a spinster.

Madge Butters corrected her old friend. "I'd say Lily indeed *chose* not to marry—*after* Jackie's death—even though she could have had her choice of a dozen men in the town. You included," Madge added. But since Albert was hard of hearing when he chose to be, he didn't respond.

It was on Wednesday that Madge Butters announced to the regulars at the Corner Store that as soon as Lindsey got the presents returned and saved up a bit, she was moving to Nashville, Tennessee, to try her hand at country music. Someone said, "All that money on a fancy education, and she goes and turns into a country singer. Whoever heard of such?"

And Madge Butters said, "Well, education's never wasted. And as for country singing, didn't Bonnie Raitt go to Harvard or some such? Besides," Madge said, leaning on her cane and sounding a bit testy. "Sarah says Lindsey mostly wants to *write* songs. But she'll sing too, and she is not *turning* into a country singer. She was bit by that bug by the time she could carry a tune. And she made up songs before she could write even." Madge paused just enough for breath and said, "When Sarah used to bring Lindsey in here, that little girl headed straight for the jukebox. Spent every cent she could beg from Sarah on it. She'd drop her money in and stand by the jukebox and sing her little heart out . . . especially on the sad ones. It was hard not to laugh, she was so cunnin'. But we bit our lips since she took it so serious. If Forrest was alive, he'd tell you I always did say that little girl's records would be on jukeboxes some day."

"Not many jukeboxes left these days, 'specially the old ones," Albert said.

Madge, who still went to see whatever country artist was at the Fryeburg Fair, used her cane to point over to the jukebox in the far corner of the room. "Ayuh, well this one's staying put."

"Speaking of staying put," the old-timer who always took the corner stool said, "don't see why the girl don't just stay put with her grandmother up there on Eden's Ridge. Seems like as good a place as any to write a song."

"Anybody knows you have to be in Nashville to do that," Madge answered.

"Now tell me how that makes sense?" someone asked.

"Don't have to make sense to be true," someone answered.

And no one disagreed.

Two

Early that September morning, the day she was to leave, Lindsey made one final trip to her room to make a last check of what she had taken and what she had left behind. She reached up to get the blue cowgirl hat that still hung on the mirror stand. It had been four weeks and two days since Katy had dragged out the box with all the reminders of her dreams. *Maybe there's a song in that,* she thought.

> Four weeks and two days and I'm still not sorry.
> Four weeks and three days and I'm feeling glad.
> Four weeks and four days and I'm startin' to miss him.

Just might work as a song. But she wasn't missing Herschel, even though she felt awful that she had hurt him and had written to try to explain. She wasn't missing anyone. Well, she was. But she would be missing them the rest of her life. That missing was a part of who she was. No doubt it was that missing that had first drawn her to those rawboned "I'm hurtin'" songs that she and her grandmother listened to when Lily wasn't around. And sometimes when she was.

During those four weeks and two days, Lindsey had waitressed at a nearby B&B that offered French cuisine, putting away "tiding over" money, as her grandmother called it. When she wasn't waitressing, she wrote. At first she wrote the notes of regret to go along with the returned gifts. And then she began to write lyrics again—always with her guitar in hand and pen and tablet beside her. Sometimes the melody came first. Sometimes the thought. Sometimes the words.

She sat on her bed looking at pictures on the mantel or going through the scrapbooks—and she strummed and sang and wrote. Or sometimes she wrote and strummed and sang—as she sat on the hired-man's bed in the hallway listening to the rain beat down on the tin roof of the old farmhouse. Or on the stone wall that bordered the apple orchard watching resident chipmunks scurry about in the last days of summer, preparing for the winter ahead. Or on the porch watching the light fade from the sky and the dark rise up out of the valley—out of Lake Pennesseewassee itself, it seemed. Or on the ledge by their pond with Fiddle grazing contentedly nearby.

She wrote a song about wishing she had known her mom and dad, wishing she could have been old enough to hold onto just one memory of her mom singing her a lullaby. Wishing she could remember her dad's strong arms holding her in the air the way he does in a photograph on her mantel. She wrote about Bobby Cummings, her high school sweetheart—"The One I Wish I Could Have Loved." She wrote about the drive home from Boston on a day of rain and fog to Aunt Lily's funeral—"The Long, Long Drive to Sorrow."

She held Katy's hand as Katy tossed and moaned and swore never to have another child. Then laughed when it was over, when Katy said she wanted at least two more. Katy named her new daughter Lindsey Elizabeth.

And then it was time to leave.

Lindsey and her grandmother rose soon after dawn the September day of Lindsey's leaving. Sarah Frost fixed blueberry pancakes with berries they had picked in late July while Lindsey finished packing her car. She had just put her guitar on top of the load in the backseat when her grandmother leaned out the kitchen window to say, "Food's on."

Her grandmother had gone all out in setting the table. In the center, a blue luster vase filled with the last of the season's wild flowers they had picked the day before. And to Lindsey's surprise, the Blue Willow family dishes that Sarah and Lily always reserved for holidays or the most special occasions.

Lindsey smiled past the lump in her throat. "Grandma Sarah, I'm so lucky to have your support on all this. I don't know how you can be so understanding considering what I put you through. I mean, all the expense. And the embarrassment must have been awful . . ."

"Pshaw," her grandmother said, standing up to go to the stove and interrupting Lindsey midsentence. Her grandmother and some of her bridge club were the only people in the world Lindsey knew who really did say that word. Sarah Frost ladled warm maple syrup into a miniature pitcher and brought it to the table.

"What would have been awful was for you to marry that boy," Sarah said.

Lindsey was shocked at such a flat-out statement. It was her Aunt Lily who would have freely offered such an opinion. Sarah Frost seldom put things so boldly. And she had certainly given Lindsey no signal that she had reservations about Herschel. Or maybe Lindsey had just not read the signs.

"Ayuh," Sarah continued, picking up the coffee pot on her way back to the table. "I told the girls at cards just last month that I thought you were being led by your head." She filled Lindsey's Blue Willow cup and her own. "I just knew in my heart he wasn't the one *destined* for you." Sarah Frost emphasized the word as she returned the coffeepot to its place on the counter.

"Grandma Sarah, no one is *destined* for anyone else," Lindsey said.

"Pshaw," her grandmother said again, using her most dismissive word for the second time that morning. Sarah Frost took her place at the table and lifted her cup with both hands to take a sip. "You can tell yourself that until the cows come back from Capistrano."

Lindsey clinched her jaws and held her breath in an effort not to break into laughter and spew coffee everywhere. Her grandmother occasionally came up with priceless mixed metaphors. Maybe Lindsey could use some of them in a song.

"That poor boy, rich as he was, just wasn't the one for you," Sarah continued, breaking into Lindsey's thoughts.

"Then why didn't you say something? *Do* something?" Lindsey asked, still astonished at her grandmother's uncharacteristically unreserved opinions.

Sarah picked up the pitcher of syrup and offered it to Lindsey. "Number one." Lindsey suppressed smiling at her grandmother's tendency to put things in a numbered list. "Number one," Sarah repeated, "you are stubborn as mud on a boot, so my saying so wouldn't have done a bit of good if you had really made up your mind to do it. And number two . . ." Sarah held up a second finger. "I was sure you would figure that out for yourself before you walked down the aisle—though I didn't think you'd cut it so close. And number three, I did do something."

"What do you mean?" Lindsey racked her brain to think what her grandmother had done to discourage her from marrying Herschel.

Her grandmother gave her a smile that seemed both shy and sly. "Well, number one, that old apple box didn't get to the front of the closet by itself. And number two—I made sure you had time alone. Most folks can figure out a lot if they have some time to themselves, and Lord knows you've hardly had that with working and making wedding plans and looking for a place for you and Herschel.

"And number three . . . well . . ." At that point she choked up and tears rimmed her eyes. All she could do was wave her hand in the air, which meant *and so forth.*

Suddenly, Lindsey knew what the third thing was. "You're the one who stood me in front of the mirror in my mother's dress and reminded me that it was the happiest day of her life. And . . ." Lindsey followed the thought until it gave her the answer. ". . . it should have been the happiest day of mine, too."

"Something like that," Sarah said, taking a breath to get back her composure.

"Grandma Sarah, do you mean you . . . that you . . ."

"Rigged it?" Sarah said. "Well, I'm not sure I'd call it that," she added—even though she had just supplied Lindsey with the word she was searching for. "But I sure wouldn't want to go through that again. You have to promise me that the next time you agree to marry someone, he's the one that really makes your heart flutter."

Lindsey was about to argue that it just wasn't that simple when her grandmother said, "Seems to me, you try to choose who to love. You wanted to love that Bobby Cummings because he was sweet and because he would have given you everything in his power; you wanted to love Herschel because he was Herschel Bosley the Third and *could* give you everything. But when it came down to it, I figure you realized you didn't *want* everything."

Sarah took a sip of her coffee, put the cup back in the saucer, then reached over and patted Lindsey's hand. "If you ask me, which you haven't, of course, you haven't really loved a man because you haven't found the man you love."

Lindsey forced herself not to chuckle at her grandmother's impossibly romantic notions. Besides, for Sarah Frost it really had been that simple—

for a while, at least. She had met Tad Frost at a Service Club for enlisted men near her home in Pennsylvania shortly before he shipped off to France. They had declared their love while dancing to Glenn Miller on their second date. Then she had written him every day when he was away as she waited for him to come back. And he *had* come back, unlike Jack Tate, Lily's beau.

Tad and Sarah had obviously been happy in those few short years they had together. Then Tad had been killed in a logging accident when she was expecting their second child. A distraught Sarah had returned to Pennsylvania to live with her family. But after Jenny was born, she'd decided to come back to the farm on Eden's Ridge and raise the two children she and Tad had been blessed with—she always put it that way—in the place, the very house, where their father had grown up. And there she had stayed, living and working side by side with Tad's twin sister, Lily. *Like Ruth and Naomi in the Bible,* Lindsey had always thought. Sarah and Lily had put their whole life into keeping the farm that had been in their family for three hundred years. And later, after the unspeakable tragedy of losing Jenny and her husband in a car wreck, into raising Lindsey.

Now Lily, too, was gone. And Lindsey was leaving. And Sarah Frost, in spite of being left alone, and in spite of Lindsey's causing a stir by walking out on her wedding—was totally supportive of Lindsey's pursuit. A surge of gratitude washed over Lindsey. She'd have to think of something mundane to say, or else she'd start crying right then and there. And the Frost women weren't criers. Never had been.

So she said how good the syrup was. And that it was nice that their flowers had escaped the frosts that had already hit the valley.

———

And then her grandmother was walking her to the car. Across the road and down the valley slope, the steam of early morning rose from the lake.

Fog from a low cloud shrouded the apple orchard and hovered over Eden's Ridge. Grass glistened from the dew that had almost been cold enough to frost. Hollyhocks, phlox, asters stood attendance on both sides of the porch steps.

"Let's take a short walk before I leave," she said to her grandmother. And Sarah knew where Lindsey meant to go.

"I'll wait here," her grandmother said. "I think you need to go by yourself."

Lindsey started, then she stopped, ran back inside and took the flowers from the vase. Then she set off through the apple orchard, which had been tended by generations of Frosts. She stopped at the spot where a Ribston Pippin, the oldest of apple trees, had stood. *That, too, is a song I will find my way to someday.*

When the old tree died, Lily and young Jenny Frost—who would become Lindsey's mom—had pulled up the rotted stump and put another tree in its place. "For the generations still to come," Aunt Lily had always said when she told Lindsey the story.

The small family cemetery was just past the orchard, surrounded by an old iron fence. Lindsey stepped inside and walked quietly past the tombstones until she came to the far corner, near the line of lilac bushes. There she stopped at the graves of her parents. She placed the bouquet of flowers, except for one black-eyed Susan, near their common headstone.

Then she stood before her Aunt Lily's grave, which was next to her parents'. The gravestone was a large chunk of pink quartz from a nearby quarry. Lily had picked it out herself long before she was an old woman.

Lindsey looked at the pink quartz headstone, at the English tea-rose bush planted nearby. Then she looked back at her parents' headstone. Kevin Dean Briggs and Jenny Lind Briggs.

I dream of Jenny with the light, brown hair,
Borne like a vapor in the summer air. . . .

Lily had sung those words to Lindsey once—substituting her mother's name for Stephen Foster's "Jeannie." That had been when Lindsey was very little, sitting beside Lily at the piano. Then Lily's voice had broken, and she had sung a funny song instead.

Lindsey stood there in the soft light of early morning, in air so sweet she could have sworn she smelled lilacs even though they were long past blossoming, and she wondered which grief weighed heavier—longing for what you have never had, never known, or losing what you *have* had, what you *have* known. She didn't know the answer. But she did know the weight of each.

She stood there remembering Jenny, the mother she had never known. And Lilian Frost, the woman who taught her not only to read notes but to *hear* the music. It was Grandma Sarah who had tucked her into bed. It was Aunt Lily who had played the soothing sounds that floated up the stairs as Lindsey drifted off to sleep.

Lily was also the woman who taught her to swim in their pond, to ice skate, to throw a softball. She was the woman who had insisted Lindsey get back on Fiddle the one time he threw her.

And even though Lily could not abide country music, she had been a good sport when that music took first place in Lindsey's life. When Lindsey was twelve, she had overheard Lily sigh in surrender one day and say, "If she's got her mind made up, might as well get her the best." Soon after that, Lily had presented her with a Martin guitar—which must have taken a chunk out of her checkbook.

Lindsey knelt down and placed the black-eyed Susan on Lily's grave. She stood and whispered, "Goodbye, Aunt Lily." Then she said a little louder, "Thank you."

Sarah Frost put on a cheerful face as she helped her granddaughter rearrange the trunk. She made sure Lindsey had her coffee thermos. Then

Sarah said, for the thousandth time, that she would feel so much better if only Lindsey knew someone where she was going.

"Well," Lindsey said, as she wedged her suitcase into the backseat of her car, "I just might try to look up Ben McBride and tell him Tad Frost was my grandfather, so he owes me dinner at least."

"He probably won't even remember Tad," Sarah Frost said quickly. "It's been so long, you know; I wouldn't bother him," her grandmother continued, "and didn't I read that he lives in Memphis, not Nashville? And besides . . ."

"I was just teasing," Lindsey said a bit defensively, surprised at the emotion her statement had provoked in her grandmother. "And besides," she said, squaring her shoulders and putting her chin up in the air, "asking favors from anyone is simply not the Frost way."

Both of the women chuckled at Lindsey's imitation of Lily Frost.

Lindsey hugged her grandmother, who held on to her much longer than usual.

"You take care of yourself, you hear?" Sarah Frost said, and might have said more had her voice not choked. Lindsey smiled. That was what Grandma Sarah always said—her way of telling Lindsey she loved her. *You have sweet dreams, you hear? You drive careful, you hear?*

"Remember what Aunt Lily always said each time I took off on a trip?" Lindsey asked as she settled in and fastened her seat belt.

Sarah smiled, then she tried to cock her head the way Lily had done. "Don't forget your way home." And they both laughed.

Then Lindsey Briggs was heading south on Eden's Ridge. The fog was lifting. The mist had burned off the lake below, and Lindsey could see for miles and miles. Almost, it seemed, to Tennessee.

For now, Lindsey Briggs burst into song, one of her own.

> Slipping out the back door
> To an early morning sunrise,

Thinking in my head there's something more.
Yeah, I'm moving down the highway
Through an early morning sunrise,
Thinking 'bout the things that I will leave.
Good things I know that I'll be missing,
Tender lips I could be kissing,
But that's the price for choosing to be free,
For making time and space for being me.

Yeah, I'm moving down the highway
In the early morning sunrise,
Drinking cups of coffee black and strong,
And eating up the highway with a song.

Three

It took Lindsey one night on the road and the better part of two days to get to Nashville. She drove through the Berkshires, through the Poconos, and crossed the Susquehanna River—she had always loved that word, *Susquehanna*. She touched the edge of Maryland and West Virginia and stopped for the night near Winchester, Virginia. The next morning she entered the Shenandoah Valley just as the fog lifted. She could see the Blue Ridge to the east and the Alleghenies to the west—a different kind of beauty than New England, but the rolling farmland, framed by the mountains, was breathtaking. And the river running through it prompted Lindsey to sing,

> Oh Shenandoah, I long to see you,
> Away you rolling river. . . .

wishing she knew more than two verses.

She turned on the radio. All day she listened to the many country stations—and just outside of Bristol, on the Tennessee-Virginia line, she found herself singing along to Ben McBride's "Ol' Boys in Memphis." The same song that had won her tickets to the Red Sox.

> They don't remember when
> The streets were bright and the bars were dark
> And the river was blood flowin' to their hearts.

Lindsey had been surprised that her grandmother thought Ben McBride wouldn't remember Tad. How could the two men in that photograph forget each other? But then again, Ben McBride had not kept in touch. The price of fame, she supposed. But she would not be like that if fame came to her. She would always come back home, back to Eden's Ridge. She'd stay in touch with her friends, even the ones who had no idea why she was doing what she did. She promised herself. And she promised all those she was leaving behind at Eden's Ridge.

Lindsey Briggs with all her CMA awards has the time for her fans. And always has the time for her friends—no matter how busy she is. Always stays in touch.

She left behind the mountains when she turned west out of Knoxville, singing along with Reba and Willie and Trisha and Lyle. Then she was driving across the high Cumberland Plateau. Not long now. She'd be in Nashville, where—she was sure—her future lay.

The phone rings just as she's heading out the door to sign her next contract with Rounder Records. "Lindsey," her manager says, "Willie just called from Austin. Plans to use your latest song as the title for his next album. And he'd like you to open for him at the Farm Aid concert."

"I'd love to, but I've got to go to my class reunion. Promised my friends."

And Lindsey Briggs always has time for her friends. Always.

"Get your mind on the road, girl," Lindsey said aloud, amused at the grandiosity of her fantasy. She turned the radio up even higher, and she and Willie were belting it out, her hand keeping time on the steering wheel, when she saw the sign for the Hermitage—"Home of Andrew Jackson." Her heart jumped. Almost there. Nashville.

Billboards, banned in Maine, seemed to fight for space alongside the road as they hawked radio stations, cowboy boots, restaurants, and tourist attractions. She was headed west, into the late afternoon Tennessee sun, and the feeble stream of air conditioning did little to counter the heat pouring through the windshield. A time and temperature update on the radio confirmed it—5:13 and ninety-one degrees. And it was September. There might be three days in Maine—all summer—when it reached ninety degrees, if at all. The rare three days *in a row* of ninety was an official heat wave. She was thankful the top wouldn't go down in Knoxville. She would have been cooked.

Lindsey shut off the AC switch and rolled down her window. The rush of hot air startled her. A chirpy woman's voice from the radio told Lindsey what she already saw, a slowing flow of traffic headed into the city on I-40 because of road construction. Expect delays. Take alternate routes. But Lindsey didn't know any alternate routes.

Then she saw the yellow-and-brown billboard for a Cracker Barrel restaurant. In smaller letters: "Old Country Store, Exit 219, *Breakfast Any Time.*" Suddenly she thought of the Corner Store and Madge Butters and cool mornings in Maine. And without giving any thought to the fact that it was late afternoon, she edged into the exit lane, hungry for eggs and toast.

In the Cracker Barrel's sprawling parking lot, Lindsey waited as a Country Music Tours bus unloaded an endless line of gray-haired travelers. She pulled into an empty slot. Maybe she'd be singing for them someday. No, that wasn't the way to think—she *would* be singing for folks who took country music tours. Or at least she'd be writing the songs they would listen to. But that was someday. Right now, she was tired. And hungry.

If she had driven a little faster she could have beaten the line that snaked back from the hostess stand. Now it would be an endless wait, but what was the hurry? Just so she got a motel room for the night. She gave her name to the hostess, who called her honey. Then she bought a newspaper, *The Tennessean,* and braved the heat again to sit on one of a dozen wooden rocking chairs that lined the front porch.

She turned immediately to the apartment rentals since the first item on her agenda was to find a place to live. For her grandmother's peace of mind, she had brought along the numbers for two college friends who lived in Murfreesboro, but Nashville was where she needed to be. She rifled through her backpack for a notepad and wrote down number after number of places with swimming pools. Already she missed Frost Pond, missed the lake that stayed cold even during three-day heat waves.

She called five places that sounded promising—promising to everyone, it seemed, since they had already been rented. She ruled out a half dozen more—she couldn't afford them. Then, for the first time, she fought off a creeping doubt. Not about Herschel and the wedding. She had never regretted calling it off. Even though she felt guilt for hurting Herschel, she knew her decision had not been rash. Late in coming, but not rash. No, that decision she did not doubt.

But had she been too quick to come here without a job, without a place to live? When her grandmother had worried about that, Lindsey assured her she would be fine. But now she was here, and she wasn't exactly sure where to turn next. It would come to her, she reassured herself, and leaned back in the rocking chair, watching two small boys play checkers on the shaded porch.

If I could go back to yesterday . . . The line ran through her head, and she scribbled it on the back of the newspaper. Then an ad in the "Roommate" column caught her eye. She circled it just as her name was called for a table.

She maneuvered her way through the crowded country store, took her seat, and ordered the Sunrise Sampler: two eggs with grits, something called "sawmill gravy," homemade buttermilk biscuits, real butter, preserves, fried apples, and hash-brown casserole with a sampling of country ham, smoked sausage, and bacon. And a cup of coffee. She enjoyed every bite of the huge meal.

Lindsey couldn't help but overhear conversations going on around her, where one syllable was stretched to two. At least. A waitress who also called her honey poured more coffee as Lindsey pulled out her newspaper and returned to the ad she had circled:

If you're a girl between 24 and whatever, love Elvis and the Carter family and can stand my fiddling—then call 555-2516 and ask for me. It's not a palace—it's home.

Another musician. A quirky musician. Lindsey liked Elvis. And she liked quirky. But there was something more in the ad. The reference to the Carter family. Their mournful "Motherless Children" had always struck a chord with Lindsey. She knew that Sara Carter had been three when her mother died—she had been raised by an aunt and uncle. The ad seemed better than a long shot.

An answering machine picked up, and a young woman's voice said in a Southern accent: "I thought I was here but I don't see me. Leave a message and I'll return the call when I get back and not one minute sooner."

"Hello, my name is Lindsey, and I'm moving here from Maine. I'd like to talk with you about the apartment . . . but I don't have a phone. I'm calling from a Cracker Barrel restaurant out on Percy Priest Drive."

Suddenly, the same voice she had heard on the answering machine said, "Don't ya just love the food there? My favorite is their pork roast, but their fried chicken is almost as good as my mama's. And the hot roast beef sandwich . . ."

In a five-minute conversation, Lindsey learned that Shannon Alene Nelson was called Gabby by her friends. That she was from Sugar Creek, Arkansas. That her apartment was "a big old place" that had been cobbled up into three tiny apartments. The landlady who lived on the main floor was hard of hearing, "which is good because she doesn't complain about the music." Gabby lived in the apartment upstairs, and J. J. Perkins, Gabby's best friend from Sugar Creek who played "every instrument in the world," lived in the basement apartment—"the cavern," Gabby called it.

"We've been best friends since we were three years old and in Sunday school together—except for fourth grade, when we hated each other," Gabby explained on the phone. "We came here together—not together-together, but to play music together. We've been dreaming about this since fifth grade. I hope you don't smoke, because I forgot to put in my ad that I don't smoke." Lindsey assured her she didn't.

"Got a napkin or something you can scribble directions on?" Gabby had asked. Then she assured Lindsey that the apartment was a cinch to find. "You can't get lost in Nashville. Just circle around and find yourself again. Everybody does."

Lindsey followed the directions on the napkin, maneuvering through traffic that had thinned out while she ate her late-day breakfast. She left the interstate and turned left off 21st Street going toward Belmont. She passed Bongo Java—according to Gabby, "the granddaddy of Nashville coffee houses. I *do* drink coffee, and their coffee is good even if it's a bit show-offy." Gabby had gone on to describe the coffee drinking habits of her grandmother and her great-uncle and about everyone else she knew.

Lindsey passed Tabouli's. "They have the best fountain coke in town." And she passed the Sterling Court Apartments, with their large balconies. "Old. No luxury but cool prestige—and a waiting list."

Lindsey found herself chuckling at the way Gabby had given inch-by-inch directions, complete with running commentary. A Mainer would certainly give different directions. "Can you tell me how to get to Portland?" a stranger might ask. "Ayuh," the Mainer would reply, leaving it at that.

In her amusement, Lindsey drove past the big X on the napkin. She did a quick U-turn and parked on the wide, tree-lined street. The house was one of many two-story houses on the block—all of which had at one time been graceful homes.

Lindsey was impressed by the spacious front porch, but Gabby had made it clear on the phone that the porch wasn't theirs to use. She walked down the gravel drive to the back entrance of the stone house. There, seven steep steps—Gabby had told her the number—led up to a concrete porch, just big enough for one white plastic chair and a wilted geranium. The glass in the storm door was cracked, and there was a hole where the door-bell buzzer was supposed to be.

Lindsey knocked hard on the wooden doorframe. She heard someone bounding down the stairs inside, and a young woman, her brown hair with gold streaks (yellow was more like it) in huge pink rollers, pulled back the curtain and smiled.

"This is it, and I'm Gabby," she said, opening the door and welcoming Lindsey in with a sweep of a hand that held a Dr. Pepper. She had a friendly, pretty face. And even with her hair in rollers, she wore mascara and lipstick. "I sure hope you like it."

Clearly, she had made up her mind from the phone conversation that if Lindsey wanted to move in, the second bedroom was hers.

She followed Gabby up the stairs. "Not much room for two-way traffic in the hallway," Gabby said, beginning the tour. She gestured toward the bathroom door. "Don't you just love an old claw-foot tub? One bathroom. We have to share a closet. Forgot to mention that. But I don't carry much baggage in the way of clothes."

In the kitchen, which was really an extension of the living room, straw-berry print curtains brightened the windows. Three mismatched chairs sur-rounded a small round table. An Elvis clock hung on the wall, his legs swinging back and forth, keeping time. "A birthday present from my daddy," Gabby boasted.

Gabby called the other end of the room the "sitting room." There was an old yellow-velvet couch and an overstuffed, over-the-hill green chair. "Yard sale finds," Gabby explained. Two guitars and a fiddle were propped in one corner of the room. An oversized poster with color photographs of a dozen breeds of chickens was pinned to the wall. "It's a thing between me and J. J.—the chickens. Ever seen Buff Orpingtons? Buttercup yellow, they are. I like the black-and-white Barred Plymouth Rocks. I could move it into my bedroom, but . . ." She hesitated. ". . . it kinda reminds me and J. J. of why we're here."

"No problem," Lindsey said with an assuring smile. She knew the chicken story would come soon enough.

Gabby showed her the available bedroom. The white iron bed and antique dresser reminded Lindsey of home. "The bedroom furniture comes with the house. And look—you get your own private balcony." Gabby pointed to the small metal landing outside the big window. "Just enough room for two people to sit close. Great place for cooling off on a hot summer night. But I do have an air conditioner—of sorts."

Gabby talked as if Lindsey had already made her decision. But she hadn't. Not quite.

Lindsey walked to the window that overlooked the gravel driveway. Below, an immense Rose of Sharon hedge was still in bloom. Two robins, making their last forays before night, flitted in and out of the thick hedge, and for a minute Lindsey was back with her Aunt Lily, bird-watching in the twilight on Eden's Ridge.

"Count me in unless there's a wait list," she said then, sealing the deal with a handshake. Then she asked, "You have many Carter family recordings?"

"Just everything they ever did," Gabby said.

Gabby helped Lindsey unpack her car, thrilled that it was a covertible. Lindsey set out the few belongings she had brought with her, among them the pewter candlesticks and two candles that Madge Butters had given her for a wedding gift and refused to take back. "I bought them for you, not for Haskell," Madge had said. Lindsey had almost corrected Madge on Herschel's name, but she suspected Madge had mis-said it on purpose.

By ten that evening, Lindsey and Gabby were drinking Red Dog beer and eating a Papa John's pizza. Gabby was entertaining Lindsey with an imitation of her high school principal when a tiny pebble pinged on the window. Lindsey, startled, looked at Gabby.

"That's just J. J. letting me know he's home," Gabby said, opening the window. She leaned out and said, none too quietly, "Come on up and meet my new roommate, and bring your bass. And some popcorn," she added as an afterthought.

Not ten minutes later, J. J. came into the room, lugging a bass guitar and balancing a huge plastic bowl of popcorn. J. J. was tall and gangly—all arms and legs—and his red hair was pulled neatly back into a short ponytail. He wore a brown UPS driver's shirt.

"Lindsey is from Maine, and she has a horse named Fiddle, but it's not for the fiddle—it's short for fiddlesticks," Gabby said as she introduced Lindsey. "And,"—Gabby turned to J. J. —"J. J. just loads the delivery trucks now, but he knows *all* the streets in Nashville," Gabby added with pride.

"And it sure beats chicken work," J. J. said, reaching out his hand shyly to Lindsey.

"Ah," Lindsey said, shaking J. J.'s hand and then reaching for a handful of popcorn, "the story behind the poster?"

"Yeah. Ever hear of liver pullers, gizzard cutters, skin rollers, or lung gunners?" Gabby asked. "Well," she said, reaching for more popcorn and not waiting for Lindsey to answer, "J. J. and I did all those things at one time or another in the chicken-processing plant near home. Decent enough pay. But . . ." She hesitated, something Lindsey had yet to see Gabby do. "I read somewhere that Patsy Cline worked in a poultry plant in Virginia—cut off chicken heads. But she made it. She had music in her, and it got her out of there."

J. J. picked up the story, "We played on Friday nights at the Hot Biscuit just down the road from Sugar Creek, and one night after we got a big hand for "Me and Bobby McGee," Gabby told me she'd been thinkin' if Patsy could walk away from chickens, we could too. And look at us now." He reached over and tousled Gabby's hair. "Just the chicken poster to remind us not to look back."

When the popcorn and storytelling were finished for the night, Gabby took out her fiddle. J. J. picked up his bass, and all his shyness vanished as he began to accompany Gabby, who could make a fiddle talk.

After two songs, Gabby turned to Lindsey, "Now, get out your guitar and let's hear how a Yankee sings country. And you might as well sing a song you wrote. We'll just follow along."

Lindsey sang "The One I Wish I Could Have Loved."

> He's the one I know I should have loved,
> The one I wish I could have loved. . . .

When she finished, Gabby and J. J. exchanged a knowing look. "You're good," Gabby said. "There's a lot of talent here in Nashville, but if you can write like that—and a voice to boot . . ." For once, Gabby let the words trail off.

"Thanks," Lindsey said. "Today I needed to hear that."

"Believe me, you'll need to hear it more when you've been here awhile," J. J. said.

Gabby cut in. "Look, you're the singer we've been looking for—my voice is kinda thin, which is sad, but I'm pretty good singing backup. Anyway, all we need is a dynamite lead guitar and we've got a band—Sugar Creek. Now," Gabby said, again not waiting for Lindsey to answer, "let's play something we all know."

At one o'clock the next morning, the three of them were still alternating harmonies, pleased with how their voices blended and enjoying each other's musical sense and sense of humor. And true to Gabby's word, no one complained about the noise.

Lindsey crawled into bed for her first night in Nashville, exhausted and elated. It was almost too good to be true. She'd call Grandma Sarah tomorrow and tell her about the apartment. And the Rhode Island Reds on the living room wall.

They were an odd match, the Harvard-educated girl from Maine and the Arkansas-born Gabby, who'd said goodbye to academics the day she walked across the stage and got her high school diploma. But Lindsey felt at home with Gabby almost from the start. Not only could she fiddle; she knew the words to every country song anyone had ever sung. She could sing Kitty Wells's hit, "It Wasn't God Who Made Honky-Tonk Angels" and then slip into Iris DeMent's "Easy's Gettin' Harder Every Day." And Lindsey loved Gabby's no-nonsense good sense. In that way, Gabby reminded her of Katy, who was half a world away in Japan and who, despite her earlier dreams of being a journalist, had proven to be a lousy correspondent.

Gabby, who had been in Nashville only six months herself—long enough to learn she couldn't afford to live by herself, even in that small apartment— never doubted that finding Lindsey was fate. "I just felt it in my bones the minute I heard your voice on the telephone," she said.

Gabby wasted no time in introducing Lindsey to what had been her lifeline: temporary office work at Vanderbilt University. "It pays the bills, and you can still focus on writing songs and singing nights. It's that or waiting tables, and that means a lot of suppertime work. You know, most of the waiters here in Nashville are singers or songwriters. You'll meet 'em at workshops and stuff. It's a small town, really."

The first two weeks, Lindsey got called for a day here and a day there at different offices at the university, but Gabby assured her she'd soon land a regular stint—maybe the medical center for a couple of weeks or the alumni office for a week. Gabby herself finally landed a long-term assignment at the Dayani Center, the university's health and fitness center, so she treated Lindsey and J. J. to take-out barbecue and a half-gallon of chocolate ice cream to celebrate the two-week anniversary of Lindsey's arrival in Nashville.

And so it was that Lindsey began a cycle of working on her songs . . .

> I've been looking for tomorrow,
> But I'm lost in yesterday.

Answering phones. Working on her songs.

> I can't get caught in what used to be—
> I don't do memories.

Filing papers. Working on her songs.

> Memories that never were
> Sometimes never die.

She and Gabby, giddy and silly in the wee hours one morning, even put their heads together and wrote,

> You got your dog,
> You got your truck,
> You got your guns,
> I wish you luck.
> You got the girls down at the bar
> You got your horse, your old guitar.
> You've got the things that make you free—
> I'll just leave you a picture of me.

In early October, Gabby took her to join the Nashville Songwriters Association on West End and introduced her around. "Best hundred bucks you ever spent," she told Lindsey as they were leaving. "You'll see."

"Good Lord, doesn't it ever get cool here?" she asked Gabby that night. They had both resorted to sleeping in the sitting room, where the tiny window air conditioner blew out a faint stream of cool air. "After Halloween," Gabby promised, but Lindsey realized it wasn't a guarantee.

In late October, Lindsey worked up her courage to call Nashville songwriter Ralph Murphy. She'd already been to one of his workshops, and she knew the songs he'd written for Ronnie Milsap and Crystal Gayle. It hadn't taken Lindsey long to learn that he was a friend to new songwriters. So while she had been raised not to ask favors, she was learning it didn't hurt to ask advice.

She dialed the number for ASCAP—the American Society of Composers, Authors, and Publishers—in their impressive, modern building on Music Square West. She asked for Ralph Murphy, and when a friendly masculine voice picked up, she said, "My name is Lindsey Briggs and I'm a songwriter."

————————

Gabby was amazed. "He saw you? Just like that? Wow. Now tell me what he looks like. What he said. What he asked."

"He asked me why I want to write songs."

"And you said?"

"That I couldn't *not* write."

"And he said?"

"He asked me why I want to write *country* songs."

"And you said?"

"I said it was just in my blood, somehow."

"And?"

"He told me when I was sure I was ready, to come back with a few songs.

"So head back now," Gabby said.

"No. If he's willing to help me, then I'm not going back until they're the best I can make them."

Madge Butters announced to the folks who always came to Butters' Corner Store for the popovers on Wednesdays that Lindsey Briggs—in her most recent letter to Sarah—had said they were still using air conditioning in Tennessee in late October. "And we've already had snow," Madge said. "Anyway, Lindsey's working at a university—there was a picture of it in the letter, and it looks real nice."

"Ayuh," someone said, "told you she'd end up at a college or somethin'."

"She hasn't *ended* up there." Madge lifted her cane slightly as if to point somewhere. "She's just working there to feed herself while she gets on her feet with her singing and writing. She's already in a little band."

"Well," someone who was about half Madge's age said as he popped a butter-filled popover into his mouth, "I doubt I'll live to see the day that girl makes a living writin' and singin'."

"Ayuh," Madge said. "You keep eating like that and you may not live to see it. But I plan to."

"What else did Lindsey have to say?" Albert Tikander asked as he waited for his coffee to cool.

"She told Sarah to tell me I should start selling Moon Pies—whatever they are."

"Well," someone said, "still don't know why that girl is so bent on being a songwriter."

"Yeah, well, I asked her that the day before she left." Madge stood up, put down her cane to lift the lid to the pickle jar, and fished out a pickled egg. "Her answer made sense to me." She put the lid back on the jar and picked up her cane again.

"Well, what was it?" Albert asked, still waiting for his coffee to cool.

"Because she had to."

Throughout October and November, Gabby, Lindsey, and J. J. performed at every open-mike opportunity there was in Nashville. They got to know other fledgling songwriters and performers. They even sang at open-mike night at the Bluebird Café, which added fuel to Lindsey's dream of singing there on one of the Sunday writer's nights. When they couldn't play somewhere, they went to listen. And since word travels fast in Nashville, they were asked on two occasions to sit in with other bands.

They had yet to book a paying gig. Lindsey and Gabby lived on off-brand macaroni and cheese dinners, pasta, and day-old bread with peanut butter and jelly. Gabby sometimes grilled peanut-butter-and-banana sandwiches in honor of Elvis. And Lindsey introduced Gabby to peanut-butter-and-pickle, peanut-butter-and-onion, and peanut-butter-and-olive sandwiches.

Lindsey needed to save money for a demo of her songs; at about four hundred dollars a song, it wasn't going to be cheap. So she found a second job waiting tables at the Calypso Café—the day shift on weekends—taking orders for black beans and rice and coconut corn muffins from young professionals and Vanderbilt students and finding herself thankful for the occasional free meal.

She was even more thankful when Gabby lined up two paying gigs on the Friday and Saturday nights after Thanksgiving at the Hot Biscuit in Sugar Creek, Arkansas, and Gabby's mom insisted they come for Thanksgiving dinner. Everyone gorged themselves on the wild turkeys Gabby's dad had shot. Lindsey ate three helpings of corn bread dressing and two pieces of pecan pie.

After dinner, the whole family sang deep into the night, and Gabby's mom and dad played mountain dulcimers. And on Friday and Saturday, Lindsey and J. J. and Gabby played to a full house at the Hot Biscuit.

"Wanna drive by Graceland?" Gabby asked as they crossed the bridge into Memphis on their way back to Nashville on Sunday afternoon. "My mom has been there thirty-two times, and I've been there six."

"More like twelve," J. J. mumbled from the backseat of Lindsey's car.

"No thanks," Lindsay said. "I like to remember Elvis before . . ." She let her sentence finish itself.

"Or," Gabby said, "we could try to find out where Ben McBride lives— even though you had your chance to meet him and blew it."

Gabby was referring to the time Lindsey had gone to see Ben McBride at the Grand Ole Opry after his induction into the Country Music Hall of Fame. Lindsey had wanted to speak to him, to ask if he remembered her grandfather. But it had been impossible. If Gabby hadn't stayed at home sick that night, she would no doubt have finagled a way to get backstage. As it was, Lindsey had inched her way out of the crowd and gone home.

"But on the other hand," Gabby said, not waiting for Lindsey to respond, "my mom has tried to find his house. He's on some dusty gravel road someplace out in the country near a place called Nankipoo or something like that."

"You mean like in the *Mikado*?"

Gabby's blank look made Lindsey realize that, as full of information as Gabby was about most things, she hadn't had the benefit of a great-aunt who directed Gilbert and Sullivan. Not that it mattered when the goal was locating Ben McBride—which might be actually possible, with Gabby's help.

What the heck, let's give it a try, Lindsey was about to say even though it made her feel like she was back in junior high.

"Come on, you two," J. J. said. "If Gabby's mom couldn't find him, then you two sure as shootin' can't. I expect her to find Elvis any day now—wherever he's hiding out."

Lindsey sighed. "You're right." She glanced into the rearview mirror, looking for a break in traffic so she could change lanes. "Just don't let me miss the signs to Nashville, or we'll end up in Mississippi."

It was just after Thanksgiving that they found the lead guitar they'd been looking for—Billy Earl Elliott, who called himself William when he played classical guitar at Vanderbilt. His wife, Trisha, was a high school teacher who made homemade soup and homemade bread for the band members of Sugar Creek at least once a week.

And for the first time in her life, Lindsey did not spend Christmas on Eden's Ridge. Sugar Creek had five gigs lined up for the holidays—something they couldn't afford to pass up. She promised her grandmother that she would get up for a visit soon, but even she didn't know when *soon* would be. Bit by bit, Sugar Creek was finding small gigs in and around Nashville, pooling money both to buy gas and to pay for five hundred copies of their first CD—which they sold to the small but appreciative audiences who came to hear them. They were saving their CD proceeds for a dependable van to replace J. J.'s ailing Volkswagen bus, and as they continued to work their day jobs, they kept reminding each other that many of the country greats had lived close to the bone for years before their breaks came.

"You gotta pay Peter Piper," J. J. explained as they headed south on I-24 for a Saturday night show at a small café outside Chattanooga. Billy Earl was beside him in the front seat of the VW, and Gabby was curled up between Trisha and Lindsey in the back. "It's exposure plus ten percent of the cover, and we get to sell our CD. They serve good barbecue, too," he added, "and my cousin's living room floor comes at no charge."

"We know," Lindsey and Gabby said in sync. "Them that do without will know better what to do with it when they get it."

"And . . ." J. J. added, circling his finger over the map of Chattanooga taped to the dashboard, "Chattanooga is home to the greatest breakfast food, snack food, and dessert ever—the Moon Pie." He smiled at Gabby. "I was waiting to surprise you with that bit of info. Maybe it will take your mind off the heater not working too good."

At least it wasn't snowing, Lindsey thought. She only knew Februarys with two-foot snowfalls and temperatures that didn't climb above zero for days. Gabby, still complaining about the cold, refused to wear a hat or gloves. She sat huddled in the backseat, a blanket wrapped around her head.

"Wake me when we get to Lookout Mountain," she said, "but only if there's hot coffee nearby. And Moon Pies."

At Butters' Corner Store, folks ate their hot cereal or eggs and home fries—and heard Madge Butters report that flowers were already in bloom in Nashville. "Good thing, too," Madge said, spooning brown sugar on her oatmeal. "Lindsey says folks there don't know how to dress for the cold. And can't drive in it too good either."

"She gettin' famous yet?" Albert Tikander asked, waiting for his oatmeal and coffee to cool.

"Well, they did play recently in Chattanooga," Madge answered. "And they sell their records—or what's that called now—a DC? And Sarah said Lindsey was all excited about seeing Naomi Judd at a Krispy Kreme Donut Shop. Saw Garth Brooks at a red light. And such as that."

"I'd sure like to be in Tennessee about this time of year," someone said, looking out at the eight-foot mounds of snow thrown up by the snowplow.

"Now I don't know 'bout that," Madge said. "They got tornadoes down there. I'd take a blizzard any day. Besides, if it don't get down to freezing every night this time of year, we won't get sap from our maples."

"Ayuh," one of the old-timers said as he poured maple syrup on his pancakes.

Spring had indeed come earlier than Lindsey thought was possible. By the first week of March, Nashville was awash with forsythia—"yellow bells, we call them back home," Gabby said. Tulips, crocus, and daffodils were color-coordinated in manicured beds throughout Nashville. Green leaves, greener grass, blue days with white clouds—all of that interspersed with thunderstorms that at night shook their apartment, jarring Lindsey from her sleep. She would sit up in her bed, frightened yet fascinated as she watched the lightning zigzag across the dark sky, making it seem for a split second like day itself.

By June, Lindsey was moaning about the heat. "It's perception," J. J. said as they packed up for a gig in Murfreesboro. "Think about how ninety-two degrees is not even body temperature. Works for me."

"Perspective," Gabby chimed in. "When we were kids, we'd sleep over at my grandma's house, Mama Lula's, on her screened-in porch in nothing but our underwear. Well, Mama Lula just got an air conditioner three years ago. Guess where all the kids still want to sleep? You'll get used to it."

As the unforgiving swelter of July enveloped Nashville, their rebuilt air conditioner quit. Gabby and J. J.—in a time-honored tradition—timed how long it took to fry an egg on the metal steps, and sometimes J. J. brought home a bucket of ice to set in front of their fans the way they did at NFL games. Lindsey and Gabby drank gallons of sun-brewed iced tea, and their tongues were a permanent orange from all the Popsicles they ate. And Lindsey, waiting to get used to the heat, grew to appreciate the steady hum of the fan that kept the air moving in her bedroom. At the beginning of August, a check arrived from Sarah Frost. "If you don't go out and buy a better air conditioner, I am going to disinherit you."

That autumn, on the one-year anniversary of Lindsey's coming to Tennessee, the water pump went out in Lindsey's car and the battery died in J. J's van—on the way back from their two-night stint in a little bar out-side Gatlinburg. The next week, Gabby's car flat-out kicked the bucket, as she put it, so she sold it to the same junkyard where J. J. scouted for spare parts for his ailing van. Gabby took a second job at Bookstar, and on nights when they weren't playing someplace, Lindsey put in as many hours as she could get at Calypso after a day at Vanderbilt and put away a little extra money for a plane ticket to Maine. This year Sugar Creek had gigs *after* the holidays, and Lindsey was counting the days until she could go home for a week at Christmas.

"At least we aren't in chickens," J. J. said one night as they polished off yet another carry-out, coupon-special pizza.

December came with a sky the color of lead. Lindsey marked the days on the calendar on the kitchen wall, counting down to December 22, when she'd be flying to Maine. Fifteen months since she'd been home. No wonder she was homesick. She couldn't wait to see Uncle Max and Aunt Priscilla and her cousins who always came up from Boston at Christmas. She and her cousins would ice skate on the pond the way they had as children. They'd probably do some cross-country skiing through the orchard. They'd feast on turkey midafternoon on Christmas day—but since the holiday fell on a Saturday, Lindsey knew her grand-mother would also have brown bread and franks later that evening. Her mouth watered at the thought of a piece of mincemeat pie at the Corner Store. And she and some of her classmates had planned a sledding party and a moonlight wiener roast to usher in the millenium. Most of all she'd be with her grandmother. She couldn't wait.

But she'd have to. She woke to a telephone call from her grandmother on the morning she was to leave. The sun shone through Lindsey's window as her grandmother said the snow was so heavy they had closed the airport in Portland, so Lindsey would have to catch a ride from Boston with her Uncle Max. Then Sarah called two hours later to say that Boston's Logan Airport was closed, too, and all flights that day had been canceled. After hours of waiting at the airport and calling airlines, the first flight Lindsey could rebook was for the day she had to come home.

Once again, she had missed Christmas up on Eden's Ridge. Her grandmother's assurance that she was fine—Uncle Max and his family had been delayed a day, but all of them made it except for the Seattle cousins—helped somewhat. At least her grandmother wasn't alone. But with Gabby and J. J. in Arkansas, and Billy Earl and Trisha in Georgia, Lindsey *was*.

Lindsey, dejected, sat on her bed and thumbed through the folders of her songs. *Twelve finished ones.* Some had gotten good responses from open-mike performances. A few people requested them when the band played in familiar spots. She remembered what she had sung at the Antioch Bar and Grill, Douglas Corner Café, and the French Quarter. They had been fine-tuned and polished at critiquing sessions and workshops. She had read and reread Ralph Murphy's *Laws of Songwriting,* and now she was pulling a few of the best to send to him.

Then she moaned in frustration and fell back on her bed. She knew that many hopefuls came, stayed a year or two, and then gave up. Now she understood why. But even as discouraged and alone and homesick as she was—Lord, she was homesick—she did not intend to be one of those who came and went. She was in this for the long haul. Sugar Creek was in it for the long haul—however long that was.

———————

Sunday night is "writer's night" at Nashville's famous Bluebird Café, which holds auditions four times a year for the first ninety songwriters who call on sign-up day. Now, if she passed the audition, she would get a spot to sing three songs on a Sunday night. The only catch was that only three people were allowed on stage—and Sugar Creek had four people. Billy Earl insisted he'd be the one to step aside. Gabby would play the fiddle, and J. J. bass or guitar, depending on the song. Lindsey could handle the rest of the guitar work.

Lindsey found auditioning for a Sunday slot nerve-racking—not at all the same as the open-mike nights they had played for occasionally—and it brought home to Lindsey how much competition there was on the country music scene. But Gabby seemed unfazed as usual. "Lord," she squealed on the drive back home, "we were damn-tootin' good and one man short. Imagine what the whole band could do."

And now the wait. It could be weeks before they'd know anything. Ages. Lindsey told Gabby not to think about it. Told herself not to think about it—she had other things to think about. For one thing, she was working on songs for the demo. And Sugar Creek was getting more and more engagements. There were even some fans who said they came out just to hear the band. Maybe things were looking up.

———————

It had rained, it seemed, for most of the month of February. And it had not been a good day. The coin machine at the Laundromat had taken their money. Then, when they got more change, the drier had overheated, scorching a load of clothes. On the way home, Lindsey's car had sputtered and stalled, leaving Gabby and Lindsey lugging a heavy load for four blocks in the biting, cold rain. When they finally got home, the key to their apartment broke in the door. They had to wait an hour in J. J.'s apartment for a locksmith.

The phone was ringing as they finally opened the door. "Maybe we should just not answer—considering our luck today," Lindsey said. Gabby, though, headed straight for it. Gabby would never *not* answer the phone, just as she would never *not* strike up a conversation with anyone she came in contact with—which was why Gabby knew everyone in Nashville, or so it seemed.

It would, of course, be for Gabby anyway. So Lindsey began unloading the wet and scorched clothes, laying them around the apartment to dry.

"It's for you," Gabby said, holding out the phone to her and looking wide-eyed. "And I think you'll want to talk to this person."

That was how Lindsey Briggs learned that she would be singing at a Sunday writer's night at the Bluebird Café. After screaming and jumping and hugging Gabby over and over, she called J. J. and Billy Earl and Trisha. Then she called her grandmother, who called Madge Butters.

"I knew it," Madge said. "If Forrest was alive, he'd tell you I said all along that girl was going to go places."

That night, Lindsey and J. J. and Billy Earl and Trisha went to Brown's Diner to celebrate. And as they waited for their chili, Gabby lifted her glass of beer.

"To Lindsey," she said.

"To Sugar Creek," Lindsey said.

They clinked their near-empty glasses together. Her eyes on the future, Lindsey Briggs had no idea she was about to collide with the past.

Four

Ben McBride pulled his midnight-blue pickup into the parking lot in front of the Bluebird Café. He turned off the engine, rolled down the window, and waited for Michael James, his lawyer, who shook his head every time he saw Ben's truck and said, "Ben, you could afford a Cadillac or Mercedes or even a Jaguar—and here you are driving a truck that's almost old enough to vote."

"Seems to me someone as old as I am should drive something old," Ben always said.

Michael's grandfather, Curly James, had played steel guitar with Ben for more than thirty years. So when Ben, about to retire, was finally convinced he needed a lawyer who'd give him the best legal and financial advice, he had chosen the boy who had sat on his knee as a child.

Ben had sold his house near Franklin ten years ago and gone back to his roots. Or close to them, anyway, buying a farm an hour from Memphis. "Ben McBride was raised in the city," the article in *Country Weekly* had said, "but was always a country boy at heart. Now he owns a hundred acres where he raises Black Angus cattle." The article had gone on to report that Ben had taken up bass fishing and wondered why he hadn't done that years ago.

All of which was true. In fact, this was Ben's first time back in Nashville since his induction into the Country Music Hall of Fame a year ago. Usually he had Michael come to his place outside of Memphis to discuss his legal affairs in between jaunts on the river. But this time, Ben had suddenly decided he would drive to Nashville. Visit a few old haunts as he waited for that magical time of year, the time when the mosquitoes aren't bad yet, the humidity hasn't found its way into the air, the river is still a little high—and the bass are off their nests and hungry.

Ben had driven the downtown streets earlier that day. Nothing much was the same. The old Ryman Auditorium was still there, but it had a new addition, and of course the Opry hadn't been there for a while. The new convention center with its green girders loomed over the street. Too modern for his taste. A Hard Rock Café over on Broadway. With hard-rock teens, country fans, and tourists in Wrangler jeans and cowboy boots all together on the streets, Nashville was a city with a split personality. Had been for years. The Athens of the South—as the city had long called itself, but also the home of the Grand Ole Opry. And now Nashville was also sleek and urban and home to the country music *industry.*

Tootsie's Orchid Lounge was still going strong. Gruhn Guitar, too. But so many places were no longer there—and so many of his friends were *no longer.* Red Foley, Carl Perkins, Jim Reeves, Webb Pierce. Patsy Cline, who once had been his warmup and who had died long before her time. His good, good friend Minnie Pearl, who had style enough to hide her style. And even Tammy Wynette—strong and fragile Tammy—whose voice was even more perfect because it was frayed.

Suddenly, sitting there in his truck in the parking lot, Ben McBride was profoundly lonesome. But then again, lonesome was a feeling he was accustomed to. Probably what led him to his music in the first place.

"Ben, you look like you're off in space."

Ben turned. A young man's face was framed by the window almost as if it were a painting. Green eyes, a mischievous smile, wavy black hair that curled at the nape of his neck. For a flash, Ben was back in another time and his steel guitar player Curly was grinning at him. But of course it was Curly's grandson, Michael.

"Hey, kid," Ben said as the young man opened the door and climbed in. Michael's dad and mother had turned away from the life on the road that both of their parents had lived. Still, it was their contacts that had helped their son Michael become a successful entertainment lawyer, working for some of the leading country musicians. Michael loved country music—a legacy from his granddad, Curly. But he wasn't country by any stretch. Even in casual dress, as he was now—slacks and a sweater with a striped collar peeking out—Michael looked "turned out."

Michael brought Ben up to date on his assets and on the trust he had established, noticing as he did so that Ben McBride was looking out the window, watching the cars go by on Hillsboro Road. Or else he was day-dreaming and not seeing the cars at all. When Michael finished, he put the papers in his briefcase. "I'll make those changes we talked about earlier and get the paperwork back to you."

Ben nodded nonchalantly. Michael sighed and shook his head at how little interest Ben McBride took in portfolios and profits. Just his music—and now his farm. Michael had heard all his life how his Grandpa Curly and Ben had started out on the road right after coming back from the war. "With nothing more than the clothes on our backs," they always said. Ben McBride and the Crooked River Boys had traveled from dusty town to dusty town, from honky-tonk to honky-tonk. It was a road they had stayed on for much of their lives. A road that had been their life. And not a road Michael—or his parents—had ever been tempted to take.

Yet, anytime he found himself in the company of Ben McBride, Michael James—a product of Webb School, Rhodes College, and Vanderbilt Law School—felt that he had missed out on something, even though he could not name what it was or why he felt that way. Maybe it had to do with the comfortable way Ben McBride still carried himself at his age. Maybe it came from hearing what a free spirit Ben McBride had always been. Or maybe it was his smile, which always seemed to carry a secret. A smile that to this day drew women to Ben—like flies to watermelon, as Michael's grandmother, Letha Jewel James, always put it, and that seemed to put men at their ease. There was just something about him, she often said. Michael had spent enough time with Ben to know it was true.

"Now that we've taken care of things, let's get a beer and listen to some of these young folks with big dreams—after I stretch these old legs a bit," Ben said, adjusting his worn brown Stetson and opening the truck door.

"Thought you'd have that girl of yours meeting us for supper—the one you told me just might become Mrs. Michael James. What's her name? I forget," Ben said as they walked across the parking lot.

"Brunhilda?" Michael asked with mischief in his eyes.

"She's your woman—you should know if that's her name or not," Ben replied as he tipped his hat to a motorist who had obviously recognized him and almost driven up onto the curb.

"Her name's Cynthia," Michael admitted. "She travels a lot with her job. In fact, I can only catch a bit of the show tonight because I have to pick her up at the airport. Promised her I would before you called me."

"You gonna marry her?" That was Ben for you, Michael thought, never one to beat around the bush.

"I honestly don't know, Ben. I thought I was. I think I am. She's a great woman. We have everything in common. Everything. We both like the same things—well, she's not crazy about country music, and my sense of humor kind of throws her, but . . . we basically want the same things. And she's beautiful."

"And do you love her?"

Michael kicked a paper cup on the pavement. "Yeah. Of course."

"Well, then, what's keeping you? You've said goodbye to your twenties—if I reckon right."

"I don't know." Michael bent down to pick up the cup and threw it in a nearby trash can. "I think maybe I'm too much like you."

"Now, what do you mean by that?" Ben asked, although he knew what Michael was getting at.

"Every time I think about asking her to marry me, I see another woman that I just *have* to meet. Maybe it's a case of the grass looking greener on the other lawn."

"*Pasture* is the term I think," Ben said, chuckling slightly at the fact that the pure country, hayseed-country, Curly James had a grandson who, in spite of his cowboy boots, was quintessentially urban. Ben was also amused at Michael's assumptions about him. Though over the years he had been linked with many women, he had been faithful during his brief marriage.

He shook his head. He wished he could tell Michael what he had learned about love. But he knew Michael would have to learn it—or not—on his own.

"Well, if she doesn't get your mind *off* other women, I suggest you don't ask her," Ben said. He turned around. "Now, let's go inside and see what the songwriters are coming up with nowadays."

As they neared the entrance, Michael saw Ben McBride's brown eyes light up in anticipation. Light up more than they ever had for woman or for bass.

The man simply loved music more than anyone Michael had ever known.

———

Sugar Creek—well three of them anyway—were on stage at the Bluebird for their Sunday night performance, their big chance. Lindsey had finished the first of her two songs and was adjusting her guitar strap when she noticed heads turning toward the entrance. She noticed, too, that the heads did not turn back toward her. She looked to see who had captured such attention.

Two men stood just behind the glass divider. The older gentleman, the taller one with the Stetson, waved to someone at the bar. He was shaking hands with the manager. Then he followed the younger man, who had found an empty table near the back of the room. It was then, just as Lindsey was about to introduce her third and last song, that she almost gasped. Almost said *Oh my God* aloud. Ben McBride!

Of course, he was not the same young, vibrant man who stood beside her grandfather in that picture or who smiled out from his album covers. But the *old* Ben McBride, whom she had only seen from a distance at the Opry, looked amazingly like the *young* Ben McBride in spite of the silver hair, leathered skin, and slightly rounded shoulders. He carried himself with a sense of ease, but ease was not what Lindsey was feeling. Ben McBride was going to hear her sing.

I can't breathe. This is not a fantasy. This is real. I think.

Suddenly she couldn't remember the opening words to the next song—even though she had written it. She had heard that such things happened to other singer-songwriters, but never to her. No, Lindsey Briggs had never been one to suffer stage fright before an audience. But Ben McBride had not been in any of those audiences.

She started to say something, but her mouth seemed paralyzed. So she turned her back to the audience and told Gabby and J. J. the key—as if they didn't know. Gabby rolled her eyes. Lindsey turned back to the audience, but still she felt short of breath.

To stall for time, she began tuning her guitar—which was totally in tune. *Remember to breathe properly when singing*, her Aunt Lily's words came back to her. Lindsey took a deep breath and let it out slowly. Finally, she felt her composure coming back. But not enough yet for her to sing—she knew she'd have to talk her way into the song.

"I've noticed Mr. Ben McBride is here tonight," she began. "Now, he doesn't know me, but he's been my idol since I was a small child, listening to his records for hours on end."

Somehow talking made her more relaxed, so she stopped tuning. "My great-aunt, a classical pianist, didn't take to country music. But . . ." Lindsey paused, resting her right arm on the curve of her guitar. ". . . there were lots of Ben McBride records at a café near my home." She leaned toward the microphone, and lowered her voice as if about to share a secret. "And my grandma was always sneaking country records into our house, especially those of Ben McBride. I was forever hooked—to my great-aunt's dismay."

The audience, visualizing such a situation, laughed, and that relaxed Lindsey even more. She knew she could sing now—but there was something else she wanted to say. "Besides, Mr. McBride was also my grandfather's friend." She was surprised that her eyes misted when she said that.

And Ben McBride, sitting at his table, felt his heart quickening. *What friend?* What *was* he hearing? Or *seeing?* Who was this young woman? Something about the set of her shoulders. What?

Lindsey nodded to Gabby and J. J. and said, "Here goes." The crowd responded with indulgent smiles at her nervousness. But when she began to sing, her voice felt rich and strong, and it transported everyone to the place she was singing about—especially Lindsey herself,

> Now I know you love this life
> Here in Middle Tennessee,
> But there's a place that I call home,
> I'd give the world if you could see.
> Just drive through Hadley's Curve,
> Then cross the narrow bridge,
> And you'll soon be climbing up to
> Eden's Ridge.

It was about that time that Lindsey looked over to Ben McBride's table. He looked as if he had seen a ghost.

———————

Lindsey finished the song and looked back at Gabby and J. J., who gave her a simultaneous thumbs-up. Then she turned around to see Ben McBride. He was looking at her, yet he seemed to be looking *through* her. He seemed to be clapping almost like a wind-up toy.

Michael James had not failed to notice Ben's response, and he had not failed to notice that this Lindsey Briggs was one of those women he just had to meet. He stopped clapping long enough to motion to her. It was a gesture that said *Come on over, Ben McBride wants to meet you.* And Ben McBride was not the only one at that table who wanted to meet her.

As Lindsey made her way to the table, Ben dropped his hands and stood there, looking dazed. His first words to her were, "Don't tell me your grandfather was Tad Frost."

"One and the same," Lindsey said as her mouth spread into a generous smile. She reached out to shake his hand. And now he recognized the likeness. The strong chin. The smile. The reaching out of the hand.

"And your name is?" Ben asked as he clasped her hand, obviously still stunned by this thing called coincidence.

"Lindsey Briggs."

"Briggs. You married?"

At that Lindsey laughed. "No, why do you ask?"

"But aren't you Max Frost's daughter? Tad's granddaughter? You look . . ." He paused.

She was taken aback that he remembered her uncle Max's name or that he even knew it. In the picture of Ben with Sarah and Tad, taken on Ben's one visit to Eden's Ridge, Sarah was pregnant with Max. Lindsey knew that Ben had not stayed in touch after that one visit.

But there had been postcards from Ben, saved in an old cigar box. Where were they now? Probably her parents had written him as well and told him about their baby. How could her grandmother Sarah have thought that Ben wouldn't remember Tad? After all these years he remembered the name of Tad's *son*.

"No, Max is my uncle. My mother was his little sister. She and my dad were killed in a car accident when I was a baby."

"I'm so sorry." Ben shook his head sadly and reached to touch Lindsey's shoulder with his big, gentle hand. Michael James, who had not taken his eyes off her, nodded in sympathy as well, but she wasn't looking at him.

"Thanks for saying so," she said to Ben.

Ben pulled out a chair for her in a manner as natural as breathing. A real gentleman—like she knew he'd be.

The next singer was getting set up on stage, and Lindsey knew that time for talking was about over. Ben pulled his chair closer and, just as she sat down, Michael put out his hand and flashed what some called his hundred-watt smile. He was about to introduce himself when Ben, suddenly realizing he had completely forgotten Michael was with him, shook his head as if to clear it. "Oh, I must have left my manners back in Memphis. This one that's gawking at you"—he nodded to Michael—"is Michael James. The grandson of my steel guitar player."

Lindsey looked into Michael's gray-green eyes and held out her hand as he sat down again across from her.

"But don't let this dressed-down look fool you," Ben said and leaned toward Lindsey as if to be giving a dire warning. "He's a suit. A lawyer to be exact. And," Ben added, "he's quite the ladies' man, so if you're not careful he'll be romancing you."

By then, Lindsey's and Michael's hands had made contact, and both of them could have beaned Ben for putting them on the spot. Before Michael could say anything, Lindsey pulled her hand away, shook her head, and laughed a soft, friendly laugh. "Sorry, but I've been down that road . . .

with a lawyer, I mean." Then she smiled at him and said, "No offense meant."

Michael James, seldom without a retort, was muddled as to how to answer. He should be offended, but he had long since become accustomed to lawyer jokes and jibes. Besides, this woman had a way of saying things without offense. Maybe it was the ready smile on those ample lips, or maybe it was the light in her brown eyes.

Michael had no chance to reply anyway, since Ben was already asking her about this place called Eden's Ridge—a place, Michael discerned, that Ben had obviously visited.

Ben and Michael had a beer, and Lindsey sipped on a Dr. Pepper, which she explained had become her favorite drink since meeting her Arkansas roommate. Ben asked questions—about Lindsey herself at first. Both Ben and Michael were impressed to hear she had gone to Harvard. Ben seemed even more impressed to hear that Harvard had not, as he put it, "got in the way of your dreams. And I gotta tell you," Ben added, "you can write, and you can sing with the best of them."

I've died and gone to country music heaven, Lindsey thought.

It was just as the music started again that Ben decided to ask what he had been afraid to ask, knowing what the answer all too often was when someone his age inquired of people in the past. So he had to lean over close and whisper it in her ear.

"And how is . . . everything, every . . . *one* on the Frost place?"

"Well, there's only my grandmother left," Lindsey whispered back. She'd no sooner said it than she noticed the color drain from Ben's face, and she realized he might have thought all these years that her grandfather was still alive.

"Grandpa Tad got killed in 1950, in a logging accident," she said—in a whisper—as tenderly as she could, since she was, in effect, breaking the news to him these many years later.

"Yes, I know," Ben said, sadness laced through his lowered voice.

She was about to ask him how he had known that, when he asked, "And Lily?"

"Aunt Lily died five years ago," Lindsey said, her whisper barely loud enough for Ben to hear. She was suddenly amazed at how long it had been when it seemed like yesterday. Then again, sometimes, it seemed like forever.

A shadow crossed Ben's face as if he were surprised that time had not stood still on Eden's Ridge. "And her husband, is he still alive?" He said it so low that Lindsey wasn't sure she had heard him right.

"Who?" Lindsey whispered back, confused.

"Lily's husband?"

"Aunt Lily didn't have a husband."

"You mean he died before she did," Ben said as if he needed to clarify her statement for her.

"No, I mean Aunt Lily never married," she said, whispering louder than she had meant to.

Lindsey might have noticed what was in Ben McBride's face, what was in his eyes. But at that moment, a customer at a nearby table looked over and shushed them. And too, Lindsey was—as much as she hated to admit it—somewhat distracted by this man, this Michael James, this lawyer who could have done a toothpaste commercial with that smile.

———————

It was midnight. Back at their apartment, Lindsey lay on the yellow-velvet couch, her feet propped across the headrest, savoring the memory of the evening. Michael James had excused himself soon after Gabby and J. J. joined them—had to pick up someone at the airport, he'd explained, seeming reluctant to leave. Ben, though, had stayed on and had insisted on treating Gabby, J. J., and Lindsey to cheeseburgers at Brown's Diner. "That place didn't become a landmark for cheeseburgers for nothing," he'd told them. Ben had laughed heartily as Gabby told entertaining stories about their temp jobs and their living conditions. And as they were leaving, Gabby had asked Ben to sign at least a dozen napkins for friends back in Sugar Creek. "My mom is going to faint dead away when she sees these," Gabby said.

In the kitchen, Gabby was prying open the jar of muscadine jelly her mother had made last fall. "Too bad it's too late to call home and tell them I met Ben McBride and that he thinks we're going to be famous," she said.

Lindsey shook her head and smiled at Gabby's interpretation. What Ben had actually said about the group's future was, "You can't keep a squirrel on the ground in tall timber."

"Wasn't going out with him just the greatest thing that's happened—besides getting to sing at the Bluebird?" Gabby said, dipping a sour pickle into the jelly and then licking it. "I bet you can't wait to call your Grandma Sarah and tell her Ben McBride remembered everybody after all these years. What do you think she'll say about that?"

"Will wonders never cease?" Lindsey said.

Gabby, thinking Lindsey was talking about pickles and jelly, said, "Don't knock it if you haven't tried it. Besides, you eat peanut-butter-and-pickle sandwiches."

"No," Lindsey said, ignoring the culinary remark, "Grandma Sarah will say, 'Will wonders never cease?'"

Gabby dipped the pickle into the jelly once again. "And," she said, drawing out the *and* with dramatic emphasis, "I did not fail to notice that Michael James sure had his radar fixed on you."

"Well, he can just unfix it," Lindsey said as she got up and joined Gabby in the kitchen.

"Good Lord, Lindsey, it's like pulling teeth to get you out on a date. All work and no play . . . don't you know who he is?"

"A lawyer," Lindsey said. She looked through the cupboards for something to nibble on. Why was she so hungry?

"Not just any lawyer. The lawyer to the stars. I can't believe you haven't heard about Michael James. He's in the top ten of the most-wanted list—

one of the ten most eligible bachelors in town. But that won't be for long, I guess. Word is, he's sort of engaged to be engaged, and darn that I missed out on his roaming years," Gabby said, making a sad face.

Lindsey pretended not to be interested in anything but her search for food—which was yielding scant results. A Moon Pie, slightly squashed, with bits of marshmallow and graham cracker crumbs breaking free of the chocolate coating. A handful of stale Fritos. She put them on the counter and opened the fridge to see what might be lurking in there.

"Everyone thought he'd settle on some big country star," Gabby said. "But she's a professional woman—and a dishy blonde, or so I hear."

"*We're* professional women," Lindsey said as she smelled the milk and decided to throw it out. "Our profession just doesn't require power dressing."

Gabby joined Lindsey at the refrigerator—or Frigidaire, as Gabby called it—reached around her, opened the tiny freezer door, and took out the rocky-road ice cream. "Even if he's been reeled in, I'd sure look back if Michael James looked at me the way he looked at you," she said as she dished the last of the ice cream into a bowl and crumbled the Fritos on top of it.

"Oh, you are exaggerating." Lindsey gave up on finding any food in the refrigerator. She vowed to reform their grocery habits as she reached for the Moon Pie before Gabby decided to eat that too.

When Lindsey called her grandmother the next morning to tell her she had met Ben McBride and he had indeed remembered them all, Sarah did not say, "Will wonders never cease?" Her exact words were, "I never thought for once he wouldn't remember." Lindsey did not remind her grandmother that was *not* what she had said when they were packing the car. Then Sarah Frost turned the subject to what a good year it was going to be for syrup. "Ayuh, these old sugar maples got lots of sap in them this year."

"I've got something else to tell you too," Lindsey said, delighted in the surprise she had in store for her grandmother. In fact, Lindsey had told Gabby that if hearing they had met Ben didn't rate a will-wonders-never-cease from Sarah, then hearing about their upcoming New England road trip—which Gabby insisted on calling a tour—*would*. Especially when she found out that Lindsey was going to stay on for a couple of weeks at the end.

"Sugar Creek has decided to take a road trip through New England. We're going to take a leave from our day jobs. We've got a little saved up, and we can camp out, crash with friends, crash with you when we're close enough by, and we might even make some money hawking our CD. And I've already told them I want some time off at the end to spend with you. Which will work great because Trisha and Billy Earl's baby will be due about the time we finish, and Gabby has to be a bridesmaid in a bunch of weddings, and J. J. says if he doesn't get some fishing in he's going to forget how."

But again, there was no wonders-never-ceasing from her grandmother. Instead Sarah Frost simply said, "It'll do you good to get home and get some real food for a change. Every time I call and get your roommate, she tells me what you live on. And tell me," Sarah Frost asked, "what exactly is a Moon Pie?"

——————

Two weeks later Lindsey, elated—to put it mildly—called her grand-mother to say Ben McBride had heard about their tour and done them a big favor. Sugar Creek had been in the midst of a practice session at Gabby and Lindsey's when a call came from the manager at Johnny D's, which Lindsey had had to explain to the rest of her band was just out-side of Boston, Massachusetts, right next to Cambridge, and was the happening place for country music in that area. It seemed there had been an unexpected cancellation just about the time the manager got a call from his old friend Ben McBride to say he should book the band Sugar Creek, which was heading his way soon. And he liked what he heard on the CD Ben sent, so could he possibly book them on a Tuesday night the last week in May?

Lindsey had to fight to keep her voice calm as she said, "I'll have to put you on with our manager." She covered the mouthpiece and in a whisper told J. J., Gabby, Billy Earl, and Trisha—who had taken charge of their bookings and books—what they had been offered. All five of them jumped up and down with more exuberance, Trisha reminded them later, than when she'd announced to Billy Earl in front of them all that the test strip was positive. All five of them banged the floor with their feet as if they were running in place. Then Lindsey composed herself and signaled for them to be quiet. Then she took her hand from the mouthpiece and handed the phone to Trisha, who said, "It seems they are free that night."

"I know Ben McBride has a reputation for helping others get started, but can you believe he did that for us?" Lindsey said when she talked to her grandmother. "I guess the CD we gave him that night at the Bluebird impressed him."

"Well, he always did have a big heart," her grandmother said.

"You can come to Boston to see us at Johnny D's too, and stay over at Uncle Max's."

"Ayuh, well, I'll probably just wait till you get up in our neck of the woods."

Lindsey hung up the phone. "If Johnny D's didn't do it, then I'd say we'll have to get on the Grand Ole Opry to get a will-wonders-never-cease from my grandmother," Lindsey said with a theatrical sigh, reaching for the last piece of pizza just as J. J. was eyeing it.

"Johnny D's. Who'd have ever thunk?"

The next week Lindsey got a letter from her grandmother that began, "Will wonders never cease?"

The wonder Sarah Frost was talking about was the vote at the town meeting that past Monday night. The town of Hadley's Curve had voted to purchase and restore the old opera house.

It had been a grand place in its prime. Aunt Lily had campaigned for years to have the town buy it from the owners, who were using it for a storage building. It had been her dream to bring it back to its original splendor, replicating the plush seats and thick velvet curtains and reviving the rich shine of the long curving banister that Lily remembered from her youth. The restored opera house could feature chamber music, plays, and musicals, still popular events of Maine summers.

Lindsey sat drinking tomato juice and read on. The voters also, by acclamation, had decided to rename the building the Lilian Frost Opera House. "It will, of course, take years of church suppers, auctions, and bake sales for us to begin to have the money for the renovations," Grandma Sarah wrote. "Still, we have put our minds to it. Just think how proud this would make Lily. The only sad thing is we didn't do this when she was alive and could have played there once again."

Later that day, Lindsey proudly called her grandmother to tell her that Sugar Creek had voted—*also* by acclamation—to do a benefit concert at Hadley's Curve. "It won't make a lot of money, but it will at least be a way I can do my part. And we're coming to New England anyway," Lindsey said.

"Tell that band of yours we'll see to it that they eat good," was all her grandmother said in reply.

Five

Two weeks later, Lindsey sat in a booth at Brown's Diner, waiting for Ben McBride. He had called the night before, saying he was coming to Nashville and would she indulge an old man by having supper with him. Lindsey had felt like a star-struck kid once again and couldn't help but gloat a bit as she told Gabby, "I'm *dining* with Ben McBride,"—saying *dining* with a playful pretentiousness since Ben had suggested Brown's.

It was one of the few nights that Sugar Creek wasn't practicing or playing. And since they were getting a few more paying engagements, J. J. had insisted that they splurge. "Everyone needs to go all-out every once in a while," he had said. To J. J., "all-out" meant dining at Logan's Roadhouse.

Lindsey had begged off, even though she felt guilty not inviting her friends to come with her to Brown's. She wanted time alone with Ben McBride, wanted a chance to hear about the grandfather she never knew. Everyone said she looked like Grandpa Tad. What had he been like—from Ben's perspective?

She had arrived, ordered a beer, and found herself watching the clock. And the door. *A watched pot never boils.* And, it seemed, a watched door never opened. An idea for a song.

She got out the small notebook she always kept with her and wrote, "watching a door that never opens." She tried to imagine the woman who would sing this song. *Works at a tavern maybe. Maybe two jobs. Maybe she's a hairdresser and keeps looking at the door to her beauty parlor. Maybe it's the door to her house. She's independent, this woman—but still she keeps looking at the door, waiting for someone.*

Lindsey wrote a few more lines and then looked at her watch—exactly the time for Ben McBride to be there. *There are three kinds of people,* she thought, *the ones who arrive early, the ones who arrive on time, and the ones who arrive late.* She had assumed Ben would be the "on time" type.

The door opened. In walked Gabby and J. J., followed by two of their musician friends. "Don't mind us," Gabby said, "but when you told us you were coming here, it made us hungry for their chili." She signaled to the other three to sit down in the booth behind Lindsey—which was, to be fair, the only empty booth. Still, Lindsey suspected Gabby would have chosen that one if the whole place had been deserted. "And don't pay us any mind," Gabby said, "we'll just sit here and pretend we don't know you."

Lindsey shook her head as if to say *honestly.* Gabby told her that Billy Earl had located a van for them to look at. "Billy Earl says its body is banged up, but it's in good condition otherwise. J. J. thinks he might have time to paint it before we leave for our tour." Gabby raised her voice a bit on the words *our tour* in hopes others might hear and be impressed.

"It's a road trip," J. J. said, trying to bring Gabby down to earth a bit. Seeing the look of concern that had appeared on Lindsey's face at the mention of his painting the van, he said, "Don't worry. I'll stick to purple, pink, and green." Then he added, as if in all seriousness, "And some orange and red flames on both sides for sure."

Lindsey shook her head and went back to her writing. When the waitress came to take her order, Lindsey said she'd wait a few more minutes. "Now quit bugging me," she said over her shoulder to Gabby and J. J. "I've got an idea for a song, and if I don't write it down now, I'll lose it." She returned to her notes about watching a door.

"Psst," Gabby said over her shoulder. "Don't look back toward the bar, but a certain Michael James has just bought a beer—I almost didn't recognize him in that getup—and now he's looking for someone."

Lindsey ignored Gabby and kept on writing, willing herself not to look up. After all, she wasn't back in junior high.

"And now," Gabby said, again in a loud whisper as though she were announcing a golf meet, "he's stopping to talk to some admirers at the bar. He's patting some pal on the back. He looks around again. He's heading this way. Play it cool. Pretend to be concentrating."

"I *am* concentrating," Lindsey muttered, keeping her head down so that Michael James, if indeed he were watching, would not see that they were talking.

"And now his radar is fixed on you," Gabby said.

Lindsey pretended not to hear Gabby and could only hope that Michael James had not heard her either. *Keep writing. Keep thinking about this woman at the beauty parlor.* She was into the second verse.

> I don't want to see you,
> Don't even need you,
> Don't even want you to call.
> So why do I keep watching that door?

And then she realized someone was standing over her. She looked down at cowboy boots, black with gold sunbursts. Her eyes slowly scanned up. Black jeans, hand-tooled leather belt with a longhorn silver buckle, black western shirt with its share of sequins, and atop the smiling face of Michael James was a Clint Black hat. Every item was obviously new. She bit her lip to stifle a laugh at what on some in Nashville might pass for natural garb but on Michael James was obviously a costume.

"Oh, hi," she said, sounding surprised and casual at the same time, as if Gabby had not been giving her a play-by-play of his movements.

"Now, if I remember correctly, you don't take kindly to lawyers, so I'm pretending not to be one," he said, grinning sheepishly. "Ben called and asked me to come here and tell you his truck broke down in Jackson—he tried to call you but no answer—so he's stuck there. He made me promise I'd buy you dinner," he added, obviously waiting for Lindsey to ask him to sit down. He held out his arms, showing off the outlandish outfit. "I even dressed for the occasion."

She lifted one eyebrow. "That's really not necessary. I'll just join my friends." She nodded toward the next booth.

"Why don't you *both* join us?" It was Gabby, looking over the back of the booth. "We can squeeze in and make room for you," she said to Michael.

I don't need him coming through that door,
Don't need that smile flashing at me.

Where in heck had that line come from? Lindsey shook her head in surrender, put her notebook in her pocket, and began gathering her things to slide into the booth with the others.

"It's going to be too crowded there. Why don't I just sit here with you?" Michael said, still standing by Lindsey's booth but nodding to the waitress that he was ready to order. "Besides, Ben would have my hide if I didn't treat you royally, considering he's stranded somewhere in that truck of his that I keep telling him to trade."

Thinking of Ben still driving a truck—and not a new one at that—brought a smile to Lindsey's face. Michael James evidently knew that particular smile meant she had acquiesced to his plea to buy her supper. He slid into the seat across from her.

"Well, you negotiated that move nicely." Gabby turned in her seat and put her head around the end of the booth. In a conspiratorial whisper she added to Michael, "But I gotta warn you before you get drawn in that Lindsey Briggs once left a lawyer standing at the altar."

"So that's the story," Michael said, turning to talk to Gabby—his back to Lindsey. "She mentioned she had a past with a lawyer, but she didn't give me the details. No wonder." And then he laughed as if he were picturing it himself. "I'll have to remember not to ask her to marry me." Then he turned, tilted his hat back slightly, and beamed his smile on Lindsey— who looked past him to Gabby.

"See if I *ever* tell you anything again," Lindsey said.

"Okay, okay, I won't say another word, I promise," Gabby said as she turned toward her friends. "Oh, look who just came in. Amilia and Celina from the fitness center." Gabby pointed to two women who were heading for a booth on the other end of the diner. "Come on, J. J., I've got to introduce you. They always say they want to meet someone who's put up with me since first grade. Come on, y'all," she said to the others at the table, "grab our water, and I'll ask the waitress to bring our chili there."

"Gabby never meets a stranger," Lindsey said, shaking her head in wonderment at her roommate.

"That's the Southerner in her," Michael said. "And what about you? You ever let a stranger become a friend?"

"Of course I do—Gabby and I used to be strangers. But I also take time for my old friends far away," she said, pointing to her backpack, which held some letters she had ready to mail.

"Except for the lawyer."

"Look, I know that was an insensitive remark I made at the Bluebird. It's just . . ."

"That you leave 'em standing at the altar?"

"I wish Gabby hadn't said that. He wasn't exactly standing at the altar. But almost. I'm not proud of it. He was a genuinely nice guy."

"So what happened? If that's not too personal a question."

Of course it was too personal, but something about Michael James made her want to be open with him. Made her want to tell him. "It's just that I realized—at the very last possible moment almost—that I have things I want to accomplish on my own. I don't want to get involved—and I certainly don't want to get married—for a long, long time. And when and if I do, it will be with someone I have a lot more in common with than I did with . . . Herschel."

"Herschel? Was that his name?" Michael said as took a large swallow of beer.

"Yes," Lindsey said. "Herschel Philip Bosley the Third."

Michael broke into laughter, spewing beer over the table, bits of foam hitting Lindsey. She found herself laughing almost convulsively along with him as she dabbed beads of beer from her sweater.

"I'm sorry," he said as their laughter subsided and he wiped the spilled beer from the table with a napkin, "but names like that give us lawyers our bad reputation. Though some might think the name *James* evokes the image of a smooth-talking thief."

"You talking about Jesse or you?" Lindsey asked, surprised to realize she was enjoying herself.

"Well, I was talkin' 'bout my ancestor, Jesse," Michael said in an exaggerated country accent, "but I sincerely hope I can smooth-talk you into letting me show you around Nashville."

"I've been here for a year and a half," Lindsey said.

"Still, I get the feeling you haven't had the time to really see our fair city and the surrounding environs—as we say."

She caught herself in midsmile. *Better stop this before it starts.*

"It's sweet . . . I mean, *kind* of you to offer, but I'm afraid I have to decline."

At that moment the waitress stopped at their table. Michael waited until they had both ordered chili before he said, "Can you give me a reason if you're going to shatter my ego like that?" He tilted his hat back even farther. Lindsey could have sworn his green eyes caught some reflecting light and twinkled.

"I can give you several," she said. And he waited for her to list them.

"Number one," she began, "I doubt that you and I have a thing in common.

"And number two." She held up two fingers to keep count. "I don't have time to get involved with *anyone*. Number three. If I *were* to see someone, then it wouldn't be a lawyer. It's not personal—we're just not on the same road.

"Number four," she added, "I'm making it a point not to date gorgeous men." That was a line she had grown accustomed to giving—a good way to turn a man down and boost his ego. Yet when she said it to Michael, she found herself slightly embarrassed, so she quickly held up her hand to indicate she had reached number five, the final point she wanted to make.

Inhaling more deeply than she had intended, she finished: "Number five. I don't date men who are already *taken*."

Michael James seemed caught off guard by her last reason. But it did not take him long to recover. "Rebuttal?"

"What?"

"May I give a rebuttal?"

"Be my guest," she said, holding out her hand as if to give him the floor.

"If you don't mind," he said, holding up four fingers, "I'll begin with number four—the gorgeous man line. It's very flattering." He looked down at his shirt. "But I'm throwing that out as frivolous evidence.

"And now to the others. May I point out that number five completely negates number three. To elaborate: Since I am *taken*—and by the way, I was going to tell you about Cynthia over our chili—then you won't be *seeing* a lawyer. We'd just be hanging out—as friends. Folks do that nowadays, you know. Don't you watch TV?"

Michael's voice became serious and sincere. "And frankly, I could use a friend to hang out with. Cynthia travels; she's gone more than half the time. Most of my men friends are married. Most of the women who are my friends are married. So it seems to me we are perfect for each other, especially since . . ." Michael held up two fingers to indicate a reference to her point number two. ". . . you won't have time to get involved with anyone for a long, long time. Probably until you are ancient."

Lindsey couldn't help but laugh, "Not until I'm at least thirty."

"So I won't be getting in the way of your getting involved if we should do something together during those rare moments when you've got some time and need to spend it not getting involved. In fact," Michael said, "it's a good idea for you to hang out with a *taken* lawyer just so you won't get involved until you really want to."

"You *are* certainly a lawyer," Lindsey said, shaking her head in fake dismay as she tried to get a handle on his convoluted reasoning, and as she found herself liking this zany Southern man more and more.

"Now number *one,* your supposition that we don't have a thing in common—I can't argue with that . . . yet." Michael took a swallow of his beer and set the glass on the table with determination. "But I know I sure like to hear you sing, and I like being with you. So what do you say?" He tilted his hat back so far, Lindsey thought it would fall off. A grin spread across his face. "Let's at least test out number one—we might find that we really can be good buddies. You name it, we'll do it."

Why not? she thought. Gabby and J. J. manage it. Besides, I like being around this man.

"Have you ever ridden a horse?" Lindsey said, suddenly feeling mischievous. "Not lately," Michael said warily, "but I do have a friend in Franklin who *has* horses. Does that count?"

"Well, no one should wear cowboy boots that doesn't ride horses."

"Then horses in Franklin it will be," Michael said, holding out his hand to seal the deal. Lindsey smiled. She really should tell Michael James that the price tag for his sequined shirt was still hanging from his collar. But for now, for some inexplicable reason, she was suddenly famished. The chili that the waitress had just put in front of them was sure going to taste good.

As for his part, Michael James felt amazingly happy in Lindsey Briggs's company. All that he could hope for was that she was not particularly adept with those four-legged creatures. He really didn't want to have to admit to her he'd never been on a horse in his life.

Ben McBride called from Jackson the next morning just as Lindsey was headed out the door. The first thing he did was apologize for standing her up. "But I have to tell you, I think Michael James paid someone to sabotage my truck so I'd have to buy a new one," Ben said, "or maybe that rascal did this so he could get you all to himself—and I've got my guesses which one of those it was."

Lindsey thanked him yet again for the favor he had done for her at Johnny D's. "All I did was pass along a tip on a good band and send the CD," he said. "Your talent got you in."

Lindsey changed the subject by telling Ben more about their plans for the upcoming New England road trip. "Trisha has already booked quite a few spots. Little places of course. We're staying with friends, camping out," Lindsey explained, "and we're really hoping our *new* van doesn't break down."

"Well, kiddo, prepare yourself for the worst. I've been there," Ben said, chuckling. "But the truth is, it'll be fun."

"The band's taking off three weeks after the tour so Billy Earl can be there when the baby comes and help out a while after. And I'm going to spend some much-needed time with my grandmother. Then, in July, we're doing a benefit concert in Hadley's Curve to raise money for the old opera house."

"What's this about the opera house?" Ben asked.

Lindsey told him about the town's vote and about their dreams for restoration—that they'd be using the new Lilian Frost Opera House for all kinds of community productions. "So Gabby came up with the idea for

Sugar Creek to do a benefit for them. Of course, I think it's a great idea, even though it will raise about enough for one velvet seat cushion," Lindsey said. "Still, it made my grandmother very happy, and Aunt Lily would have appreciated the irony that some of the money for the opera house will be coming from country music. Besides," she added wistfully, "it's something I can do."

Silence at the other end of the line. "Did we get disconnected?"

"No, just thinking," Ben said. "You know, I've got time on my hands. Fished out every lake in Tennessee, Arkansas, Mississippi, and Missouri. Frankly, I'm bored. If you think it would help, I could come up and join you—my way of honoring . . . an old friend. Might raise enough for two seats that way."

This time the silence was at the other end of the line.

"Lindsey-gal, you there?"

Oh my God. Am I hearing right? Ben McBride coming to Hadley's Curve for a concert—and all for his buddy, a wartime friend who had been dead over forty years? "Do you really mean it?" Lindsey asked.

Ben laughed that laugh of his. "Lindsey, one thing I can say about me. If I say it, I mean it. Now you just let me know the date, and I'll be there with my hat on and whatever band I can drag up out of the hills here. But before I forget why I called, I better tell you that I called my lawyer this morning—and by the way, I hear you have a date to ride horses. It's my guess that you'll leave that poor boy in the dust."

Before Lindsey could protest that it wasn't a *date,* Ben said, "Anyway, I told this lawyer of mine I want to record 'Eden's Ridge.' That is, if you like the idea. And if so, we'll need to get it registered with a publisher if you haven't already."

Lindsey's head began to swirl, and she would have sat down to keep from fainting if she hadn't already been sitting down. "Do you really mean it?" she said again.

Ben laughed. "You are a doubting soul," Ben said. "Come by it naturally, is my guess. But yes, I not only mean it, I mean to record it. Always said I'd recorded my last album. But when I heard that one, I knew I had to get back in the studio one more time and sing that one and a few others that have been rolling around in my head while I'm out fishin'. And maybe we could do a duet on the album. I've found one I'd like us to sing together. And we could throw some of my old band in with yours on it. We could even sing it at the concert."

Now I know I'm dreaming.

Before she could find any words, Ben told her what he'd be offering Sugar Creek to do one or two songs with him on the album, but she barely heard through the buzzing in her head. They would eat well for months. As soon as they hung up, Lindsey pressed the one preprogrammed number on her phone. Which of those mind-boggling bits of news would she tell first?

"Grandma Sarah," Lindsey shouted, her voice an octave higher with excitement, "you are never, ever, in all of your life going to believe this."

Six

L ate April, and already a summer heat had come to Middle Tennessee. Sugar Creek would be leaving for New England in one week—eight days to be exact. They'd do a couple of spots in western Massachusetts, one place in Connecticut, a tiny place in New York, several in both New Hampshire and Vermont before Johnny D's, and then they had numerous engagements in Maine, mostly along the coast from Portland to Bangor. Lindsey and Gabby sat on the metal landing outside Lindsey's bedroom, drinking Dr. Pepper floats and talking about the trip. Lindsey had already told Gabby that in Maine folks say *spider* instead of *skillet*, and that when a waitress asks if you drink your coffee *regular*, that means with cream. Milkshakes are basically what the name implies: flavored, shaken milk. If you want ice cream in yours, you have to ask for a frappe. And groceries are put in paper bags, never sacks. A baby is never cute; it's cunnin'. And on this warm evening in Nashville, Lindsey told Gabby that even though it'd be May when Sugar Creek got to Maine, there would still be the likelihood of a frost. Or even the rare May snow. "Poor man's fertilizer is what we call snow that comes after the grass has greened."

She explained to Gabby, whose folks had recently brought over early garden produce—English peas, radishes, and green onions—that folks in Maine often wait until the first full moon closest to Memorial Day to put in their gardens.

"At least mud season will be past when we get there," Lindsey said. "There are lots of back roads that have to be closed until then, including the road to Patch Mountain—close to our farm. But then about the first week of May the grass seems to turn green overnight, and it's the greenest green there is. So when we get there, the lilacs and apple trees will be in bloom, and the flowering crabapples," she told Gabby with the awe she always felt at that time of year in Maine, blackflies and all.

"Aaa-yay-uh," Gabby said, practicing the Maine talk that Lindsey had tried to teach her. "Can't wait to see it," she said. "And it's not long now. And of course the next time you get married, I'll be there too."

"Aren't you the funny one."

"But I bet this time you don't back out."

"What do you mean *this* time?"

"This time—with Michael," Gabby said, dipping her spoon into the float for some ice cream.

"What in the world are you talking about, Shannon Alene Nelson?"

"You and Michael. You'll end up getting hitched."

"We're just friends. I've told you that," Lindsey said in exasperation.

"Just-friends don't spend so much time together."

"Look who's talking. You and J. J. are like Siamese twins and have been—"

"But I'm talking about spending so much time with a just-friend when one of the just-friends is supposedly in love with someone else."

"Well, if you and J. J. let each other out of your shadow, you might find somebody. But Michael and I don't spend *that* much time together."

"Oh, no?" Gabby said. Before Lindsey could answer, even if she'd had anything to say, Gabby said, "I tell you what. Let's just replay these last few weeks." She made the move with her hands of someone filming. Then she made the "cut" motion.

"Cut to: Lindsey and Michael on their first outing. Lindsey floats on a galloping steed, followed by Michael, about to bounce off the horse."

Lindsey, trying to view Gabby's performance with disdain, couldn't help but chuckle as she remembered Michael hanging onto the saddle horn with both hands, hollering—in a bumping voice—to Lindsey, who was ahead of him, "I hope you realize I'm just hanging back so I won't show you up."

"Cut to: Lindsey and Michael at Brown's—why, there's a table there that might as well have your name on it."

"You *know* that Michael and I just get a quick bite to eat after our shows and, as I recall, I often beat you and J. J. home."

"Cut to: Lindsey and Michael at Mule Day in Columbia."

Lindsey looked down at her Mule Day T-shirt from that outing.

"Yeah, you sure did come home glowing, and I don't think it was because of the parade and the mule sale."

"The sun," Lindsey said.

"Yeah, sure," Gabby said.

"And now—can we have a drumroll, please? Last Friday night, Michael, our only groupie, can't take his eyes off you the whole time you're singing. Why, it was almost embarrassing just having to watch him all moon-eyed over you."

"He just likes *our* music," Lindsey protested, although she had been caught in Michael's gaze and found herself thinking, *Am I fooling myself?* . . .

"Yeah, well, tell that to someone who'll believe you," Gabby said, getting up to crawl through the window. "I've got to go try out my new hair color—dusty rose. But may I remind you, just-friends don't sit and pine when the other one is out with his fiancée."

"I am *not* pining," Lindsey said. But Gabby had gone into the bathroom by then and wasn't listening.

Lindsey sat there, telling herself that Gabby certainly had a fertile imagination. But she wouldn't have much to imagine for the next few days, anyway. Cynthia was home. Had been all week. And Lindsey had to admit she missed Michael. Good friends miss each other. Good friends share special times together. Lord, she was sounding like a Hallmark card. But last Friday night had certainly been . . . *special.*

They had come back to the apartment to a surprise birthday party for Lindsey that Gabby and J. J., with some help from Michael, had planned. The band and a few other friends had eaten chocolate cake and drunk good champagne—Michael's contribution.

Then, after everyone else had gone, Gabby and J. J. had sat on the floor playing Monopoly, while Lindsey and Michael took the last of the champagne outside on this same balcony. It had been a clear night, and she had named what few constellations were visible through the city glow of lights, explaining that her Aunt Lily had taught her all the constellations —"and much more."

"Tell me about the *much more,*" Michael asked, and she found herself talking about her music lessons, the Scrabble games. Aunt Lily had even taught Lindsey the ballroom dances of her youth. "She'd push back the furniture, put on the old phonograph, and suddenly our parlor was transformed into a huge ballroom . . ." Lindsey found herself talking on and on—maybe it was the champagne—and Michael hung, or so it seemed, on every word.

"Now it's your turn," she said.

"Some other time," he said. "This is your birthday. Your night." Through the open window they could hear J. J. complaining that Gabby was taking everything he had.

"Good thing they aren't playing strip poker," Michael said.

"Sshh, don't give her any ideas," Lindsey answered, putting her fingers to Michael's lips to quiet him. She must have left her fingers there only a second, but it was long enough to feel the warmth. Long enough to feel something move through her. *The electric force between any given charged particles is much stronger than the gravitational force—ten to the thirty-ninth.* Physics again! That's what she got for having such good physics teachers. Now she *needed* a strong gravitational force—to hold her back, to keep her grounded.

She left her fingers on his lips long enough for Michael to reach for her hand and hold it there. He closed his eyes as if to remember this moment. Then he opened them and smiled that mischievous grin. *And those green eyes, the color of the swamp that Gabby took me to last Thanksgiving.*

She wanted to lean into him, to move toward him, to bring her lips to his. *No, don't go there.* She pulled her hand away, "This champagne has made me a tad tipsy." She stood up. "Let's go in and see what Gabby and J. J. are up to."

But that had been last Friday night. Cynthia had come back Saturday and would be back for a while, Michael had said in what seemed a studied casual manner. Six days since she had seen him. So here she was, on a Thursday night, sitting on the landing again—but this time holding a half-empty Dr. Pepper float and sitting alone.

Probably for the best that Sugar Creek was leaving in eight days for New England.

No, *definitely* for the best.

Two nights later, Gabby and Lindsey lay sprawled out on the floor, having eaten all of an extra-large pizza—even though they had planned to save some of it for J. J. when he got home from tinkering with the "new" van at a friend's garage. Lindsey couldn't resist trying out a few lyrics about day-old pizza and day-old love. It was the kind of nonsensical writing that comes from too many hours of trying too hard and not knowing when to stop.

"No more music, no more writing," Gabby finally said. "We're out of here for a while. We're not staying home on our only free Saturday night in ages. Besides, we've got something to celebrate. We've taken all this next week off to get ready—and then New England, here we come."

They didn't even bother to comb their hair. And Gabby insisted that they each wear a Razorback T-shirt. She tossed Lindsey one from her collection:

1994 Arkansas Razorbacks National Champs, with a ferocious red razorback hog snarling under the lettering. It was nine-thirty when they drove into a parking lot off 12th Avenue. They locked the car doors and walked toward the Pub of Love. It was in a squat, nondescript building, but it had a group of regulars and a bartender who knew them all.

"Well, it looks like the upscale crowd is out in force," Gabby said, looking across the street at the Pub's chic neighbor, a restaurant and nightspot named after its location: 12th & Porter. "Wonder what group's playing there tonight? And where do people get all that money to blow on food and drinks?"

"Hey, speaking of Michael," Gabby said, even though no one was, "look!" She pointed across the street. He was standing outside. And the woman next to him had to be Cynthia.

"Well, whadaya know." Gabby poked Lindsey in the arm. "I think we are finally going to meet—ta-da—*the girlfriend.* Hey Michael, yo. Over here," Gabby yelled across the street.

But Michael didn't seem to hear, so Gabby let out a loud, Razorback yell, "WOOOOOOOOOOOOOO-eeeeee pig, Sooey."

Of course Michael heard that and turned. Everyone on the street heard that and turned. Lindsey's face also turned—as red as the razorback on her T-shirt. Michael peered hard and then broke into a delighted smile and waved. The tall, blonde woman in the tailored black pantsuit turned to see what the commotion was. She seemed slightly annoyed at the disturbance.

"C'mon, let's say hello," Gabby said, taking Lindsey by the hand and pulling her toward the street.

"No," Lindsey said, standing her ground, "you've said enough already." She gave a quick wave to Michael and then pulled Gabby toward the Pub, all the time looking at Michael from the corner of her eye.

Michael hesitated, his body seeming to lean as if he were going to walk across the street, until Cynthia took him by the arm and steered him inside the restaurant. She never looked back.

"Well, I wouldn't say she's a get-down, get-funky kind of girl, would you?" Gabby said as they ordered two beers at the bar. For Gabby it was a statement, not a question. "Nice clothes, though. I can't buy 'em, but I know 'em. Good hair, too. Bet she went to Vandy."

"Ole Miss," Lindsey corrected her. "Tennis team, Chi Omega, business major. Originally from Chattanooga—the right side of the tracks."

"You sure know a lot about her," Gabby said. She took a sip of her beer. Lindsey shrugged. "She is his girlfriend, after all."

Gabby reached for a handful of peanuts. "You know, I think this is the first time I've seen Michael in a suit. And that suit had to be at least a Brooks Brothers. I had almost forgotten he was a lawyer. My grandpa always said, 'You can take a lawyer out of a suit, but you can't take a suit out of a lawyer.'"

"Ayuh," Lindsey said, imitating her Maine grandmother, but somehow she didn't feel like keeping up the frivolity. She let the drone of the crowded bar replace the need for conversation.

———————

Later that night, Lindsey sat at the kitchen table working on the lyrics to the song she had begun at Brown's the night she had waited for Ben McBride. The night Michael had walked over to her booth in that cowboy costume and brandished his smile at her. The night he had convinced her they could "hang out."

> Don't want to see him anymore,
> So why do I keep watching the door?

She was still working on that same song. She needed two more lines.

> Don't need him for anything,
> So why do I hope that phone will ring?

She frowned and crossed out those lines. This obviously wasn't the night to write a song. She closed her notebook and slammed her pen on the table. She looked up at the Elvis clock. Twelve exactly. She turned on the kitchen radio, set to their favorite station. Reba was singing, "Till You Love Me." But that particular set of lyrics was just a little too close to home, and somehow too beautiful to listen to tonight. She turned off the radio and opened the notebook again. She heard a melody in her head.

"It's midnight and," she wrote. And what? The woman in this song can't sleep. The woman writing the song about the woman who can't sleep can't sleep either. She could hear Gabby's soft snore. She wished sleep came as easily to her. She looked up at the clock again and watched Elvis swinging his legs back and forth. She wondered what it would have been like to have seen him when he was young.

In the '50s, Gabby's mother saw Elvis singing from the flatbed of a truck on a football field in DeQueen, Arkansas. In the late '40s, Lindsey's grandmother met Ben McBride when he was still singing on the flatbeds of trucks as well, right before his career started to take off. When young Ben McBride paid that one visit to Maine, he had sat on the porch swing and sung for Sarah. "A private concert just for me and Tad," her grandmother had boasted recently as they made plans over the phone for the summer concert.

"Where was Aunt Lily?" Lindsey asked. "Oh, she had left on a date," her grandmother said.

"Who with?" Lindsey suddenly wanted to know. "I think it was Jim Ellingwood, but can't remember for sure. Lily had so many suitors back then."

But obviously, none of those suitors had suited her great-aunt Lily. Lindsey had never known either her grandmother or Lily to have something remotely akin to a date—even though there were certainly some eligible, elderly gentlemen in Hadley's Curve.

It would be good to get back to Hadley's Curve. Lindsey could not imagine *not* having Maine to go home to. Suddenly she wanted to call her grandmother just to hear her voice—but of course it was too late, and even later in Maine. She'd do that the first thing in the morning.

Just then the phone rang. She flinched as she always did at late-night phone calls—even though she had grown accustomed to Gabby's sister in Arkansas, who worked a late night shift, calling at any hour.

She was reaching for the phone when Gabby, not knowing Lindsey was still up, came tearing out of the bedroom. "You get it," Lindsey said. She stepped out of Gabby's way and headed for her bedroom.

"Well, well," she heard Gabby say, "if it isn't Charming Prince Michael." Lindsey's heart jumped. She stopped and turned around. She knew now she *had* hoped he would call. Had sat there waiting for his call just in case. In case what? Why wasn't he with Cynthia? Then she remembered something he had said a week ago about Cynthia taking a red-eye to somewhere this weekend. *He put her on the plane and then called me. Such gall.*

"Yes, you did wake me," Gabby said. "After all, it *is* after midnight. By the way, a funny thing happened on our way home from the Pub. Our coach turned into a pumpkin. Our coachman is gone too, but I did see a mouse scurry across the floor before I went to sleep. Did you by any chance find a glass slipper?" Gabby asked as she motioned furiously for Lindsey to come to the phone.

Lindsey shook her head no, put her hands to the side of her face, and closed her eyes—which meant for Gabby to tell him she was sleeping.

"She says she's sleeping," Gabby said. Lindsey threw up her hands in exasperation and went into her room, closing the door behind her.

She didn't hear the rest of what Gabby said to Michael, but it wasn't long before Gabby was in Lindsey's room, the clothes she had worn earlier that evening in her hand.

"Good going, Gab," Lindsey said, her voice heavy with irritation.

"I can tell that you two are going to drive me nuts," Gabby said, putting her Razorback T-shirt back on. "First he wakes me just as Alan Jackson was asking me to dance. Then you expect me to lie and say you're asleep when you're standing right in front of me."

"What did he say?" Lindsey asked as she unzipped her jeans.

"He said he was still hungry and wanted to know if you wanted to go for a donut. And that has made me hungry. Wanna go to Krispy Kreme?" Gabby said, stepping into her jeans.

Lindsey stepped *out* of her jeans. "Well, I guess that answers that," Gabby said. "Then I'm gonna go get J. J. to go out with me."

"Gabby, did you ever think that J. J. might not want you to wake him up anytime you take a notion?"

"No, I never did think that," Gabby said, an unfamiliar edge to her voice. "Just like I never did think that he shouldn't call me any time he wants to, and you know why? J. J. and I are *best* friends. And you and Michael are *just* friends," Gabby said as she turned and left the room.

And then she hollered as she headed out the door, "Or so y'all both tell yourselves."

———

Lindsey looked at the clock. Two-twenty-two in the morning, and she had not been asleep. Instead she lay there listening to distant thunder getting closer and closer. Gabby had called from Krispy Kreme at one-twelve to say not to worry about the coming thunderstorm because there were no tornado warnings. Gabby watched out for storms. And she watched out for friends—even when her friends were difficult.

And why was Lindsey being difficult? And why couldn't she sleep? And why had it upset her to see Michael, finally, with Cynthia? Certainly not because Cynthia was taller, blonder, and more beautiful than Lindsey had ever imagined. But she and Cynthia were not in competition, so that should not bother her. Still, the encounter—even from across the street—had left her unsettled. Michael's phone call had left her unsettled.

The thunder rolled in even closer now. She'd leave the windows open until the rain came. Too hot to close them. She might even let it rain in. She loved the smell of rain.

Another rumble of thunder. Then she heard something else. The strumming of a guitar—or rather the attempt at strumming a guitar. Who? What? At least she knew the *where*. It was outside her window.

Lindsey went to the window and looked out. Standing in the gravel driveway below was Michael, once again in the western costume, complete with cowboy boots and the Clint Black hat he'd had on that first night at Brown's. And making the most discordant sounds she had ever heard—on a beat-up guitar.

> Ain't got me a dog or a pickup truck,
> Don't like whiskey. Ain't it just my luck
> Not to hail from a holler in Tennessee?
> Oh Lord, I'm a country boy wannabe.

Lindsey couldn't help but break into laughter. *This is what I love about this man.* Even the casual use of the word *love* surprised her. And scared her.

Michael finished, flipped what must have been the world's cheapest guitar behind his back, and tipped his hat to her. *He is beyond tipsy.* Lindsey thought as Michael reached under the hedge and pulled out a green-and-white box of Krispy Kreme donuts. "Now, Rapunzel," he said, bowing, "I've come bearing a gift. And since your hair isn't long enough, may I please scale the trellis to your castle?" He pointed to the rusting metal fire escape folded up under the landing.

It took all her willpower not to make a sweeping gesture to bid him welcome. But she knew, somehow, this was a turning point. She knew she was headed for heartbreak if she invited him up.

She said in a loud whisper, "Go home, Michael James. You're going to wake the neighbors."

"That's exactly what I'm going to do if you don't beckon me to your tower. I'm going to stand here and play my gee-tar and sing loud enough to wake even your landlady." He placed the box of donuts back under the hedge and swung the guitar around from his back with a flourish—but it caught against the hedge.

Lindsey laughed. Then the first of the raindrops hit the landing. "Michael," she said, "go home before you get drenched."

But Michael James finally had his guitar back in place. "Now my next selection," he said, addressing the trees and bushes as if they were an audience, "is to honor the woman on the balcony who's going on tour in a week, going as far away as Maine." And again he began strumming and this time actually hit the chords right, if amateurishly, as he sang,

> From this valley they say you are going
> We will miss your bright eyes and sweet smile,
> For they say you are taking the sunshine,
> That has brightened our pathway awhile.

The rain was coming down steadily now. Then a jag of lightning lit up the sky.

"Michael! Go home before you get struck by lightning."

Michael stopped singing. He took off his guitar strap, reached for the donuts, and held them up to her. "Probably not too soggy to eat if I get them to dry land soon."

She was about to tell him to go home one more time when he leaned his guitar up against the bush and took off his hat. Flashes of lightning brightened the sky, and she saw the rain on his face. The hair on the nape of his head curled even more because of the rain. She saw his wide smile. And then the smile faded, "It suddenly dawned on me that my best pal is leaving for

Maine in a week. Can I come in and talk about that—and other things that have dawned on me?" He didn't seem the least bit tipsy now.

She closed her eyes. *Do you, Lindsey Briggs, know what you are about to do?* She motioned for him to go to the door. And then his playful tone was back. "No," he hollered through the loud rain. "Unlatch that screen," he said, indicating the window at their landing. "I didn't stand in the rain catching my death of pneumonia to go through a door. Let that ladder down. I'm scaling that wall and coming through your window—like any self-respecting cowboy would when he's on the run."

She unlatched the screen, released the hitch that held the fire escape, and watched it drop. Soon Michael was climbing up the metal ladder, a ruined guitar in one hand and a wet donut box under his arm.

"And what are you running from, cowboy?" she asked as he came through the window. Seeing how drenched he was, she didn't give him a chance to answer. "Stand right there," she ordered.

She rushed to the bathroom, grabbed towels, and rushed back. She handed one to him, put one on the puddle on the floor, used another to wipe off the guitar and the donut box. It dawned on her what they must look like—she in a T-shirt that reached almost to her knees, he in dripping cowboy garb. She waited for him to say something funny. He could always find something funny to say. But all he did was dab his hat with the towel—which was now sopping wet itself.

"You are crazy, Michael James," she said. "You've got to get out of those wet clothes. Take off those boots and go into the bathroom, and I'll find something for you to put on."

"I've got to warn you, I don't wear pink," he hollered from the bathroom as she looked for something that would fit him.

She tapped on the door, and when he opened it she turned her head so she wouldn't see him and handed him a black sweat shirt and sweat pants. "From our newly laundered selection," she said. "Lucky for you it was Gabby's turn to do J. J.'s laundry."

He opened the door and stood there, dry except for his hair. "I feel like the spy who came in from the cold. Or the rain, I guess."

"So you were a medieval prince, then a cowboy, and now you're a spy?" she asked as he followed her into the kitchen. She took the donuts from the soggy box and put them on a plate.

"Well, not really a spy. A detective. A private investigator dressed up as a cowboy."

She put the plate of donuts on the table and motioned for him to sit down.

"And what? The lady of the castle isn't eating?"

"The lady of the castle wants to go back to her chamber to sleep."

"Now that's where you slipped up, oh ye fairest of ladies. Thou didst not slumber."

"Oh didst I not? Pray thee, how canst thou know such things?" she asked as she sat down across from him. And it dawned on her she had never been this happy—dare she use the word *giddy?*—in the company of any other man. And it dawned on her, too, that she was playing with fire. Or lightning. She'd seen too many of her friends let their lives get sidetracked by a man. She had almost done that herself.

"Yonder light was shining." He pointed to her bedroom as he bit into a chocolate-covered donut.

She smiled slightly, shook her head, got up, opened the refrigerator—or the Frigidaire, as Gabby called it, or the icebox, as J. J. called it—and got out the milk. "You *are* crazy, Michael James," she said again as she poured a glass of milk and put it in front of him.

"Am I?" He took the milk with one hand, her hand with the other, and looked up at her. There was no playfulness in his voice now. The warmth from his hand moved up her arm, moved through her neck, moved to her head. She felt almost dizzy.

She fixed her gaze on the Elvis clock. She couldn't hear the ticking as Elvis's pelvis swung back and forth because of the pounding of the rain on the windows and on the roof and on the landing. Or maybe it was the pounding of her heart.

Michael held on to her hand and stood up. He tilted her chin with his other hand to force her to look at him. "Lindsey, was I crazy to come here tonight?"

"Yes," she said, finally looking straight on into his eyes. *And you, too, Lindsey*, she said to herself. *You've gone stark raving mad.*

And as he ran his hands through her hair and brought her face to his, she felt her heart flutter. Lord, what an old-fashioned word, but that was the word that fitted.

"You should go home, Michael," she said. "I know," he said. But there was no conviction in either voice. And when their lips met, a bolt of lightning seemed to light up all of Nashville, Tennessee.

"Oops," Gabby said as she stood in the doorway, taking in the situation. They had not even heard her coming up the stairs.

Lindsey quickly pulled away from Michael.

"I don't suppose you'd believe it if I told you she had something in her eye," Michael said.

Gabby obviously wasn't fooled. "I would have called to say I was coming home, but of course I didn't know you two were . . . and besides, I don't use the telephone when it's storming . . . in fact, J. J. and I have been sitting in the car and I thought the lightning had passed, or I would have stayed in the car because my cousin's cousin on my mother's side of the family got struck once when she ran from the car to the house. But don't mind me. I'm just going to dry off, grab a donut—can I have that pink one?—and I'll go down to J. J.'s so you two can . . . take care of Lindsey's eye. Or whatever."

"No," Lindsey said as Gabby headed into the bedroom to get into dry clothes. "Stay here. Michael was just leaving—weren't you, Michael?"

"If you say so," Michael said.

"I say so," she answered.

—————

Gabby must have sensed that this was not a night when any more talking should be done. She had gone straight to bed after Michael walked past her and out the door. And as Lindsey packed, she could hear the deep sleep in Gabby's breathing.

Lindsey would get a few hours sleep and then, she had just decided, she'd leave for Maine a week ahead of the rest of them. She'd fly standby with the frequent-flyer ticket her Uncle Max had sent as a way to help her out. Gabby and J. J. and Billy Earl would understand; they had even talked about her going early to be what J. J. called their "advance man." They didn't have any engagements until then, and she had not taken any jobs for the next week—so why wait? Gabby could explain to Michael. Or else Lindsey would leave a very light, casual message on his answering machine. *Hi, this is your old pal Lindsey, off to Maine. Be back when I get back. Have a good life. Have a good wife . . .*

Why was she so stewed up over Michael and Cynthia, anyway? It was just as well there was a Cynthia, even though it would have been easier on Lindsey's ego if she hadn't been quite so beautiful. With no Cynthia, she might have let down her guard, might have been vulnerable, might have succumbed to this man named Michael James.

But who was she kidding? She *was* vulnerable. And she had almost succumbed—no, she *had* succumbed. Thank goodness Gabby had come in when she did. Or so Lindsey told herself.

Seven

Lindsey had been in New England for six weeks. During that time
Sugar Creek had appeared at Johnny D's, and the Boston *Phoenix*
music critic had written that they were still a bit green but without doubt
a band to watch.

Sugar Creek had also been well received in their other New England
gigs—or "venues" as Gabby had taken to saying. The band had stayed with
Lindsey's grandmother on the Frost place whenever they were in range and
with Lindsey's Uncle Max when they were in the Boston area. Otherwise
they'd stayed in cheap hotels, bunked with a friend or two along the way,
and even tented out some. Then the band, except for Lindsey, had headed
back south.

J. J. and Gabby, after dropping Billy Earl off in Nashville to await the
birth of the baby, had continued on to Arkansas, where they had arranged
to play at the Hot Biscuit for a couple of weeks. And fish. And be in weddings. Then the two of them would return to Nashville, where they (and
Billy Earl if things went as planned) would ride to Maine in the luxury bus
Ben had hired for the occasion. Ben was paying for the trip up and for
what he called "other incidentals."

They'd be okay. Sugar Creek was on the rise—as J. J. liked to put it. "Nobody can keep us within our banks now," he'd add.

Lindsey, as planned, had stayed on at Eden's Ridge to help plan the Ben McBride concert coming up in three weeks. And also, she had to admit to herself, to ground herself again in the comfort of being *home*.

The apple blossoms that had perfumed the ridges and valleys in May had fallen now, turning the orchard grounds white, like snow almost. The blackflies, which make it unbearable to be in the woods or gardens except on days with a brisk breeze, had come and thankfully had gone. Sarah swore they always left on the twelfth of June.

Lindsey helped her grandmother with the annual spring-cleaning that always took place in June. Scrubbing and waxing the wood floors, beating the old rugs, washing the walls—in fact, washing anything that could be washed. She helped the young 4-H girl who took care of Fiddle give his stall a good mucking. She brushed out the last of Fiddle's winter coat and rode for hours, marveling at the view of the far ridges and the valley and of Lake Pennesseewassee below—the view she had grown up with and had been told often not to take for granted.

She also put in countless hours working with the Opera House Restoration and Renovation Committee—something she and her grandmother had taken to calling the R&R Gang—as they planned for the Ben McBride concert on July 8. Sarah had declined a spot on the committee, insisting she'd offer her opinion and home-baked cookies when she thought either was needed. Lindsey visited her paternal grandparents, old neighbors, childhood friends, childhood haunts. She spent a day helping Katy's mom shop for gifts to send to Katy in Japan—and picked up some tiny T-shirts with Maine insignias for Billy Earl and Trisha's newborn, Eli, who had thoughtfully made his appearance as soon as his daddy reached home. During all that—as busy as she had kept herself—she had somehow *not* managed to get Michael James from her mind.

Because getting him off her mind was her intention, she had not returned his many phone calls. *Why confuse the situation by talking about it?* At first, her grandmother had written brief messages: "A young man calling himself Michael James called." Or "Michael James called and asked you to call him back." Then her grandmother had taken to writing down longer messages word for word as Michael gave them to her: "Michael James would be overjoyed if Lindsey Briggs would deign to return at least one of his many phone calls." They progressed to, "Michael James is so distressed his buddy hasn't returned his calls that he's taken to writing country song lyrics."

Every time Lindsey returned home to find one of his messages scribbled on her grandmother's kitchen tablet, she felt her heart warming. She almost called him to tell him the truth—that she had felt herself drawing too close to him, so she had to pull away. But if she did so, she knew, Michael would give one of his famous rebuttals, cast his smile her way, spin his web around her. Another idea for a song,

> I love being with him
> But I really don't love him,
> Don't want to love him,
> I simply won't love him,
> So I'm not returning his calls.

"It just seems so rude that you haven't returned that young man's phone calls," Sarah said to her as they drove home from Hadley's Curve early in the afternoon. Lindsey didn't answer her grandmother, who had obviously fallen for Michael's charm. Not that it was a false charm. That's what was so charming about it.

It was a day that was not turning out as planned. Lindsey had decided to have a morning of leisure, sleeping late, maybe riding Fiddle. Then she'd spend the afternoon in town doing errands and stay on for the early evening R&R committee meeting. But her grandmother had suddenly booked a midmorning appointment with Carolyn to get her hair "fixed." And then decided she wasn't up to driving, so she'd asked Lindsey to drive her. She had tried but failed to talk Lindsey into getting her hair done as well.

When they left the beauty shop, Lindsey had suggested they stop in at Butters' and have lunch with Madge. But Sarah had looked at her watch and said no, she was too tired and needed to go home and lie down—after a quick stop at the store for milk and eggs. It was on the way home, seemingly out of nowhere, that Sarah had brought up the issue of Michael's phone calls.

"Oh, now you two are on a first-name basis," Lindsey said, not replying to her grandmother's concern for her lack of manners.

"Yes, well, we've talked enough now, considering you're never available." Sarah paused for a few moments, but Lindsey did not fill the silence with an answer. Then with a mock tone of confusion in her voice, Sarah said, "Now I know we've been over this, but I'm having a hard time getting it in my head." She patted her stiff pale blue hair with her fingers as if she were try-ing to organize information. "Help me get this straight. This young man is a wonderful friend, a wonderful friend—so you don't want to talk to him," she said. "Is that it?"

Lindsey took a breath of deep frustration and let it out. "It's not that I don't want to talk to him. It's just that I've got a long list of things to do. I'm meeting myself coming and going. Friends understand such things, and Michael and I *are* friends, but that is all we are. Just friends."

"It doesn't sound like 'just friends' to me. It doesn't even sound like friends at all—on your part. Friends return each other's calls."

"Grandma Sarah, I—"

But her grandmother was holding up two fingers, already embarking on one of her lists. "Lindsey, there are two reasons for not returning a friend's call, and being busy is not one of them."

As they drove up to the house, Lindsey waited for her grandmother's phi-losophy on this one. She must have gotten her own tendency for listing from Sarah, the ultimate list maker. Lindsey pulled the car to a stop and turned off the key.

"One reason not to return a personal call is if you simply don't like the person—and that is obviously not the case with this young man," Sarah said as she opened the door and got herself situated to get out. "So I'm to conclude it is the other reason," she added, as she pulled herself to a standing position.

"Which is?" Lindsey asked, getting out and reaching back in for their bag of groceries.

"That you *do* like him," Sarah said, grasping the step railing to climb to the porch, then ambling into the kitchen.

Lindsey, following her, shook her head as if her grandmother were definitely mistaken. "Now," Sarah said when they were in the kitchen, "I'll take care of the groceries, and you go sit on the porch and let me know if you see George and Ruth go by."

"Grandma Sarah," Lindsey said, trying not to sound exasperated, "George and Ruth go by every day at one. We can set our clocks by them." In fact, her Aunt Lily had been known to do just that. "Besides," Lindsey added, "I'm heading back to town to run those errands—just as soon as I help you with these groceries. I'll grab a burger at Butters'."

"No, that will just tire you out. I'll go in with you tomorrow and help with the errands. Let me fix you a good meal. Go sit on the porch."

It was not like her grandmother to interfere so much with Lindsey's schedule. Of the two women who raised her, Sarah had definitely been the less assertive one. But today she was being downright bossy. Come to think of it, her grandmother had been acting strange all day.

Right after breakfast, she had said, "Let's get this place picked up." Even though there was precious little out of place. Then Sarah had proceeded to make her way back up the stairs to, as she put it, "get the guest bedroom ready."

"Ben isn't coming for weeks, Grandma Sarah," Lindsey had said as she helped her grandmother put on clean sheets. "I'll make sure this room is ready by then."

"Well, I would like to go ahead and get it ready," her grandmother had said. "Would you mind vacuuming?"

So Lindsey had vacuumed, and then she had driven her grandmother into town for her hair appointment, and now—on Sarah's orders—she was sitting on the porch waiting for a lunch that was taking forever.

She was about to go inside and see what her grandmother was puttering with when Sarah stepped out on the porch, "Don't you want to wash up a bit, put on some different clothes—since you've got that meeting?"

Lindsey looked down at her cutoffs and at her puffin T-shirt from Butters' store to see if she had gotten something on them. No, they were clean. What had gotten into her grandmother? Lindsey looked back up to catch Sarah looking past her toward the road.

"Are you expecting someone?" Lindsey asked, thinking one of Grandma Sarah's bridge club friends might be dropping by.

"No," her grandma said, her face lighting up suddenly, "but a car just turned into our driveway. You stay here and see who it is. I've got some food to take care of." Sarah Frost turned and scurried back into the house like a mouse trying to find a place to hide.

Lindsey looked at a red Lexus crawling up the gravel driveway. Probably some New York tourist needing directions. She stepped down from the porch to save them the trouble of getting out. Then she felt a tremor pass through her. Michael.

She stood there frozen—even on a summer day—as Michael James braked to a stop and hopped out. Even though he had on jeans and a black T-shirt, he wiped the smile off his face and took on an official pose. "Ma'am, I'm from the telephone company, and it seems your phone is out of order. It only receives incoming calls."

It was all she could do not to run to Michael, put her arms around his neck, and hold on tight. Why didn't she? Instead, she stood her ground. "Michael, what in the world? . . ."

". . . am I doing here? Came to check on a buddy." He turned and looked around him. "So this is Eden's Ridge?" He looked over at the orchard, then across the road and down at the ribbon of lake in the valley. "That must be Penta-sa-what's-it."

"Pennesseewassee," she said, and finally smiled the way he always made her do.

"I can see now why you had to write songs about it—about all this."

She still couldn't believe he was there. Then the penny finally dropped. "Grandma Sarah knew you were coming, didn't she?"

He smiled playfully as he continued to look out over the valley. "Now, you'll have to ask her that." Then he looked into her eyes, and his smile faded. "Can we take a walk? Can we talk?"

They walked down to the pond, both of them avoiding any mention of the phone calls or the night she left. Michael asked questions about the tour, the upcoming concert, any songs she had written since he had seen her. "Ben says you two are going to sing a duet. I'd love to be there."

She found herself almost saying, *I'd love for you to be there.* She found herself almost saying, *why don't you just stay here for it?* Then she found herself almost saying, *you and Cynthia should come up for it.* But she said none of those things. Instead she reached down and picked up a small white stone and threw it across the field.

"Great arm."

"You should have seen my Aunt Lily throw a softball even when she was seventy," she said, smiling wistfully at a snapshot memory. They reached the pond, and she picked up a few more smooth, round stones to skip across the water. Soon they were in a contest for the most skips, and she almost forgot to remember that she had to stop having these times with him.

The last stone he threw seemed to skip forever. He rubbed his palms against each other to indicate he was quitting while he was ahead.

"And now, Ms. Briggs, it's time for you to explain why you've been avoiding me."

"I'm not avoiding you," she said, looking out over the pond, avoiding his eyes. *You're avoiding falling in love with him, Lindsey Briggs. Don't forget that.*

"Yeah, well tell that to someone whose brains wouldn't fill a thimble, as my Grandma Letha Jewel would say," he said, following her gaze across the pond, without a hint of the usual playfulness in his voice. "You left over a week early, didn't even say goodbye."

"It was a sudden decision," she said, still keeping her eyes on the water.

"Was it my singing?" he asked. And she knew not to look at him because he'd have that sly smile on his face. Still, she couldn't help but laugh.

"You could have called before you left." This time there was no smile in his voice.

She didn't answer.

"And you could have returned my calls," he said, adding to his list of complaints.

"Yes, I could have. And Cynthia could have answered, and what would I have said? Do you realize, Michael, that we never once talked about how Cynthia feels about us? Even though there is no *us*, except that we somehow ended up spending so much time together."

"And why do you think that is?" Michael asked. The man can ask more questions than a four-year-old.

"Why do I think *what* is—that we've never talked about how Cynthia feels? Or that we somehow found ourselves spending a lot of time together?" She would put the question right back to him if that's how he wanted to be. Besides, that way she didn't have to think about the answer. Whatever it was.

"Either. Both," he said.

"You tell me."

His eyes seem to stay on her eyes forever. Then finally he looked away, looked up toward the orchard and said, "Okay, I will. After all, I didn't come all this way just to skip stones." He took a deep breath, then let it out.

"Cynthia has always known I spend time with you—with the band. She knows I love your music. But to be honest, the more time we spent together, the less I brought it up to Cynthia. She's not particularly interested in country music. Sees it, amusingly, as one of my idiosyncrasies. And the other question—how did you and I find ourselves spending so much time together? I told myself it was exactly as I had laid it out. You don't want to be involved. And I am involved with Cynthia. And she's great, of course.

"But then you and I have such fun doing a simple thing like eating at Brown's. And it's just so . . . relaxing after a long day to go hear you sing and then drive you home—and be entertained with the latest episode of *Life with Gabby.* Or I found myself wanting to hear more of your stories about growing up on Eden's Ridge. You grew up without parents, and still the stories of your childhood comfort me. That's really something." Michael paused, waiting for her to comment, but for a moment Lindsey couldn't think of anything to say. "So," he continued, "it was fun, relaxing, entertaining. Comforting. That's what I told myself. Then that night, after I saw you and Gabby outside 12th & Porter—Cynthia and I had been shopping for a . . . ring."

"You . . . you what?" Lindsey sputtered. "You go shopping for a ring, take her out to dinner, give her the ring, put her on a red-eye to wherever, and then come over to my house and try to seduce me?"

"No! You're all wrong—that's not the way it was. I mean, it's the way it sounds, but—"

"You mean you didn't buy her the ring? You didn't give her the ring? Or you didn't put her on the plane? Or you didn't try to seduce me?" Tears of both hurt and anger welled in her eyes, and she turned away, unwilling to let him see her cry.

"I mean that if you'll just listen long enough for me to tell you—"

"Michael, I don't need you to tell me anything. You don't owe me an explanation." And even as she said it, Lindsey asked herself why people said that when they didn't mean it. He had come this far, and there must be a reason for that too. And that scared her. She did not want him to love her, did not want to hear him say he did because she did not want to love him. She *would not* love him.

Even though she might already love him.

"Lindsey," Michael said quietly, "I'll get in my car right now if you'll look me in the eye and tell me that it meant nothing to you."

"That *what* meant nothing to me?" *Why am I playing dumb?*

"You know exactly what I'm talking about, Lindsey Briggs—I'm talking about what happened between us."

"Nothing happened between us." *Another lie.* "There is no us, Michael. We're just friends who got carried away. Sometimes that happens. You and Cynthia are an *us.*"

"Lindsey," he took her by the shoulder and turned her to him. She felt her knees grow weak. *Don't betray yourself. Don't fall into the arms of this man. Your dreams are within reach. There's no such thing as once-in-a-lifetime love. You've always known that. Don't forget it now. There will be another man, another Michael.*

"Look at me and tell me that all I am to you is a friend."

Why was he doing this to her? It took all her strength to find the right tone, a forced calm, as she looked at him straight on and said—in the same gentle tone, she recognized, as the one she had used to tell Herschel she wasn't marrying him. "Michael, that *is* what you are to me—a friend. A valued friend. But nothing more." Once again she turned and looked into the woods.

"And what if I told you Cynthia and I are no longer together? What if I told you? . . ."

Don't fall. Don't succumb. Don't give in to these feelings. Send him away. In a month—at least in a year—you'll be glad you did. And with her last bit of resolve she swirled around to face him. "Michael, I know my grandmother invited you here. I know you came a long way, but I need you to leave." Somehow she managed to say every word and not look away—all the while, willing the tears not to come.

She watched him walk back toward the house, get into his car, and drive away, heading to Nashville. To Cynthia, for sure. Spurned men always go back to the other woman. He'd do that now, even if he had had second thoughts before. She managed, somehow, not to run after him and tell him she would take what he had come to offer, whatever it was.

Back in her front yard, her voice choked with tears as she called to her grandmother through the kitchen window, "I just remembered I've got an appointment in fifteen minutes."

She got into the car and drove out too fast for Sarah to come to the porch. She turned right, drove the length of Eden's Ridge, turned left, and followed the road down the hill toward Hadley's Curve. Halfway down the hill, she pulled in at the old Congregational church—where nearly two years ago, she had made her most fateful decision.

The front door was locked, but she knew where they hung the key to get in the back way—she suspected 'most everyone knew where the key was. She took it from its prominent hiding place, went inside, and sat there on the front pew. Sat there for most of the afternoon, tears streaming down her face. Conversations echoing in her head. Snatches of songs flitting through her memory. But one kept coming back, and finally she sang it, her voice first shaky and tearful, then stronger, bouncing off the church walls. It was the old Shaker hymn she had learned as a child.

> 'Tis the gift to be simple, 'tis the gift to be free,
> 'Tis the gift to come down where we ought to be. . . .

When the song was over, she gathered herself together and drove into town for her meeting.

When Lindsey came home in the fading light of day, Sarah Frost had finished her supper and was sitting on her porch rocker. In her lap was the country music magazine Lindsey had sent her when Ben McBride was inducted into the Country Music Hall of Fame—the one with Ben on the cover.

Lindsey felt drained. And she felt like chiding her grandmother for inviting Michael up without asking—or telling—her. But she had decided if her grandmother would simply let it go, she would too. For now. And for now, she needed to keep the conversation away from Michael.

"My stock in Hadley's Curve has skyrocketed," she said as she plopped down on the porch steps. "The R&R gang persists in thinking I twisted Ben McBride's arm to get him here." And in the way that humor often injects itself into the heart of pain, Lindsey found herself able to entertain her grandmother by imitating Madge and Albert, two of the committee members, arguing with the seriousness of UN delegates over whether to use red-skinned or brown-skinned hot dogs at the concession stand.

Sarah responded to her granddaughter's stories with enough laughter to bring tears. She dabbed the corner of her eyes with her embroidered handkerchief—the only woman Lindsey knew who still used one. After Lindsey assured her she was not hungry, that she had eaten a tuna sandwich at Butters' on the way home, Sarah began turning the pages of the magazine as if looking for the article on Ben McBride—even though, from the magazine's wear, it was obvious Sarah had read it several times before. At any rate, her grandmother didn't seem intent on more conversation, which was fine with Lindsey. She and Grandma Sarah had always been comfortable with silence. Now Lindsey needed the silence to think. Or maybe she needed the silence so she wouldn't have to think.

The chickadees and finches were out in number, and there was a lone warbler she didn't recognize. Neither did Sarah, apparently, who broke the silence by saying, "Wonder what bird that is?"

"Aunt Lily would know," Lindsey said, almost as if Lily were still among the living. Sarah nodded and said, "Ayuh."

Lindsey realized she had missed these evenings on the porch, these even-tides, as Aunt Lily called them. As a child, Lindsey had thought the word was *edentide*, named—she had bragged to her first-grade classmates—after her great-great-great grandfather, Eden Frost.

She realized now that Lily had muffled a laugh as she explained to young Lindsey that it was *even*-tide, the period of balance between daylight and dark, a short span that gives one both time and reason to ponder—as her Aunt Lily had put it.

But on this evening, on this porch, Lindsey simply could not let herself ponder. So while her grandmother read her magazine, she closed her eyes and listened. And she could almost hear her Aunt Lily's piano music drifting through the open window the way it had so many summer evenings of her childhood.

She opened her eyes and looked out over the valley, where the falling sun had earlier lit up the horizon with a cast of gold, then a hint of peach. And now the valley and hills were flushed with a rosy haze.

She started to mention the colors to her grandmother. But Sarah, immersed in the magazine article about Ben McBride, seemed light years removed from Lindsey. Just as Michael seemed light years from her, even though they had been together down by the pond that very afternoon. She could still feel him near her. Could still smell the subtle hint of aftershave when he stepped close and took her by the shoulders.

No, she could not let herself think about Michael, even though he seemed to be hovering wherever her mind took her. Once again, she willed him from her thoughts.

And now Sarah was turning pages, trying to find the second section of "Ben McBride: The Man behind the Legend." "I'll never understand why magazines don't just put an article all in one place," she said.

Lindsey almost reminded her grandmother that she had read that article enough to have it memorized, but she thought better of it. While her grandmother obviously looked forward to Ben's visit with joyful anticipation, Lindsey had also detected a certain anxiety. She suspected both feelings were linked to her grandfather. Seeing a man who had been her husband's friend would surely bring back memories of the happiest times in Sarah Frost's life. And yet even seeing Ben McBride's picture in the magazine also had to make Sarah painfully aware that she and Ben had grown old while Tad had, in a way, remained forever young.

Sarah found the second part of the article just as the phone rang. Lindsey jumped up and ran inside, reaching it before the third ring. Of course it wasn't Michael. Why would it be?

After the call, she got herself a soda, a Moxie for old times' sake. Then she poured her grandmother her nightly thimbleful of sherry—a ritual Sarah and Lily had developed by the time Lindsey's memory began—and returned to the porch.

Sarah laid the open magazine face down on her lap to take the glass of sherry. She took one sip, put the tiny glass on the wicker table beside her chair, and picked up the magazine again. Lindsey thought how cute she looked sitting in a tall rocker—a tiny, plump woman who always wore a dress and nearly always had pink fingernail polish on her spotted, chubby hands.

Then it came. "So that wasn't who you hoped it was?" Sarah asked nonchalantly, keeping her eyes on the magazine.

"It was Albert. He said he had a good price for the red-skinned franks. Besides, I wasn't hoping it was anyone."

"The way you raced to that phone didn't look like a woman who wasn't hoping it was *anyone*. I take it, though, that you sent your young man packing—after he came all this way."

Her grandmother's voice hinted of disapproval. "He sure seems like a special young man."

Lindsey shrugged and took a long drink from her soda bottle as if Michael James were of no consequence to her.

"I have to tell you—if I were a spring chicken, I'd set my cap for him," her grandmother said, putting her fingers to her lips to hide a girlish grin.

"Yeah, well, you'd be welcome to him, if you could beat out Cynthia," Lindsey said with a rueful smile. "But I don't plan to get involved with *anyone*—Cynthia or no Cynthia—even if he is special."

"That sounds like a case of closing the barn door after the horses are out," Sarah said.

Somehow Lindsey had known she was going to say that.

Lindsey blew her breath into the night air. Then she took another swallow of her Moxie. Why was her grandmother riding her about this when she had not said one word about walking out on her wedding?

"It would just be too complicated to fall in love right now, Grandma Sarah. I have too much to do for my career."

"Always the practical one," Sarah said. "Like Lily."

Again Lindsey detected a tinge of disapproval in her grandmother's voice. Then Sarah picked up the magazine, flipped another page, and proceeded to read while Lindsey sat there—missing Michael. If they were still "just friends," she could have shown him around: Snow Falls, the caves, the quarry where she'd learned to swim. They could have climbed Patch Mountain now that the blackflies were gone.

But that wasn't possible now. And she needed to remember some of her own lyrics:

> Don't need a man to make me smile,
> To make my life worthwhile.

After a while, Sarah Frost closed the magazine. This time she put it on the wicker table instead of her lap. She picked up her sherry glass and held it in her hand, taking the tiniest of sips as she looked out over the ridge at the sinking sun.

Lindsey slapped at a mosquito on her leg, then set her soda bottle down,

got up, and went inside to find the long fireplace matches to light the cit-
ronella candles in buckets on the corners of the porch. She was putting the
match to the last candle when her grandmother said, "If Michael is that
once-in-a-lifetime love, are you going to let it slip away?"

Lindsey blew out the long match with a frustrated sigh. She started to
tell her grandmother—yet again—that she really didn't believe in that kind
of love when her grandmother, almost as if reading her mind, said, "There
is such a thing, you know—even though your generation doesn't seem to
believe that."

Lindsey sat back down on the top porch step. She assumed her grandmother was talking about herself and Grandpa Tad—"the only man I ever
kissed or wanted to," she was known to say. Maybe, too, she was talking
about Aunt Lily and Jack Tate.

Lindsey started to tell her grandmother that she was right, that she,
Lindsey, did *not* take such a romantic view of love. She didn't want it,
didn't need it complicating her life, her plans, didn't need the pain, that's
for sure—if what she was feeling was anything close to the pain of love.

Maybe she was more like Aunt Lily. She might have loved Jack Tate with
all her heart, but you could tell Lily didn't *need* love. Didn't *need* a man.

But Lindsey did not want to diminish the belief in love that Sarah still
clung to after all these years. So she decided to let her grandmother's
proclamation float into the pink evening air.

Sarah Frost finished her sherry. Then she picked up the music magazine
yet again and looked at Ben McBride's picture on the cover. Looked at his
leathered and wrinkled but still handsome face. Looked at his full head of
hair—not quite all silver.

"The camera doesn't do him justice," Lindsey said, noticing her grandmother had once again put the magazine in her lap. "It doesn't capture
how when he laughs, his brown eyes glimmer. He must have taken over
any room he entered when he was a young man."

"That he did," Sarah said, putting her right hand to her blue-gray curls and seeming almost to blush. "Of course, I never gave a thought to any man but your grandfather, but every woman in Hadley's Curve was sweet on Ben McBride back then. And they liked his kind of music, too—well, not Lily, as you know, but most folks. Some called it honky-tonk, some called it hillbilly, and some called it country-western. And now, you tell me, we have to call it just country. But whatever they called it back then, they kept wearing out Ben's records on the jukebox at the Corner Store. Hank Williams, too, and Eddie Arnold and Ernest Tubb. But it was Ben they were most sweet on. Liked him, and liked the way he sang. It was like—what was that I read? . . ."

She flipped through the magazine until she found what she wanted. "Here it is." She quoted, "'a voice edged in a rough, smoky-blue sadness.' Or at least that's how this reviewer describes it, and that's about right." Sarah flipped the magazine closed and plopped it back in her lap.

Lindsey gestured to the magazine in her grandmother's lap and asked, "Did you see in that article where they asked Ben why he never married again? He said it was because even when he married the first time, the woman he loved was already in his past."

"Ayuh." Sarah nodded and rocked once or twice in her rocker. It seemed she wasn't going to add more to that answer.

"That article came out just after I got to Nashville. But Gabby—who sees and hears everything—said there was considerable speculation as to the identity of this mystery woman and what might have happened to her—especially since everyone assumes Ben McBride could have had the woman of his choosing."

"Ayuh," her grandmother said again, staring into the orchard where the apple trees, caught in shadow, looked like a thousand dancing arms. Then she added, "Just about."

Over the years, Lindsey had learned to read her grandmother's pauses and the pacing of her words. This last comment carried with it the weight of gravity.

Lindsey tried to lighten the mood by feigning shock. "Grandma Sarah, don't tell me *you* are Ben McBride's mystery woman?"

She fully expected Sarah to say, "Pshaw." Instead, Sarah picked up the magazine again, opened it determinedly, then closed it just as quickly. She breathed in the evening air and let it out slowly.

Then she said, "Lindsey, it's time for you to hear this story."

Part Two

And maybe one day
In some faraway time,
We'll sit by a dance floor
And sip one more wine.

—MARK DIX, "THIS OLD SONG"

Eight

July 7, 1948

Ben McBride had been raised with courtly Southern manners, so he wasn't one to swear. But he had already said *damn* a couple of times as he drove along the dusty back roads between the Maine villages of Mexico and Sweden. Or was he between Naples and Paris? Or maybe Norway and Italy? He had seen all of those names on a sign a few miles back. His war buddy, Tad Frost, had told him if he ever wanted to pay a visit, it would be easy to find him. "Just make your way to Hadley's Curve and then ask anyone there to point you to Eden's Ridge. Can't miss it."

Ben had asked for directions when he filled up with gas at Hadley's Curve and had learned that Mainers tended not to use more words than they had to. "Take a right at the four corners"—"connahs," they actually said—"then a left at the next Y, climb a bit, and that's Eden's Ridge. Can't miss the Frost place."

He had driven for miles, turned back, retraced, turned back again, and he hadn't come across a road that looked like a four corners unless that cow path counted as a crossing. And he hadn't come across a road that looked like any letter in the alphabet, much less a Y. Face it, he was lost. He had a good mind to forget the whole thing and just make his way to Bangor, where he would be playing the next night.

Still, you don't get this close to a war buddy and not go see him. In the waiting time between battles, the time when death and fear of death hover like a dark cloud, Tad Frost had talked about his home in Maine, talked about the farm and the fields and the stone walls and chunks of granite large enough to slide down.

Having grown up in Memphis, Ben could not picture such a place as being home. Well, Memphis was no longer his home, either, for that matter. His home was the road. Even though traveling from town to town left him bone-weary at times, it was a life that suited him. He loved the smell of car exhaust and greasy hamburgers. Loved singing on the backs of flatbed trucks, or in small tents or town halls. Loved the honky-tonks, where songs floated into the blue air of smoke and ladies' perfume.

Yeah, he loved being on the road, but he much preferred knowing what road he was on. Besides, the road he truly loved was the highway—a road that went from town to town. He had no desire to spend time on a dirt road that led to nowhere. How could anyone choose to spend his life in such a place? Life would be too slow, too still, too quiet.

"Damn," he said again, his usual good cheer tested. His seemed to be the only car for miles—and he himself the only living thing, except for a few cows and sheep. Heck, they could probably give more complete directions than what he had gotten in Hadley's Curve. He smiled at the thought of stopping to ask the sheep how to get to his friend's place on Eden's Ridge.

Here he was driving down a dusty road in a rattletrap of a car, which was all he owned in the world. He had spent his last dime cutting his first record and traveling to every little town on the map, it seemed, to promote it.

Here he was driving between towns called Peru and Denmark and Stockholm, and the only thing he knew was that he was still in Maine. He thought. He shook his head and said to his car, "Bertha, I think we are tee-totally lost." Then he began to sing a refrain from his first recording,

I knew even then I loved you,

But I've been on the road so long

That my life's become a honky-tonk song.

As usual when he began to sing, his tiredness lifted the way sun and wind lift fog. And Ben McBride drove down the road to wherever, singing—and looking for that darn Y in the road.

———————

Ben McBride would always remember the first time he saw Lilian Rose Frost. What he noticed were her eyes—blazing out from under a wide-brimmed farmer's hat. And spitting fire—because Lily, in her green Ford truck, had been forced to swerve to make room for his Hudson, leaving one of her wheels sunk in the sandy roadside, and leaving her not the least bit pleased.

Lily put her hand full to the horn and Ben McBride, not realizing what had happened, stopped. By the time he had backed up to see what her problem was, she was out of her truck and heading in his direction. She was dressed in farmer coveralls. The worn straw hat covered all of her hair except for some light brown strands that had found their way out.

"I don't know about where you come from . . . Tennessee, is it?" she said, looking at his plates. "But here in Maine, we don't hold to taking our half out of the center of the road."

"Goodness, ma'am," Ben said in his Tennessee drawl, "I called myself movin' over."

"Movin' over?" she said incredulously. By now he was trying to decide exactly what color those eyes were. Blue as a bottle of bluing—no, not that exactly. But what?

"Cow manure! You were hogging the road like you owned it."

Ben's response was to throw back his head and laugh. He caught a brief flash in those eyes of hers and thought for a moment that she was going to laugh too. But she didn't. And didn't intend to, either. That much was obvious from the set of her jaw.

He opened his door, stepped out, and took off his brown Stetson as if he were in the company of a lady, even though this woman certainly didn't talk like a lady.

He looked over her situation. "Ma'am, no matter how you got in this predicament," he said, nodding toward the wheel in the sand, "I think I need to help you get unstuck." He put his hat back on to shield his eyes from the July sun.

"I am *not* stuck," she said, throwing her head back, squaring her shoulders, turning, and marching back to her truck. She climbed in and slammed the door.

He noticed the strong set of her chin and the high cheekbones that gave her an even more determined look as she fastened her eyes on the road ahead.

"Well then," he said, stepping toward her truck, about to ask her for clarification on the directions to the Frost place. Was it left at the next four corners, and then a right at the fork? Or was it the other way around? But before another word could come from his mouth, she pressed the starter pedal as if to dismiss him. She revved her engine, spun the tires, and took off, spitting sand and gravel and leaving him in a swirl of dust.

Ben climbed back into his heap of a car, restarted the engine, and drove on down the road. Somehow, even though he didn't understand why, he felt less weary, and it didn't matter so much that he was lost. He began singing "Sioux City Sue," a Gene Autry song that was part of his repertoire—tapping the happy rhythm with his left foot.

Nine

Ben McBride ended up at the same place where he had filled his tank and asked for directions over an hour before—noticing this time that the name was Butters' Corner Store. He went inside for a cup of coffee and a piece of pie. He couldn't get that woman out of his mind, but it wouldn't do to ask anyone here about her. So he simply asked for directions. Once again he headed out in search of the Frost place, and this time he found it, not ten minutes from the Corner Store. He had actually driven past the house shortly after his encounter with that blue-eyed woman who accused him of squeezing her off the road. How could he have missed it? The name *Frost* was even on a mailbox right by the road. She certainly had distracted him.

A large stretch of lawn slanted up from the mailbox toward a white farmhouse. Flowers surrounded the long front porch. A big barn was attached to the house—like barns often were in New England, Ben had noticed. He eased up the graveled drive and brought his car to a stop in the wide turnaround between the house-and-barn and the few sheds. He stepped out of the car and stretched, half expecting Tad to come out of the barn, brushing hay from his clothes, or to see Tad's wife, Sarah, coming out of the kitchen in a gingham house dress and apron, wiping flour from her hands and arms. He certainly expected a dog to bark—he was under the impression that all farms had at least one dog.

But the only sounds were the strains of piano music floating out of a window of the house. Chopin—if he remembered correctly. He walked toward the house. He knew it wasn't Tad. Maybe it was Tad's wife, but Tad had not mentioned that she played. Certainly not like this.

Then he remembered the sister, Tad's twin. The one Tad had talked so much about, the one who was supposedly such a wonderful pianist. If Ben remembered right, she had gone off to Juilliard—young, about sixteen. She had been there when the war broke out. Hadn't her fiancé been killed at Pearl Harbor? What was her name? A flower name. Daisy? No. Iris. Maybe that was it.

Ben moved closer to the porch. He tiptoed up the steps, not wanting to disrupt the music. Suddenly, he found himself thinking back to his own days at the piano keyboard with Miss Dorothy Jean Langley—the old-maid piano teacher, everyone had called her. A sweet old lady who had taught him for many years and taught him well. But she had a rigid sense of timing—and of propriety. If he stretched the rhythm of a piece out of sync with the metronome, the way he had heard the jazz players do on the radio, she would pound on the wall with her hand, pulling him back into a stricter tempo. And if he was one minute late for a lesson because he'd been sitting under the ancient magnolia tree listening to the old men and their guitars, Miss Dorothy Jean had been less than happy, to put it mildly.

Maybe Tad's sister still lived here with Tad and Sarah. He remembered she had come back to teach music and look after things while Tad was gone. Yep, she might still live here, keeping time and passing time the way music teachers do.

But this was not the strictly correct, music-teacher music Miss Dorothy Jean had played. Whoever was playing now had the kind of gift that—as his friend, Tater, would have put it—could make the angels toe-dance.

He would wait until the music stopped before he knocked. It was simply too beautiful to disturb, but neither could he stand *not* to see who was playing.

After all, the door was open.

At the piano sat a woman so absorbed in her playing she didn't even hear the creak of the screen door as Ben stepped inside the hallway. He walked as lightly as he could in his cowboy boots and stood in the doorway to the parlor. There, he suddenly felt like the intruder he was. But he had been so drawn to the music. Now, he simply could not bring himself to clear his throat or make any other sound to draw attention, so entranced was he with what he heard. And saw.

The woman sat tall and regal at the carved mahogany upright, her fingers moving across the keyboard with the lightness of butterfly wings. The long, falling summer sunlight streamed into the room, hitting the crystal prisms of a hurricane lamp. And from the prisms, rainbows of light skipped across the piano keys, flickered on her white cotton sleeveless blouse, on her tanned arms, and on the rich, honey-colored hair twisted into a bun at the nape of her neck.

Years later, Ben would look back and think *that* might have been the exact moment he fell in love. But he didn't think in those terms as he stood there trapped by his long-time fondness for Chopin and by the beacons of light flying about hair that now seemed to him the same warm color as a glass of sherry.

Ben McBride was too captivated by the woman and the music to hear or see what was happening outside—although later they would tell him about it. A green Chevrolet drove up the lane and parked in one of the far sheds, next to a truck of the same color. A young man in overalls and a short, pregnant woman in a gingham dress got out of the car and walked over to the old Hudson, puzzled looks on their faces, wondering who this visitor was. The man then looked at the Tennessee license plate and his face lit up. He grabbed the woman's hand and pulled her toward the house and onto the porch just as the woman at the piano hit the final notes.

With the spontaneity that he would always be known for, Ben McBride clapped loudly and honestly. The woman jumped and turned abruptly. Their eyes froze in startled recognition.

Ben was about to laugh heartily at the coincidence of it all when a scowl came across her face. "Who are you, and what are you doing in my house?" she demanded, just as Tad and Sarah Frost stepped into the hallway.

"Ben, you son of a gun," Tad said, reaching out and then clapping his old friend on the back twice. "So you're the 'fool' who ran my sister off the road earlier today. Good thing we got here when we did. She's handy with a gun."

"Lily," Tad said, *"this* is Ben McBride."

Lily, Ben remembered then. That's her name.

Lily, whether from being startled or confused or still irritated at the earlier encounter on the road, had not removed the scowl from her face.

"Well," Ben said, smiling widely at Lily, "we've managed to skip the introductions until now."

Lily did not return the smile. Ben hesitated to put out his hand, because he knew a gentleman shouldn't offer his hand first to a lady—but, considering her earlier behavior, was she really a lady? To be frank, he wasn't sure of anything except that he was enjoying every minute of being in her presence. Even if the feeling did not seem mutual.

"I should have known she was your sister. Same blue eyes. Same . . . easygoing nature," Ben said, his teasing eyes never leaving Lily's face.

Tad laughed the way he had always laughed at Ben's impertinent sense of humor. Then, realizing he hadn't introduced his wife, he put his arm around her and said, "Ben, this is Sarah, and this," he said, putting his hand on her plump belly, "is our son, Maxwell. But we call him Max."

Sarah blushed and said, "Honestly, honey, it might be a girl!" Then

Sarah told Ben how pleased she was to meet him. "Tad has talked so much about you," she said.

"Well, don't believe it all," Ben said, and he and Tad grinned with the joy of seeing each other again. Ben decided that he *liked* Sarah, liked her friendly, easy manner. But his fascination was with the other woman. Lily.

"Ben's the one who's on the jukebox at the Corner Store," Sarah said to Lily, who had busied herself by picking up the sheet music.

Before Lily could reply, Tad put his hand on Ben's shoulder and said, "Now, let's get down to business. How long can you stay? Overnight? A week? A month?"

Ben laughed and explained he had to head back later that evening.

"Well, then you must stay and eat with us," Sarah said before Tad had a chance to offer the invitation himself.

"In fact, we just might make you play and sing for your supper," Tad said. "Don't you think so, Lily? Maybe the two of you could even play a duet."

Lily felt her face grow warm, the same feeling she had experienced on the road when Ben McBride tipped his brown cowboy hat to her and then looked at her with those eyes the color of his hat and flashed a winning smile. Keeping her gaze on the sheet music in her hand, Lily said, "Sorry, but I don't know any duets with a banjo."

Lily had actually meant it as a matter-of-fact statement, but she realized it had not come out that way and had not struck the others that way, either. In fact, Ben McBride found himself—for the first time—a bit irritated with this pretty, vibrant, and testy woman. Something about the way she said *banjo* made it sound like one of the lesser creations of the universe. Ben McBride knew better. He named all his instruments, and his banjo, Betsy, was a real queen.

Tad smiled, shook his head, and looked at Ben as if to say, *I can't do a thing about this sister of mine.* But by now Ben McBride, never changing his smile, had locked his eyes onto Lily's in a test of wills. "Well, ma'am," Ben said as he walked past her toward the piano, "I guess I'll just have to go solo. And I don't have my banjo with me, so," he continued, affecting the countriest of accents, "if you don't mind, I'll use your pie-an-o."

He sat down at the piano bench, pushed up his shirtsleeves for effect, and started playing chords in four-four time. He forced his face into a frown as if he were searching for the words to a song. "For the life of me," he said, "I can't find any inspiration at the moment."

He stopped chording and let his long fingers rest on the keyboard. Suddenly, Tad remembered that his friend had studied classical music for years, and he remembered hearing him play once when they sheltered in an abandoned house in a small French town they had recently liberated. Tad remembered, too, that he had somehow not gotten around to sharing that memory with his sister. She was in for a surprise.

Tad sat down on the deacon's bench, reached for Sarah's hand, and gently pulled her to sit beside him. Tad, for one, was going to enjoy every moment of this.

Ben McBride closed his eyes for a brief moment, took a deep breath, and began playing the "Reverie" from Schumann's *Scenes from Childhood*. His big hands moved deftly across the keys. And Lily Frost, watching them, wished to goodness she was sitting down by Sarah and Tad. But she didn't move one inch from the spot where she stood, partly out of stubbornness, partly out of embarrassment, but mostly because she was mesmerized—maybe by the music, maybe by the man.

The room was silent when he finished. Finally Sarah spoke. "That was wonderful. Don't you think so, Lily?" (Sarah would admit years later that she, like Tad, took a bit of enjoyment in Lily's comeuppance.)

"Touché," Lily said, looking Ben in the eyes and not answering Sarah directly. Ben thought he saw the hint of a smile at the corners of Lily's mouth.

Then, never breaking her stride as she turned and walked from the room, Lily said, "Sarah, I got things pretty much in control in the kitchen while you were gone. We need to eat a little early, as I'm introducing the musicians tonight at the opera house."

The three of them were left alone in the wake of Lily's departure. It was an awkward moment until Ben said, seemingly in all seriousness, "It must have been the hat. She hated the hat."

And the three of them laughed.

Had Lily Frost not written it in her journal much later, no one would know that her heart leapt as Tad invited Ben to stay overnight—or longer. No one would know her heart fell when Ben said he had to leave that night, or that it lifted again when Sarah insisted he at least stay for supper.

"I didn't mean to cause friction in the Frost household," Ben said to Tad when Lily had disappeared from sight.

"Well, Lily usually has her say, but this time I think she got a bit carried away, taking aim at you, and then at the banjo. But then again you did run her off the road, and believe me we heard all about it—and you," Tad said laughing. Then he shook his head and said, "I love that sister of mine, but she is a bit of a prude about music. We were raised to be—and it *took* with her. Didn't take with me so much." He winked. "Lily wants to save *culture* here in Hadley's Curve."

Sarah intervened as if she needed to explain, saying it almost in a conspiratorial whisper. "Tad and Lily's ancestors were 'gentleman farmers,' people of letters, you know."

Tad laughed good-naturedly. "At any rate," he said, "Lily's giving a concert this weekend at the opera house—we really do have one here. It's only the second concert she's given—the other was when she came back from Juilliard near the end of the war—so that may be why she's a bit on edge."

"I like a woman who speaks her mind," Ben said, smiling at the memory of Lily earlier that day.

Tad patted his war buddy on the back, and pleasure filled his face as he said, "Well, Lily does that. Still, you got the best of that encounter. That doesn't often happen when someone takes Lily on." Then Tad chuckled in that quiet way of his and said, "Lord, I wish you could have seen the look on her face when you hit those first few notes."

Ten

At Sarah's insistence, the meal was served in the dining room. Ben and Tad fell easily into conversation over ham, potato salad, beet greens, and the first peas from the garden, with a promise of coconut cream pie for dessert. They kept their war stories to the lighter moments, beginning with the one about how Ben had lied about his age. Only seventeen at the time of Pearl Harbor, Ben, like so many of the boys wanting to be men, had "fudged a year," as he put it. Now, he claimed to have trouble remembering what age he really was.

Sarah was obviously beside herself that Ben McBride, whom she considered famous because he had a record on the jukebox at the Corner Store, was sitting at their table. Lily, who had changed into a blue blouse that brought out the color of her eyes even more, said little as Tad and Ben reminisced and then as Tad and Sarah pumped Ben for information about his life.

Ben, for his part, did his best to ignore Lily's reserve as he entertained Tad and Sarah—and Lily, too, he hoped—with funny stories of his rained-out, washed-out, snowed-out, iced-out performances on the backs of pickup trucks, in tents, in smoke-filled joints or roadside cafés barely large enough to turn around in. Since the release of his first record, though, they were actually doing some shows in more substantial venues.

"Letha Jewel James, the wife of my steel guitar player, Curly, tells everyone in Frog Jump, Tennessee—where she's from—that one day the Crooked River Boys will fill as many seats as Roy Acuff. Lord, I hope she's right," Ben said as he stuck his fork in a piece of ham. "I mean, for years Roy's been drawing a crowd as big as Sinatra—fifteen thousand or so anywhere he goes in this country. Now, I don't see that happening to us any time soon, but we have filled a few school auditoriums here and there."

"What a glamorous life you lead," Lily said.

Sarah, not picking up that Lily was being droll, said, "I was just thinking the same thing."

"Now, I've got to rid you of that notion," Ben said, ignoring Lily and looking at Sarah as he wiped his mouth with the napkin, set his fork and knife down, and began a litany of life on the road, of not knowing where they'd be playing next, or if they'd get paid, and if that pay would pay for a flea-bitten room or if their car would get them to the next town. Yet there was a gleam in his eyes as he talked that no one at the table missed—not even Lily, even though she seemed *not* to be looking at him. *It's a hard life,* that gleam told everyone, *but it's my life, and I'd choose it again.*

Lily took a bite of beet greens and looked Ben's way long enough to notice that he seemed embarrassed at all the attention. That surprised her, and she found herself warming to him in spite of herself. His eyes caught hers for a minute, and she looked back down. If she wasn't careful, those brown eyes would draw her like a snare. Good thing this man of the road would be taking to the road again. And soon.

Because *that* was obviously what he was. Charming. Gifted. But still a man of the road. Tad had always said so when talking about Ben McBride. "The free spirit who kept us going in dark times," Tad had called him.

Now that she had met him, she could see what Tad meant about his spirit, and about his being a man who would not stay long in one place.

She could kick herself for not being more genial, but something inside said, *beware, Lily. Guard your heart on this one.*

"Well, like I tell the folks at the Corner Store," Tad said after hearing the miles Ben had traveled in one year, "you are on the road to fame."

Ben smiled. "Well, I don't know about the road to fame—so far it's been the road to Alexandria, Louisiana; Smackover, Arkansas; Tahlequah, Oklahoma; Parsons, Tennessee; Red Bird, Ohio; Ten Sleep, Wyoming—"

"Speaking of Wyoming," Tad said, suddenly remembering something, "Lily, I picked up the mail this morning. You got a letter from that beau of yours out in Wyoming. I forgot and left it on my desk."

Lily frowned, but Ben also thought he detected a slight blush as she said, "Montana."

"What?" Tad looked confused.

Lily was sure her face must be flushed. Why had she bothered to correct her brother? She wanted to say, *he is not my beau; he's just a pen pal.* But somehow that sounded juvenile, and besides, she didn't want to explain anything in front of this man who had a way of making her feel—what was the word? Light-headed? No, that wasn't it. But it was close.

Good thing it was time to serve the pie. She rose and, as Sarah cleared the plates, Lily went to the kitchen, walked quickly to open the kitchen door to the outside, and inhaled deeply of the soft evening air. Then she brought the pie into the room, put it on the sideboard, and began cutting four pieces.

"Well, this gentleman from *Montana,*" Tad said, correcting himself, "is obviously smitten with this sister of mine—even though he has never met her."

Sarah, who had picked up on Lily's discomfort, sat back down at her place and gave Tad a kick under the table to let him know he had ventured into unauthorized territory. And the four of them were suddenly silent as Lily lifted a piece of pie and put it on a small plate.

Ben watched her as she did the same with three other pieces. *I too am smitten with this woman,* he thought, *and I have just met her.* He never took his eyes off of Lily as he said, "I can't say as I blame him—this gentleman from Montana."

Ben thought again that he noticed a slight flush on her long neck, and he found that all the more appealing because Lily Frost was obviously a strong, independent woman who had learned how to camouflage uncertainty and embarrassment.

Any glimmer of shyness quickly vanished, though, and once again there was that confident set of her jaw as she said without looking at either of them, "Well, how nice of you *boys* to talk about me as if I'm not even here."

Many years later Ben would laugh and say she set the dessert plates down in front of them hard enough to shake the meringue off the pie. Sarah, laughing too at the memory all those years later, would say, "Now, that is exaggerating a bit, Ben."

But at the table that day no one laughed. "I do apologize, but I was not talking *about* you, ma'am," Ben said. "I was talking *to* you. You just weren't looking at me. I mean, you were looking at the pie you were cutting."

This definitely was not going the way Ben would have liked. And it definitely was not his usual experience on first meeting a woman. Ben did not consider himself a woman chaser, but he was not unaware that women swarmed around him like bees to honey—or that was how Letha Jewel put it.

Sarah, ever the peacemaker, filled the silence by asking Ben if he wanted another piece of pie—even though he had taken only two bites of the piece on his plate.

Sarah Frost always said that Tad's obliviousness was one of his many charms. And on this day, she realized that in the excitement of seeing his friend, Tad had no clue as to what was or what was *not* going on between his sister and Ben. Tad took his last bite of pie and said, "Too bad you can't be around this weekend to go hear Lily play at the opera house." He beamed with pride at his sister. "She could have played at Carnegie Hall if she wasn't so in love with the farm."

Lily shook her head at her brother's bragging, and Ben saw the softness in her as she said to him, "My brother does tend to exaggerate."

"You forget that I heard you play, ma'am," Ben said. "I don't think he's exaggerating." And again he saw the tinge of rose on her cheeks.

Before she had time to reply, Tad said, "Hey, maybe someday you'll come back and perform at the opera house yourself, Ben."

Ben laughed his deep, rolling laugh at what he took as a wild thought. "Maybe someday," he said.

"No, someday you'll be too big to sing here," Tad said, "so we'd better snatch you up quick. Of course, we'd have to fit you in between the operettas and the chamber music ensemble and such, but you could arrange that, couldn't you, Lily?"

Lily didn't respond to her brother's teasing. Instead she turned to Ben and said in all sincerity, "I do have to ask you, though, how you of all people can abide that honky-tonk music when you can play the way you do."

Sarah sucked in her breath as Lily threw down the gauntlet yet again, even though she was much sweeter about it this time. Tad looked at Ben, waiting for his answer. Knowing Ben, Tad expected it to be amusing.

Ben did not immediately reply. He found himself wanting to say to Lily, *if you really want to know how I came to love it, I'll tell you all about it. I'll tell you about the old men under the magnolia tree. I'll tell you how Miss Dorothy Jean Langley sighed deeply one day and said to my mama, "That boy's got shade-tree music in his soul, so you might as well accept it and buy him a banjo or a guitar—or both."*

He wanted to tell Lily that his music was about the same thing that poetry and opera are about, about searching for light in the dark, searching for a way through the pain of the world. Ben wanted to tell her how singing and being on the road was his way of finding the light. That it was the light in his life.

139

But he probably wouldn't find the words if he really tried to say them—those were things he saved for his songs. So his eyes sparkled and he, as Tad had expected, resorted to an easygoing answer. "Well, ma'am, I think of my music as poor man's opera. Besides," he said and grinned mischievously, "it's just the music to be singing when you're heading down the center of a gravel road, running ladies into a ditch."

Sarah held her breath again.

"Maybe you have a point there," Lily said. And once again, Ben noticed a smile tugging at her mouth.

Sarah, in a desperate attempt to switch the conversation from their roadside encounter, turned to Ben and said, "Speaking of opera houses, have you sung at the Grand Ole Opry?"

"No, ma'am," he said, "but it's a dream of mine to do that someday."

Sarah turned to Lily and said in a sweet but instructive voice, "The Grand Ole Opry is the Carnegie Hall of country-western music."

At which point Ben's face lit up even more. "Speaking of Carnegie Hall," he said, "Ernest Tubb played there last year—to a full house. So it's not just country folk who listen to us anymore."

Lily, who knew very well what the Grand Ole Opry was, since so many around her sat glued to their radios on Saturday night, had no idea who exactly Ernest Tubb was, but she thought it best not to say so.

"Anyway," Ben continued, "I guess Mr. Tubb was a bit nervous, so the first thing he did when he came on stage was stand there like a rabbit caught in a hunter's flashlight and look around him, gawking at the size of the place. Yessir, ol' Ernie stood there so long the crowd was about to lose patience. Then he looked out on those people with their fine gowns and tuxedos and opera glasses, and he brought the house down before he sang a note by saying, 'Lord, this place could sure hold a lot of hay.'"

And finally, maybe because the story touched the farmer in her, or maybe because she had finally succumbed to the gentle manner and the warm brown eyes of this supper guest, Lily Frost laughed, a full, rippling laugh that Ben would take with him that night and carry with him always.

Then the four of them were laughing, and Ben and Lily's eyes met once again as Sarah and Lily rose to clear the table.

———

While Lily and Sarah cleaned up in the kitchen, Ben and Tad lingered at the table with cups of coffee. Ben finally got Tad to talk about himself, about his dream for bettering what he called *the home place*. A place that Tad had described in detail during long dark nights in muddy foxholes—the pond, the orchard, the rocky fields and fine timber, and the family cemetery where generations of Frosts were buried. Ben had thought, even then, how different he was from Tad Frost. And he thought that same thing again as they sat over their coffee in the Frost dining room.

Ben listened as Tad, with a look of complete satisfaction on his face, talked about expanding the orchard, thinning the timber, starting a herd of sheep, and clearing a house site for him and Sarah and the son who was due in a month or so. Then Tad drained the last of his coffee and asked, "Ever think you'll find the right girl and settle down?"

"I'm not the settlin' kind, Tad. You know that," Ben said with a slight shrug. Ben had often wondered if he were too much like his father, who had left one day right after breakfast when Ben was a boy and had never found his way back.

Tad smiled and shook his head in puzzlement. "Still the same old free-to-come-free-to-go-nothing-but-me-my guitar-and-the-road McBride," he said.

"That's me, I guess."

Ben saw Lily's shadow on the kitchen wall just before she stepped into the room. He realized she had probably heard the conversation, and suddenly he felt embarrassed, even though he wasn't sure why.

"I've got to pick some flowers for the stage tonight, so you'll have to excuse me," Lily said. Then she looked at Ben and said, "I'll say goodbye to you now, Mr. McBride."

Ben stood, and Lily seemed to hesitate. He thought for a minute she was going to hold out her hand, and he wished she would. When it became obvious she was not going to, although she seemed suddenly to be at a loss as to what to say or do, he said, "Goodbye, ma'am, and thanks for the best meal I've had in a long, long time."

Tad, still sitting, said, "Don't you think you two ought to at least get on a first-name basis?" But by then Lily had turned and was already back in the kitchen.

———

There was the sound of a door closing, then Ben looked out the dining room window to see Lily outside, striding across the yard to a nearby field of wild flowers. He watched as she began picking daisies, black-eyed Susans, and some white ones and purple ones he couldn't name. It was as if an invisible string pulled his eyes toward her.

Why did this woman draw him so? It wasn't just her looks. He'd had his share of pretty women. No, it was something else. Her independence? Her spirited manner that barely let him glimpse any vulnerability she might have? That rare smile that he couldn't see enough of, and couldn't forget when he did? She was a woman who—as Tater, the old man who had taught him to play the guitar, would have put it—*would walk up to the devil and ask him for a light*, yet who blushed at the mention of a pen-pal boyfriend.

The sound of Tad's chair scraping the floor brought Ben back to the table. "Gotta go do the chores and check on a sow about to farrow. Why don't you come along?"

"You go ahead," Ben said.

Tad laughed, saying, "No stomach for it?"

"No, that's not it," Ben said. "I'll join you. It's just that I think I need to make peace with your sister."

They both looked out the open window to the field where Lily, by now, had gathered a big handful of white and yellow and purple flowers.

"Well, now's the time then, before her date gets here," Tad said. Then he shook his head in bewilderment. "He writes for our paper. The editor's son. And he's been sweet on Lily for years. Lots of men after that gal, but she's being mighty picky. I think maybe it's Jack getting killed and all. Or maybe she's just too strong-headed for any man." Tad scratched the back of his neck. By this time he had walked through the kitchen and was heading off toward the barn, all the time walking backward, all the time talking to Ben, who had followed him and stood in the back doorway.

"When I get back, you've got to get your guitar and play for us." The farther away he got, the louder he talked, so that Ben—and maybe Lily too—could hear. "Too bad Lily's going to miss your picking and singing— that would win her over for sure."

Lily Frost *did* hear that last part, and she could have swatted that brother of hers. But at the same time, she found herself smiling to herself at his comment.

She looked toward the house and saw Ben McBride caught in the pink and gray light of the sunset, walking jauntily through the tall grass and flowers—toward her. She really did feel her heart beating. Why was this? There were plenty of men around to give her attention, and certainly men more suited to her taste than this city man who wore cowboy boots and sang honky-tonk songs even though he could play Schumann by memory.

And now he had put on that brown felt cowboy hat again. She chided herself for feeling like a giddy schoolgirl over a man Tad had said was a modern troubadour, a country-western-music vagabond.

Just then a ruby-throated hummingbird darted to a nearby clump of bee balm. And she remembered that once Tad had likened Ben to a hummingbird—whose wings were constantly moving even when it stayed in one place to sip the nectar from a flower. Was the hummingbird a warning?

She kept her attention on the vetch and cornflowers and daisies and Queen Anne's lace she was picking, pretending not to see Ben until she was in his shadow. She looked up as if she were suddenly aware of him. He pushed his hat to the back of his head and said, "Ma'am, I cannot leave without apologizing for my bad road manners and for any other bad manners I have exhibited. Your brother means a lot to me, and I surely don't want any ill will with his sister."

Lily straightened up, flowers in one hand, but she did not look at him. "One would think," she said, looking around her as if she were searching for just the right flower to add to the bouquet, "that with all of your *experience* on the road, you'd be a better driver." Then she looked him straight on, and this time her smile appeared and stayed there long enough for Ben to know it was a peace offering.

"And," Lily said, looking off into the distance this time, "I know that you and Tad went through things in the war that he does not talk about. I don't take that lightly."

Ben didn't answer that. He wasn't expected to. Instead, he followed her gaze out over the valley and the long narrow lake below toward the ridge across the valley. The view that Tad had described time and time again. Then he looked west toward the pond, and his breath caught. "My Lord, what a sunset," he said.

Lily nodded and quoted dreamily,

> She sweeps with many-colored Brooms—
> And leaves the Shreds behind—

Oh Housewife in the Evening West—
Come back, and dust the Pond.

"I should've known you'd be a member of the Emily Dickinson fan club," Ben said. "Recognize that one from high school. Now I know what it means." He turned slowly in a circle to take it all in. The lavender and orange afterglow of day threaded the western sky, shimmering on the tin roofs of the barn and sheds, turning the bed of zinnias in the side yard into fiery balls of red, yellow, and pink.

Again, there was silence between them, but for the first time it was a tranquil silence. The frogs at the nearby pond took the fading light as their cue to begin their nightly chorus, a mourning dove called from within the woods, the chickadees sang their closing song of the day. There was the sound of a cardinal.

"Just listen to all the birds," he said finally. "Of course, we've got one bird in Tennessee that can make every one of those sounds," he added boastfully. Then he noticed Lily was obviously in a deep place in her heart at this moment, and he wished he hadn't been so glib.

"We have the rare mockingbird up here too," she said, coming back to the present, her eyes meeting his again. He thought she was going to say something more, but she was distracted by yet another birdsong. "Hear that?" Lily asked, her eyes brightening. Then she spotted it. "There. A scarlet tanager."

Ben looked where Lily pointed—at a lilac tree he had noticed from the house. Sitting on a crooked limb crooning his song was a tiny bird, red as a cardinal, but with black wings and tail. He sang in a low *chip-burr*.

"He's got a different voice, that's for sure," Ben said.

"My father always said he sounded like a robin with a sore throat, but he's so beautiful no one minds." For a minute Lily seemed again to be someplace back in time. Then she said, "It was our father who taught Tad and me to identify birds by their markings and their calls."

Ben watched as a dull, greenish yellow bird with a yellow underside and dark, brownish wings, joined the scarlet tanager. "That's the female tanager," Lily said. "She's not nearly so flashy, of course. Lady birds never are. Still, she has her own beauty."

Like you, Ben almost said. Lily's high cheekbones and clear, sun-warmed skin glowed in the fading light. *You sure have your own beauty, lady,* he wanted to say. He had found it easy to say flattering words to women all his life, but he knew this time it was different. This time he meant it so deeply that he could not say it.

Instead he reached for one of those pretty white lacy flowers, broke the stem, and handed it to Lily. "Why thank you, suh," she said, and he laughed at her attempt at a Southern accent.

They turned and began a slow walk back to the house. Grasshoppers jumped out of their path, and barn swallows darted in front of them. Ben looked to the right and saw, at the edge of the field, the small, fenced cemetery nestled under a row of lilacs. There was an uneven line of tin markers and marble and granite tombstones. Ben thought about Tad's elderly parents, who had died of the flu only weeks apart while he and Tad were in a muddy field in France.

"We tried to get Tad to come home when . . ." He didn't have to say *when your folks died;* they both knew what he meant. "He could have gotten a hardship discharge, but he wouldn't. Said that you could take charge of things here. I know what he meant now."

"Tad was right to stay over there in France," Lily said, fixing him with a blue gaze. "And after all, our parents were gone. They wouldn't have known he was here."

"I wonder about that," Ben said. "An old man I once knew—the one who taught me to play the guitar—told me that when you die, your spirit turns into a bird. Maybe these birds were once all people." Ben's words were half in jest, but half in earnest.

Lily stopped suddenly and looked toward the cemetery. Ben had obviously touched a memory that took her out of the present. "I came here after we buried my mother and father, and the most peculiar thing happened. Hardly anyone ever sees a saw-whet owl, since they're nocturnal. But that evening a saw-whet owl, not even as big as a robin, sat on their tombstone. Just sat there. Didn't even move when it saw me. I had only seen them in pictures in my father's books. But there the owl was, perched on that tombstone. Never saw him again, but still . . . it was such a strange thing."

"Or maybe it wasn't," Ben said.

Ben and Lily had both just had the thought that they could stay in this field talking a long time when a new black Oldsmobile that had probably been shiny before it made its way up the dusty ridge pulled up into the big gravel circle. Lily looked at her watch. "Oh, my goodness, I had no idea of the time."

She turned to Ben and said almost as if in apology, "I really do have to rush." And before Ben could find *his* way of saying, *Don't go. Stay here and sit on the porch with me,* Lily took off almost at a run. Then she stopped quickly, turned, and walked back to Ben, who still stood knee deep in grass and flowers. She stopped and held out her hand. "Goodbye, Ben McBride."

He wasn't accustomed to a woman with such a firm, confident handshake, and he certainly wasn't prepared for the feeling that went through him when she put her hand in his. "Be careful as you head on down the road." This time he detected only pure earnestness in her tone.

"Goodbye, Lily Frost," he said, memorizing her face. That was the first time he had called her anything but ma'am.

He watched her, trying again to name the color of her eyes, as she ran through the tall grass in strong strides. She stopped as she got to the car and seemed to fiddle with the flowers. A tall man in a suit walked back from the doorway, where he had said hello to Sarah. He nodded at Lily, opened the door for her, and just as she started to get in, it came to Ben.

"Cobalt," he hollered above the noise of the engine.

Turning to look at him, she called back, "What?"

He noticed she had tucked the cornflower into the top buttonhole of her blouse.

"Your eyes are cobalt blue."

A smile crossed her face and stayed there. Then she turned and eased her long legs inside the car.

———————

The Oldsmobile sped down the road, churning dust in its wake. Lily Frost's date talked on and on about the program they were going to hear that night. But she wasn't thinking about the string quartet. Instead, she was thinking about the feel of Ben McBride's hand, warm and strong, clasping hers.

Ben watched as the dust settled behind the trail of the car. He felt a sudden emptiness that he was not at all accustomed to. He walked toward the barn to join his friend. Later Ben would get his guitar, and Tad and Sarah would sit on the porch holding hands while the plaintive sound of Ben's voice singing an old blues song Tater had taught him floated through the last light of day.

———————

"So," Lindsey said, amused—even somewhat delighted—at the story her grandmother had just finished telling her, "Ben and Aunt Lily were slightly attracted even if they didn't hit it off exactly." She finished her Moxie and put the empty bottle beside her on the steps.

"You might say that," Sarah said, looking down at her hands in her lap, looking at the pink nail polish. The color she had worn the first night she met Tad—a story she had told Lindsey time and time again.

"I can certainly picture Aunt Lily giving Ben a piece of her mind about country music," Lindsey said. And then she laughed at a memory that came to mind. "Remember the time she told the football coach off good and proper for 'letting' her star cellist sprain his thumb the night before a concert?"

"Ayuh," Sarah said and chucked softly.

"Just recently," Lindsey said, "Ben said he'd heard Aunt Lily play Chopin and what a touch she had. And," Lindsey added as she suddenly remembered, "he also mentioned her blue eyes. I guess she did make quite the impression that one time he saw her."

"He didn't see her just that once," Sarah Frost said.

"What do you mean?" Lindsey asked.

"That's what I'm about to tell you."

Eleven

December 28, 1949

Lily Frost sat inside Butters' Corner Store the Wednesday after Christmas, sipping hot chocolate and sharing a laugh with the regulars about the recent Christmas pageant. At the most sacred moment, one of the wise men, a four-year-old, had looked down at Lily, the accompanist and director, and said in a voice much bigger than he was, "Miss Lily, I need to pee."

Lily Frost enjoyed herself at the Corner Store. Good neighbors, good food, a warm place to be. Then, just as she ordered a hamburger and a Moxie, someone put a quarter in the jukebox, pressed five numbers, and there Ben McBride was, again.

I seem to have gotten myself in a bind. . . .

Everywhere she went lately, it seemed she heard his records on jukeboxes and radios, and the local bands had taken to playing his hits at the dances at the Grange.

I think I'm doin' fine,
Then that blue-eyed lady walks across my mind.

And there Ben McBride was, walking across *her* mind. There he was tilting back his head to laugh at her as she gave him what-for for running her off the road. There he was drenched in the golden light of late afternoon, standing in the parlor doorway as she turned around from the piano. There he was in the violet light of a late summer evening, standing in a field of wild flowers, listening to bird songs, and appreciating Emily Dickinson.

She didn't really believe she was the blue-eyed lady he sang about. He probably had a woman in every town—whatever the color of her eyes. Still, when she heard it, something passed through her, something similar to what had passed through her that day she took Ben McBride's hand.

Get hold of yourself, Lily, she said. *You're acting like a star-struck schoolgirl.* It had been a year and a half, for goodness' sake, and still not a week went by, not even many days, that Ben McBride didn't walk across her mind with that smile of his and those eyes brown as chestnuts, eyes that laughed and looked forlorn at the same time.

It hadn't helped that every couple of weeks Ben had sent picture post-cards addressed to *The Frosts on Eden's Ridge.* Sent them from places like Monroe, Louisiana; Hope, Arkansas; Broken Bow, Oklahoma; Prairie City, Iowa; Wichita Falls, Texas; Horseshoe Bend, Idaho. Brief, sunny notes to explain the picture on the other side. "Yep, the sky here is dotted with oil wells." Or, "Can you believe they have watermelons this big?" Or, "Our fourteenth show in as many nights. Bed bad, hot dogs good."

The record ended just as Madge Butters put Lily's hamburger and home fries and a bottle of catsup in front of her and said, "Sure is nice of you to give Walter and June them tickets to hear Ben McBride over to Lewiston tonight—even though I don't see why you had to miss it just 'cause Tad and Sarah are gone to Pennsylvania."

Forrest Butters, who had just come inside from adding oil to Lily's truck, said, "Now Madge, you know Lily's taste don't run to *our* kind of music." Forrest picked up a rag to wipe the oil from his hands. Then, in the spirit of good-natured teasing-in-earnest that can exist between those who have known each other their whole lives, Forrest added, "Why, if Lily here had her way, she'd stuff this jukebox with songs by all them high-brows, like that deaf guy. What's his name? Beetle-oven?" Forrest could never resist a good tease. "And what's the guy you always play, Chopsticks? And Shoe-something or other?"

"Oh come on, Forrest, you are stretching the truth," Lily said with a friendly, forced frown as she took the first bite of her hamburger.

"Well, anyway," Forrest said, "Walter was in here earlier and said you'd think it was Christmas all over again the way June and that son of theirs got excited 'bout them tickets."

"Ayuh," someone just taking his place at a booth said in agreement. Then he looked outside into the early dark of winter days that Mainers have made peace with and noticed it had begun to sprinkle. So they returned to the subject that was never far from their minds during the long Maine winters: the weather.

It had been the warmest December on record, so warm that they were the only part of the state to have snow cover—and that only because of a six-inch snow the day after Christmas. Forrest reminded them that the thermometer outside his store had reached sixty-one degrees on Christmas Day. He would also lay claim, later, to have been the one to say, "I don't care what the radio said about this squall going out to sea. That's not what the sky is saying. There's rain, ice, and snow in them clouds sure as I'm standing here before you." And Lily had reminded Forrest that he was in fact *sitting*.

As the day slid deeper into the winter night ahead, anyone walking into Butters' Corner Store at that moment would have been warmed by the sound of laughter.

———

Ben McBride's converted school bus, white with a small winding river painted along the sides, seemed to be the home of the Crooked River Boys

153

these days. It had been over the considerable protest of the two married band members that Ben had set the first concert of their new tour in Lewiston, Maine, only three days after Christmas.

But Ben McBride, they had learned, in spite of his easy style, was a driven man, determined to ride the current wave of country music's popularity. Roy Acuff, the "King of Country Music," was host to the Grand Ole Opry on radio station WSM out of Nashville. WABI in Bangor, Maine, featured a weekly coast-to-coast program of country-western music, and WBZ out of Boston had a morning show hosted by Bradley Kincaid, the "Kentucky Mountain Boy."

"We've got to strike while the iron is hot," Ben kept telling his band. So they set out from Nashville in the daylight hours of December 26, taking turns driving and, just a few hours ahead of their scheduled performance, arriving dog-tired and bleary-eyed.

But the truth was that Ben had added Lewiston to the front of their schedule because he wanted, needed somehow, to see Lily Frost again. He had put four first row tickets in an envelope and sent them to Tad Frost. Surely Tad and Sarah would come. And they'd insist that Lily come as well. But in case Lily might insist on staying home to baby-sit, he had even inserted a note that said, "Can't wait to see that kid of yours."

Lord, he was being crafty. But he had found himself thinking of Lily Frost wherever he was. The truth be known, he was totally perplexed as to why he had thought of her every day for a year and a half. Thought of her hair, the color of papershell pecans or the color of sherry, depending on the light. Whether that hair was tucked under a straw hat as she drove around in that old green truck or twisted in that neat knot as she sat at the piano, wisps of it still found their way free and flew about her neck and face. He thought of her sitting at the piano, so lost in her music that she didn't notice he was there. He too, had been lost in her music, and in the tendrils of hair at the nape of her neck.

He thought of the smile that sometimes tugged at her mouth when she was trying to be serious. And her eyes. Honest eyes. Beautiful eyes. But still, no one thing to explain why he just couldn't forget her. No, he didn't understand it at all.

Had he imagined that she felt what he felt when he took her outstretched hand in the field that day? Had he imagined that she had to turn her eyes away, toward the house, as if she too had to look away from what was happening between them? Had he imagined that? He didn't know. What he did know was that he wanted to see her again. Nothing would come of it, of course, but maybe if he could see her again, see her for the *ordinary* woman she surely was instead of the one he had made up in his mind, maybe it would stop her from running around in his head. And in his dreams. And even through his songs.

He told himself if Tad and Sarah and Lily failed to show, he would let it be. But undoubtedly they would come, he told himself. As he and the boys prepared for the show, he asked a stagehand time after time if anyone was sitting in those seats yet. Just as he was being announced, the stagehand pointed to the audience and signaled yes. They had come.

The curtain opened, and Ben McBride stepped out on the stage wearing jeans, a black shirt with fringe and sequins, a string tie, and the dark brown Stetson that had already become his trademark. He took his place at the mike and began singing a song that had already become known as his opener.

> Well, it's three in the morning,
> And I'm almost where I want to be—
> Just outside of Little Rock
> And headin' for Tennessee.

He would sing it through once, then step back and say, "Take it away, boys." And while Curly James was showing his stuff on the steel guitar, Ben McBride would look down at the front row and find Lily Frost, who had plagued him for these many months, smiling the smile that was on her face the last time he saw her. Life was looking good.

To be truthful, Lilian Frost would tell Sarah much later, her heart ached to go to that concert. She might have gone had Tad and Sarah been there, because nothing would have kept Tad away, and his going would have given her an excuse.

As it was, the tickets, delayed no doubt by the Christmas rush, had not arrived until the very day of the concert. Tad and Sarah and their toddler, Max, had left on Christmas Eve morning to go to Sarah's folks in Pennsylvania—their first Christmas back there since Tad had won Sarah's heart at the service club right before he shipped out to war. They had wanted Lily to go, said they'd get their neighbor Victor Lamentov to keep an eye on things. But Lily had cited her duties as pianist for the Christmas services at the church to beg off going. She actually looked forward to having the time to herself. Besides, they would be back the day after New Year's.

And even though she wasn't in Pennsylvania, Lilian Frost wouldn't be going to the concert either. Didn't choose to. No matter how much she wanted to. Which is why, on receiving the tickets, she had quickly offered them to June and Walter before she changed her mind.

By the time she pulled her pickup under the shed, a mix of rain, sleet, and snow was falling, and she found herself wishing she had done the chores *before* going to Butters' store for supper. She jumped out of the truck and ran inside. She took off her wet coat and boots, then she looked at the clock on the kitchen mantel. Ben McBride would be up on stage singing in a few minutes.

She went to the large hallway, opened the lid to the firebox of their Russian stove, and put pine kindling to the smoldering coals. When the kindling took flame, she added a few pieces of slow-burning oak. Later she would fill the box so that it would keep the downstairs warm through the night.

She untied her scarf, and her hair sparked and flew in many directions. She pulled a pale blue sweater over her head and stepped out of her tan wool slacks. She put on the barn clothes hanging on a peg next to the stove—long-handled underwear, an old flannel shirt, old army-green wool pants, and an old, worn, man's mackintosh—and pulled on her barn boots.

She started to the barn, but then she stopped in the kitchen and turned on the Philco battery radio they kept on the mantel. Madge had said Ben McBride's show was going to be broadcast over the Lewiston station. Might as well see if she could pick it up. Tad would want to hear about it.

She turned to WLAM and tinkered with the radio until she heard, coming through the static, "Well, it's three in the morning,/ and I'm almost where I want to be. . . ." That was Ben McBride's voice all right, a voice as rough-edged as pine bark, but not one sliver off-key. There he was singing his songs about life on the road, just where he wanted to be. Singing twangy songs about two-timing love, and drinking to the gills, and driving—always driving—from some place to another but never, ever getting there.

Without thinking, she picked up the radio to take it with her. Then she thought better of it, put it down on the table, and walked out the door that led through the wood room and into the barn.

Lily climbed up to the loft, reached for the hay fork, and in the soft yellow light of the one dangling bulb, she began tossing down the hay.

———————

Of course, what Ben McBride saw when he finally stepped out of the bright lights of the auditorium was not Lily Frost at all. In her seats, instead, looking like they were in heaven, sat a pasty-faced boy, a puny man, and a double-sized woman wearing a loud red-and-green plaid with matching plaid glasses, which also matched the man's bow tie. Christmas square dancing outfits.

Ben's heart sagged. Then he told himself that was that. He told himself it was just as well—it wouldn't have led anywhere, anyway. For all he knew, Lily Frost might be married by now. Then, before a larger and more enthusiastic crowd than he had expected, Ben McBride threw his heart into the next song,

> That woman keeps on keeping me awake,
> And when I sleep she's right there in my dreams.

———————

Lily gave hay to the horse and sheep, thickened the hay beds under the chickens, lugged water from the trough in the barn cellar to the buckets in the stall. She and Tad usually did the chores together, so it had taken her longer than she thought it would. She came into the kitchen to hear Ben McBride singing,

> An old man folks called Tater
> Taught me to play his old guitar
> Underneath an old magnolia tree.
> And when his life was ending,
> He called me by his side
> And he gave that old guitar to me.
> Tater said, "Boy, sing when you are burdened,
> When you see trouble's gonna start.
> Yeah, them dark clouds will be lifted
> By the songs inside your heart.

Then he sang the chorus again and the audience sang along with him. Sounded like a huge and happy crowd. But with the weather, she told herself, it was just as well she hadn't gone. That and other reasons too.

When the song about Tater was done, Ben announced over the wild applause that he'd sing one more number.

Give me a sun and a moon and an open road and I'll be happy all my days,
Give me the wind and the rain and a blinding storm, and I'll still find my way,
'Cause I'm a roaming man, a wandering man, with a song to keep me company.
Give me my old guitar and my old, old car and I'll be on my way.

Lily turned the radio off with a determined twist of the knob. She had worked up a sweat in the barn and was beginning to feel a chill from cooling down. Before this night was over, she was going to treat herself to a long, hot bath. But she still had work to do.

Keeping the thick wool stockings on her feet, she filled the wood box next to the stove in the kitchen. She lugged armload after armload of wood from the wood room to the huge box in the hallway. Then she added more wood to the glowing embers of the hall stove and the kitchen fireplace.

"I'm a wandering man, a roaming man," she muttered to herself.

It was late before Ben McBride and the Crooked River Boys finished signing autographs. The weather had taken a distinct turn for the worse, and a cold rain bit through their clothes. Ben was doing well enough by then to put them up in motels—a step above the flea-bitten ones they had stayed in when they were just starting out, and a distinct improvement over sleeping on the bus. Good thing he had booked the accommodations early in the day. With this weather, there'd be no rooms to be found

M. L. ROSE

tonight. They just might sleep for two days since they didn't have to be in the Boston area until New Year's Eve.

Ben McBride, though, was not with them. He had suddenly announced he had old friends to see and told his band that if he wasn't back by the next day to go on to the motel in Boston without him—he'd get there in time.

He had negotiated the purchase of a rusty old tub of a car from the motel owner and set out in rain that would soon turn to ice and snow. Driving with such bad visibility would have been hard enough if it had been a road he knew well. Hell, he might never find that place on Eden's Ridge on such a night. He'd had a hard enough time finding it a year and a half ago in the clean light of a summer day.

———

Lily put her hands close to the crackling fire and shivered. Finally, she could treat herself to that bath. In fact, she wanted a bubble bath. Hadn't taken one in ages. She'd leave the door open to let in warm air from the fireplace. Warm. Warm room, warm bath, warm music. That's what she needed.

What she really needed was an antidote to Ben McBride and his music. She took the Philco battery radio into the bathroom with her, put it on the wicker stand, turned it on, and moved the dial toward a Boston station.

I was 'bout to say I love you,
She needed to hear it so,
But I knew that if I said it,
She'd never let me go,
So I said I'll call you later
And I gave that miss a kiss,
And I headed for the highway
And I gave that miss a miss.

Damn, if it wasn't Ben McBride again. This time it was a record. That voice, as blue and ragged as her old haying jeans. She quickly turned the knob and finally found the station she was looking for. Sinatra. More like it. See, she wasn't a music snob. She loved Frank, and he was often slightly off-key.

Just as she started the water running in the tub, she sneezed. She would surely catch cold if she didn't get rid of the chill she was feeling. She smiled as she remembered her mother saying to her father, "Reuben, sounds like you got a cold coming on; why don't I fix you a little toddy?" And of course her mother would fix herself a little one too, to "keep him company."

Lily had to use a stepstool in the kitchen pantry to reach the top shelf. She wasn't sure the bottle was still there, but it was. Almost half full.

She poured some of the whiskey into a striped juice glass. She looked at the label and noticed that underneath the name it said "Tennessee Sippin' Whiskey." Lord, a man from Tennessee on the radio. Tennessee in his songs. Tennessee in her whiskey.

She took a swallow. And almost choked. She added some hot water and a generous dose of honey and tried it again. Better. She felt the warmth sliding down. She took the bottle with her just in case.

As water filled the old porcelain claw-foot tub, Lilian Frost poured in Ivory Flakes, undressed, twisted her thick hair up off of her neck, and secured it as best she could. Her mother used to say, "Lily, your hair has a mind of its own just like you do."

She topped her glass off with more whiskey. Then, with the glass in one hand, she stepped into the tub and lowered herself into the deep suds. She took another swallow of the amber liquid, lay back, and relished the warmth flowing through her and the mountains of bubbles rising around her as Frank Sinatra crooned "Night and Day" from the radio beside the tub.

She took another swallow. A bigger swallow. Of course, she would have forgotten him altogether. McBride that is. But there were those *postcards*.

Tad kept shaking his head in puzzlement saying it wasn't like Ben to write.

And every time she walked into Butters' Corner Store, there he was on the jukebox. Every time she turned the radio on, there he was. And of course, Tad and Sarah had all of his records, and they played them *all* the time. Lily hoped they'd eventually wear out. All those songs about lonely old men in Memphis—and lonelier women—about loving and leaving and driving and drinking and dreaming. And then he seemed to be expanding his range, adding songs about the country and cows.

What a phony, she said to herself, or maybe she said it aloud. In spite of those jeans and cowboy boots Ben McBride wore on the jacket covers, not to mention the hat that he had taken off to her that summer day— taken it off and smiled, laughed really, even though she was giving him a piece of her mind—in spite of all those country airs, Ben McBride, city-born and raised in Memphis, Tennessee, wouldn't know one end of a cow from the other. And singing it doesn't make it so.

She quaffed a bit more of her drink—deciding she liked the word *quaffed*—and sank farther down until the mountain of suds covered all but her shoulders and head.

Sinatra was followed by Glenn Miller's orchestra with "String of Pearls." She and Jackie had danced to that very song. Good dance music. Jackie was gone. Glenn was gone too, but his music was still there. She remembered how sad she had been when she heard Glenn Miller had died in a plane crash. It had seemed like a personal loss.

And she had had her fill of loss. Lost Jackie at Pearl Harbor. Dear, sweet Jackie. She had lost other schoolmates too, who would have chosen to spend their lives in these Maine hills but were instead killed in places with names they might not have known how to pronounce.

Lost her parents, who had been middle-aged when they had Tad and Lily. Lost them in the outbreak of flu that hit Hadley's Curve especially hard during the early years of the war. Lost her father, who had taught her to love bird songs and the sound of words and left her with shelves of books. Lost her mother, who had taught her the love of music and pointed her toward Juilliard. And left her the piano.

Lily took another sip of her drink, and sank back down into the suds, and the warm liquid moved down her throat.

"String of Pearls" was finished, and now Ella was singing,

> Will love come my way
> On a rainy day? . . .

And even though Lily Frost seldom cried, hadn't cried for years, she felt tears rolling down her face.

> Or will it ever come at all?
> I glimpsed its face for a time and place
> but I was headed for a fall. . . .

"Get hold of yourself, Lily Frost," she said, definitely aloud this time, wiping her tears away with wet, sudsy hands. She took another drink of the Tennessee Sippin' Whiskey. Probably that was what Ben McBride drank.

She was sure feeling sorry for herself. Why, she even felt like she had lost Ben McBride too. Or maybe she felt she had *lost out* on something. But what? Why would she be so preoccupied with a man who galled her, had from the first? It even galled her that he could play the piano.

According to Tad, Ben's mother had suffered a harsh economic setback when her husband took off early in Ben's life. Still, even on a seamstress's earnings, she had managed to pay for his music lessons. What had gone wrong? Why was he living his life on the road, singing music that was far beneath him? Tad's take was that Ben was a good man who had rambling in the blood.

And even if she had liked Ben McBride—which of course she *had not* at all, she *did not* at all . . . Lily took another swallow. She just might stay in this tub all night. She sang along with Ella.

Will I be one to know
The feeling only love can bestow? . . .

She'd have to remember to load the stove in the hallway, the one Victor, their old Russian neighbor, had helped her father build. Then she remembered she had already fed it for the night, so Lily Frost settled back in the tub and sang loudly,

Will the love the poets extol
Come to me and then will I know
The kind of love that sings to the soul? . . .

She sipped and sang through that song, another by Frank Sinatra, and one by Mel Tormé before deciding she'd better get out of the tub or she'd shrivel. She caught the chain of the plug with her toes and pulled it out. She had pretty toes. She just might polish them with some of Sarah's pink polish. She stood ever so carefully, feeling somehow wobbly.

She looked at herself in the mirror above the sink. She knew, when she took the time to think of it, that she had a pretty body. Jackie had told her so the two times they had "gone all the way," or so the expression was. But all the way to what? It had been nice. Sweet. But certainly not fire and flames. And that was the only man she had *known*. And she knew she was supposed to feel guilty, but she never had.

She poured another shot of whiskey and told herself she was just thankful she would never see Ben McBride again, never see those eyelashes long enough to sweep the floor.

Speaking of sweeping the floor, she had noticed earlier the kitchen floor needed sweeping. She'd put her robe on and go find the broom. She was sure glad she hadn't gone to that concert.

Twelve

Thick flakes of wet snow clung to Ben McBride's Stetson and his sheepskin coat. He stood knocking hard on the door frame. There were lights. He smelled wood smoke from the chimney. Surely someone was home. For thirty miles he had sat behind the wheel of a Packard that had seen better days a long time ago, but which he'd bought for a song— well not really a song, but for a pittance.

The old car had inched along in the snow like a blue-tick hound, its two faded-yellow headlights glued to the rutted road. For hours he had followed the trail to the Frost place. Finally located the house and pulled up near the porch. Noticed there was a light on in the kitchen. Someone was up even though it was late.

In spite of the cold, he had taken off his hat before he knocked. Now he put his hat back on and knocked several more times, harder. They *had* to be home. He was trying to decide what to do when the door flew open so suddenly it startled him.

He blinked against the flood of light that spilled out from the house, forming a rectangle around his feet. Standing in the open doorway was Lily Frost, wearing a chenille bathrobe the color of a Georgia peach, and holding a broom in her hand almost as if it were a shotgun. Her hair, he would recall years later, was "wild, just plain wild, golden brown tendrils going every which way."

She blinked to make sure she wasn't hallucinating. Ben McBride. The famous Ben McBride. Tall and handsome and warm-eyed Ben McBride. Even under his dripping Stetson, she could see his eyes were still brown as a puppy's.

"Whoa, ma'am," he said, backing up and putting his hands into the air in surrender, "I give up."

Lily blinked again and leaned against the doorframe to steady herself. "The things you see when you don't have a gun." Then she stood there looking at the broom as if she were trying to remember what it was doing in her hands.

"I wouldn't advise you to go out riding on that thing tonight," he said, gesturing to the broom. "Bad visibility for the best of drivers."

Lily had a blank look. She didn't get the joke. "What are you doing at my house?" she asked.

Ben laughed and said, "Do you ask that question all the time?" Then he found himself suddenly feeling the need to explain why he *was* there, even if he didn't think she was in a particular frame to listen. "I shouldn't just show up so late, I know, but I just couldn't get this close without coming to see . . . my old buddy." He had almost said *you*.

"Your old buddy is . . . in Pennsylvania at Sarah's folks. Took a bus on the twenty-third," she said, slowly and too carefully. "I could have told you that if you had called . . . but then again, you couldn't call . . . because we don't have a phone." She smiled, thinking that was a clever thing to say.

Then he realized, this woman has gone and gotten herself tipsy.

"So you're here alone?" he asked, and immediately regretted what she might think was the implication.

"Just me and Frank Sinatra, Mel Tormé, and Maughn Vonroe . . . Vaughn Monroe," she said, gesturing toward the parlor with a flourish.

Not just a little tipsy. This lady has gone and gotten herself rip-roaring drunk. She didn't seem to notice the cold, the heavy snowflakes clinging to Ben's jacket, or the fact that she was dressed in only a bathrobe.

Ben stepped toward her, gently loosened her grip on the broom, and turned her around by the shoulders. "Let's get you out of this weather, ma'am. You might catch cold."

"Not to worry," she said, letting him direct her through the hallway into the kitchen. Then Lily stopped suddenly, and Ben bumped into her, almost toppling her over. He caught her, and she turned to face him. "Mistletops . . . mistle*toes*," she said, pointing upward toward the doorway to indicate why she had stopped. A neat cluster of mistletoe hung above their heads. Lily closed her eyes and puckered her lips.

Lord, he had dreamed of kissing this woman, dreamed of putting his lips on hers. But not like this. He wanted Lily Frost to know exactly what she was doing if she ever kissed him. He tenderly turned her around again, guiding her gently toward the harvest table, and said, "I never kiss on a first date."

She teetered ever so slightly, steadying herself against the table. Her bathrobe draped open, exposing smooth skin and cleavage.

"Have a seat, Mr. McBrode, McBroom, McBen . . . ," Lily said, picking up her empty glass and waving it toward him and then toward the deacon's bench behind the kitchen table.

Ben McBride stepped toward her, took the lapels of her bathrobe, pulled them together and cinched the corded belt by tying a square knot. She looked surprised.

"No, ma'am," he said, "*you* have the seat while I take off my boots."

With exaggerated ladylike movements, Lily lowered herself onto the bench. She put her hands in front of her eyes as if Ben were going to undress. Then she spread her fingers and peeked to watch him take off his coat and drape it across a ladder-back chair near the fireplace.

Ben took off his hat, pulled off his cowboy boots, and placed them on the hearth. Then he stood by the fire warming his hands and thinking about what he had come upon. Usually, he had no tolerance for pie-eyed drunks, having had a father who was one. His mother's recollections and his few faint memories of the man who left home when he was three had been enough to warn him away. But Lily, he recognized, was not even a drinker. He found himself thinking she was both sweet and oddly comic. He turned to face her, putting his hands behind him to the fire.

The flickering orange and yellow light from the fireplace glittered against his black sequined shirt. Lily squinted at Ben. "My, but you are spruced up," she said with a giggle. "All flinge . . . fringe and gritter . . . glitter."

"You spent Christmas all by yourself?" he asked, ignoring her comment.

"Just me—and the Christmas tree," she said, gesturing toward the parlor.

"Oh, in there with Frank and Mel and Vaughn?"

Ignoring his quip, she pointed toward the barn. "And the sheep and horse, and the chickens and our pet sow—just like in the stable in Bethlehem. I kept waiting for the three wise men to show up, but I guess they got lost. No stars out, you see," she said, pointing toward the ceiling.

She laughed at how funny she was. Then she wondered if she was making as much sense as she thought. She knew she had had a lot to drink, but she was, darn it all, clear-headed enough to be muddled as to how he had appeared out of thin air. Or out of the thick, snow-laden air, to be more precise.

"You always wear that brown hat even with a black sequined shirt?" she asked.

Actually he did, but he thought he'd avoid a fashion lesson, so he said, "Well, I left my black hat at home." Then he sneezed. Lily jumped up, almost tripping on the long bathrobe. "The *cure* is what you need. Cure for a cold. Takes away the chill. I had a teensy little dose when I came in earlier," she said, closing her fingers to show a minute amount. "Now, where's that bottle?"

Lily disappeared into the bathroom, came out with an almost empty bottle of Jack Daniels, and reached into the open cupboard for a clean glass. "I'll pour you a little *medicinal* toddy," she said, collapsing back down on the deacon's bench with a thud and patting the bench for him to sit down beside her. But Ben remained standing. "And I'll have one to keep you company," she said.

She poured her glass half full and was remarking about how pretty the color was when he took the bottle from her, "Let me, ma'am." He poured a slight finger of bourbon into the other glass, and with a quickness of hand took hers and handed that one to her instead.

"To the prevention of colds," he said. They raised their glasses in a toast. She drained the small amount in her glass. *Lord,* he thought, *she's going to have a headache tomorrow, if not worse.*

Lily put down her glass, looked directly at him. "I think," she said solemnly, "that I am *not* glad to see you, Ben McBride."

"I won't stay long then," he said, "but I think I *am* glad to see you, Lily Frost." There, he had said it, even if she was so tipsy she probably wouldn't remember. He *would*. He would remember everything about her forever. He knew that now.

Their eyes locked briefly. Then she said, "I still don't get it."

"Don't get what, ma'am?"

"This whole country-western-honky-tonk . . . phe-nom-e-non," she said, resting on every syllable, "everywhere you turn on the radio. And every song on that jukebox at Madge and Forrest's store. Walter and June—I gave them the tickets—they're cra-a-a-zy about it. Seems everybody 'round here is crazy about it. Just 'scapes me . . . *es*-capes me," she said, correcting herself.

So that was Walter and June, whoever they are, in the front row, Ben thought. Now he could smile about it, though earlier that evening it hadn't seemed the least bit amusing.

Lily put her glass to her lips before she noticed it was empty. She plunked it on the table and reclined on the deacon's bench. She stretched out her legs, tucking her bathrobe carelessly around her, and wiggling her toes in the air. "I was going to paint my toes tonight," she said. "I think I have pretty feet."

She sat up and examined her toes. "What about you? You think I have pretty feet?"

Ben found himself suppressing a laugh of delight at her out-of-character behavior. He sat down at the end of the bench and playfully picked up her left foot, "I pronounce this foot the most beautiful foot in the kingdom."

"Tad never told me how pretty you were," she said. "Do you ever sing about *loving* the woman and *leaving* the road? Why don't let's you and me dance? Frank's just in the parlor waiting to serenade us. Good old Frank. See, I'm not a music prude after all. Frank and I go way back together—even if he gets a tad off-key sometimes."

Lord, he'd love to dance with her, hold her in his arms, swaying to music. But not like this. "No, ma'am," he said, "let's get you up to bed."

He let go of her foot, took her by the hand, and pulled her to a standing position. Then, standing behind her, he more or less pushed her up the stairs, steadying her as she steered herself toward her bedroom and her bed. She fell down on top of the cream-colored bedspread, and was immediately asleep. He thought about putting her under the covers, but he knew that would be an ordeal. He went into the next room and pulled a comforter and a quilt off another bed. By the time he got back in Lily's room, she had fallen asleep, a half-smile on her face.

Ben tucked the covers around her and tiptoed downstairs. He put the screen on the fireplace and wondered if he should leave. But there was no way anyone—even a vagabond like himself—should be out on the road tonight. Besides, he didn't want to leave Lily alone in that condition. Well, he didn't want to leave her, period.

He found some more quilts, took off his wet clothes, and lay down in the hallway on a sofalike thing that he would later learn was called a hired man's bed. It was just across from a huge brick stove of some kind, which had the hallway nicely warm. He hoped it would stay that way through the night. He probably should put more wood in it, but he didn't know beans about such things.

On the other hand, he suspected Lilian Frost could survive on her own in Alaska. She could survive anywhere. Why had he thought seeing her again would make it easier to forget her? He was certain now there was nothing ordinary about her. And the way he was drawn to her was not at all ordinary for him.

Ben McBride went to sleep with a feeling of gladness for reasons he couldn't quite name. But he knew it had to do with the woman sleeping in the room above him.

Thirteen

B en woke up late the next morning to the smell of coffee and bacon. He was surprised Lily was up already. He'd have bet she'd be in her room all day with the curtains pulled.

He slid out of bed. The house was warm. Lily must have fed the stove while he slept. He pulled on his jeans and put on the same black sequined shirt. He'd need to go out to the car and get some clean clothes.

He realized he was both eager and anxious about seeing Lily this morning, and why was that? He usually wasn't at all shy around women. And *she* was the one who had been three sheets to the wind. But he stuck his head into the kitchen like a schoolboy coming to class tardy.

Lily was standing with her back to him at the black cast-iron stove. She was dressed in loose-fitting jeans and an oversized green-plaid flannel shirt with the tail out. The baggy clothes could not hide her square shoulders and the long angular lines of her body.

If he were an artist, he would paint her. If he were a truck driver, he would give a wolf whistle. He considered doing just that to gauge her reaction, but he thought better of it. *Do that, McBride, and you won't get any breakfast for sure.*

"I see the lady of the house has risen early," he said. She looked over at the clock. Ten might be early for him, but it was late for her. She would tell him as they ate breakfast that she had already seen to the animals, gathered the eggs, and prepared breakfast. She didn't tell him she had also taken some BC Headache Powder.

But she told him none of that at that particular moment in the first meeting of the morning. Ben McBride watched her as she turned to face him. Her eyes were a tad bloodshot and pallid, but still blue as a May morning. He saw a look of hesitation on her face he'd not seen before. Then slowly, slowly—that reluctant smile of hers.

"Thank you," she said, and she found herself suddenly thinking that his eyes were the brown of a creek in mud season. She felt color rising to her cheeks, so she turned quickly to tend the bacon and found herself staring at all things brown. The tin of coffee beans she had just ground. The jar of molasses.

"For what? I didn't do anything."

"That's why I'm thanking you," she said, transferring the bacon from the cast-iron spider to the plate with studied efficiency. Did she really tell him last night that he was pretty? She took the coffeepot and poured coffee in the two cups sitting on the table. She winced at the noise when she set the pot back on the burner.

Ben smiled. He had begun to know something of her ways, and he knew that come hell or high water, she would not mention last night again.

She took an egg out of a yellow stoneware bowl. "Fried or scrambled?"

"Over easy," he said.

Then quiet again—a country morning quiet, maybe a hangover quiet on her part, and also a clumsy quiet—which he broke by saying, "Mind if I wash up after breakfast once I get some clothes out of the car?"

She smiled at the sequined sunburst pattern across his shirt and said, "Please do." That broke the awkwardness, and they both laughed. Then, faking a nonchalance she didn't feel at all, she cracked the egg she'd been holding, dropped it into a thin layer of bubbling bacon grease in the spider, and asked what she had wondered since she woke up. "What time do you have to leave?"

"Well, we've actually got a breathing spell for two nights. Then on New Year's Eve we play in Massachusetts at the Hillbilly Ranch—somewhere around Boston. Supposed to draw big crowds. And it's on the radio . . . WCOP." Why did he say that?—she wouldn't listen to his music. And besides, what he wanted to say was that he wasn't in any hurry to leave.

She almost closed her eyes in gladness that he didn't have to be anywhere for two days. Then he added, "But I suppose I should be gettin' on, though, join the boys where they're puttin' us up."

She found herself wishing it had snowed a foot. As it was, the roads would be slow-going, but not impassable. She searched her mind desperately for a reason for him to stay, even though it was surely best for both of them if he left right after breakfast.

He searched his mind desperately for a reason not to leave.

"If you want to stay for the day . . . I can show you the orchard and fields . . . how they look covered with snow . . . since you've only seen the place in summer . . ." She was fumbling. She looked at the cowboy boots sitting near the fireplace. "I'm sure we can find some boots around here that fit you."

And so, on December 29, 1949, after a breakfast of bacon and eggs and coffee and home fries and toast, Lily Frost tended to the dishes, glancing out the window as she did so to watch Ben McBride gingerly make his way to his car to retrieve his travel bag. When she set the cleaned spider back on the stove a bit too hard, the noise caused her to wince again. She had certainly—what did they call it?—tied one on last night. She couldn't believe she had let her guard down in such a way. Good thing that Ben McBride, whatever else he was and was not, was a gentleman.

By the time he reached the front door, she was standing there, broom in hand. "Not again," he said in mock exasperation, putting his hands into the air in surrender. She laughed and then handed him the broom, suggesting he brush the snow off the windshield and pull his car into the shed behind her truck.

————————

After breakfast, they bundled up and went outside for a walk. Yesterday's ice and rain had yielded to large wet flakes, which in turn had, when the night grew cooler, given way to about three inches of snow as fine as powder. With each step their boots sank until they reached the layer of crust below. The few apples remaining on the orchard trees gleamed particularly red against the white backdrop.

As they tromped their way through the orchard, Lily named the many varieties for Ben and told him about her great-great-great-grandfather, Eden Frost, who had claimed the land all those years ago. And she told Ben how each generation had done its part to keep it. She stopped next to an apple tree set off to itself, its bark gnarled, its trunk twisted by wind and time. It was a Ribston Pippin, she told him, and the legend was that her grandfather had been born under the tree. Her great-grandmother had continued to pick apples at the first signs of labor—and hadn't been able to make it back to the house in time.

The winter sun was bright now, and already the wet snow was sliding off the twisted branches of the old tree—branches that seemed to Ben as feeble and brittle as ancient bones. Two-by-four props already held up its thickest limbs. Ben thought of people he knew who were so old they stood erect mostly by willpower and pride.

Lily told him how she and Tad had climbed on its branches when the tree was hardly strong enough to hold them. Then she brushed the clinging snow from one of its winding arms and seemed lost for a moment in her own thoughts.

They walked through the woods and came back by the pond. When they got to the field where they had stood a year ago that past summer, Ben stopped. "This is where I saw that sunset," he said. "What's that poem again?"

She quoted,

> She sweeps with many-colored Brooms—
> And leaves the Shreds behind—
> Oh Housewife in the Evening West—
> Come back and dust the Pond.

There had been no hesitation, no groping for what poem he was talking about—even though it had been a year and a half. They were again caught, it seemed, in the reverie of the poem.

But Ben McBride was never one to let a somber mood last long. That was the way he lived his life. He suddenly smiled as if a light had turned on in his head. "I think this calls for some music . . . Miss Frost," he said, "has a lady of your refinement ever been to a square dance?"

"As a matter of fact," she said, "we learned that in school, and I have been known to attend one from time to time. As I told you last night, or think I did"—and at this mention Lily felt color rise to her cheeks—"I am *not* a prude just because I don't care for . . ."

"Well then, a square dance it will be. To Miss Emily's poetry."

"Whatever do you mean?"

"I mean, Miss Emily's poems fit songs. 'Amazing Grace' for example," Ben said as he sang, "She sweeps with ma-ny colored brooms," to the tune of the old hymn.

Then he stopped, faced her, and said in all seeming seriousness, "I'm taking you up on your offer of that dance last night." He bowed before her as she'd seen Southern gentlemen do in the movies.

"Well, I swan," Lily said, trying to mimic a Southern belle from those same films and glad for the comic relief. She hoped he'd think the flush of her cheeks was totally from the cold. "When was it, Mr. McBride, that you last danced in snow?"

He scratched his head. "Can't rightly recall, ma'am," he said with a look of pure pleasure on his face, "but I'm sure there's nothing like a do-si-do in the snow."

Then he took her gloved hand, walked her to an imaginary spot, stood to face her, and began singing. He sang the first verse to the tune of the song "The Yellow Rose of Texas."

"She sweeps with many-colored Brooms—and leaves the Shreds behind—now, do-see-do," he yelled, and they circled each other back to back. He sang another line and hollered, "Now allemande left with your left hand, go left to your partner. Then right. Come back to your partner and do-see-do. Now hinge." They turned to face each other, stepped forward, and joined hands. Their eyes met, but Ben hollered out, "Swing your partner," swinging Lily heartily as he again sang, "Oh Housewife in the Evening West—Come back and dust the Pond."

"Now, promenade home and make an arch," he said, and they stomped their way through the snow to the home spot of this dancing circle, clasped hands raised above their heads. Snow, as fine as stardust—Lily remembered later—glittered in the air for a moment. They stood almost nose to nose. Lily was warmed by his hands, even through her gloves. How could that be? She thought she might melt, just like a top layer of snow hit by the bright winter sun. Dissolve and become nothing but a pool of water.

They looked into each other's eyes. "Thank you, ma'am," Ben said, bowing slightly again. Then, suddenly, Ben McBride stood back and flashed his smile. "Now we're going to introduce Miss Emily Dickinson to the tango."

He slowly took off his gloves and threw them with a flourish under a nearby fir. Then he removed his coat, folded it carefully, and placed it on the snow. She found herself giggling. She hadn't giggled since she was a teenager, for heaven's sake.

Without a word, he stepped up to her and began unbuttoning her coat. One button. Then another. He slipped it off her shoulders and cast it ceremoniously on top of his.

"Wait." He looked around, made his way to a nearby white birch, and broke a small twig off a low-hanging limb. He bowed and presented it to Lily. "A rose. A lady must have a rose stem in her mouth if she's going to tango."

He put the twig in her mouth. "Now keep your chin up and look forward," he said.

"I know how to tango, Mr. McBride," she said. With the twig in her mouth, though, it came out muffled.

"Juilliard," she said, when he seemed surprised. "And you? Who taught you?" She wondered what the answer was.

"I just watch and learn. Now, Maestro," Ben said, motioning over to a tree, "some good tango music, please."

As he sang Emily Dickinson's words to a tune that would later be popular as "Hernando's Hideaway," Lily Frost and Ben McBride—in a sunlit spot in the winter woods of Maine—marched back and forth in the dramatic promenade of the tango. Pounding their footprints into the snow. At the end turn, they each put one hand into the air, gave a kick of snow, and Ben shouted, "Olé!"

After several turns, finally Lily pushed him away so she could have room to laugh, the twig still in her mouth. Ben laughed too. Then Ben McBride's laughter stopped as his eyes locked on hers. And her laughter, too, ceased. There was only the silence, and the slow *chee-zay, chee-zay* of the boreal chickadees in the nearby branches.

Ben reached over and took the birch twig from Lily's mouth. Then he took Lilian Frost's face in his hands. They kept their eyes open as he brought his lips down to meet hers for a quick, soft kiss. Then another. And another. Then they closed their eyes.

The next kiss was slow, lingering, full of sweetness and longing. A kiss that if she did not stop, Lily remembered thinking, would ignite into flame.

So she pulled away, feeling more shy than she had felt on her first kiss in seventh grade. And feeling as if she wanted to never stop kissing this man. Wanted to melt into him. *Think of something to say. Think of something to do.*

Finally, it came to her. "Have you ever been on ice skates?"

They trudged back to the house, where Lily fitted Ben with a pair of Tad's skates. With the old, wide, wooden snow shovel they pushed a space of snow aside on the shallow inlet of the pond—the only place where they could be certain the ice was thick enough. "Besides, if you fall in," Lily said, "the water here is three feet at the most. Out in the middle is another story."

Lily had the fluid, graceful glides and turns Ben expected. She found herself laughing at Ben's exuberant moves—and his flailing falls. Soon they were both laughing with the joyousness they thought had been left behind in their youth. Or in the war.

Ben and Lily, not noticing how time had flown, did not head back to the house until midafternoon. Only then did they notice the blanket of clouds spreading over the early afternoon sky. By the time they went inside, the sun—which had made the snow shine like satin—had disappeared, bringing the winter dark even earlier.

"More snow ahead," Lily said, looking at the sky as they tromped their boots in the wood room before taking them off and stepping into the kitchen.

"I suppose I should grab my things, get on my way," Ben said in what sounded like both a statement of intent and a question for Lily.

"You've got to get into some dry clothes, at least," she said, and they both smiled that he had fallen so many times on the ice.

She heard herself saying, "You might as well stay for an early supper—breakfast was so late, and we seem to have skipped lunch . . . and I've got some leftover chicken that needs eating. Otherwise, you'd have to stop before you got any distance down the road."

She heard herself saying, "You could even stay for the night."

What in the world are you doing, Lily Frost? she asked herself. And to Ben she said, "What I mean is—it might do you good to get a good night's sleep before you get back on the road . . . since I saw to it you didn't get much last night." Had what she said made a lick of sense?

He smiled. She did, too.

And so it was that Ben McBride felt he had once more been reprieved.

And Lily Frost found herself wishing it would start snowing and snow forever, keeping the world out and them in.

Fourteen

After Ben had changed into a pair of dry jeans and an old pullover sweater, they did the barn chores together. Ben took to them, Lily thought, as if he were born to it. Or maybe that is what she wanted to think.

They fetched apples and carrots and squash from the root cellar and green beans from the canning shelves. Lily showed him how to tend the hallway stove while she told him that the area around Eden's Ridge was heavily Finnish and English, but that a small community of Russians lived not far away. Victor and Katrina Lamentov had been their neighbors for years, and Victor had helped her father build this wonderful stove.

In spite of the heat thrown out by the stove, Ben and Lily decided they wanted an open fire as well, so they soon had maple blazing in the shallow Rumford fireplaces in both the parlor and kitchen. While Lily cut the carrots and then made the crust for the potpie she'd make from the leftover chicken, Ben sat on the deacon's bench behind the pine harvest table coring the apples for baking—with the deft touch he had learned from the whittlers under the trees during his childhood.

Once supper was in the oven and on the stove, Ben looked down at his ragged sweater splintered with the hay he had handled in the barn. "Mind if I wash up a bit and put on another shirt?" *Hell, McBride,* he said to himself, *this isn't exactly a date you're having, so why are you spiffin' yourself up?* But he realized he wanted to do it anyway.

"Just as long as you don't put on one with sequins," Lily answered. She flashed him a quick look with her eyes that seemed to catch the flame of the blazing maple logs.

"Well now, ma'am, there's lots of women who get their hearts a-flutter when they see a bit of sparkle on the shirts." He could have bitten his tongue the minute he said it. How could he have uttered such a silly thing?

"Lots of women jump on a chair when they see a mouse, but I'm not one of them," she said with much the same authority she had used on the road that summer day—but this time, he thought, with a touch of humor.

———————

Ben McBride washed up, shaved with his Old Spice shaving soap, and put on his trusty jeans and a red-and-black plaid flannel shirt. He couldn't believe it, but he was . . . what was the word—*giddy?* Curly would have said *as giddy as a young colt in spring.*

Then it was Lily's turn in the bathroom. She'd have time to take a quick bath before the food was ready. *A sober one this time,* she told herself. And a short one. *Get in, wash off, get out.*

Just as she was about to rinse off and step out, the sound of a piano floated across the hallway, through the kitchen, and then to Lily. Debussy. "Clair de Lune."

It wasn't a record. It was Ben, touching those keys with the *feel* of every note, every chord. She closed her eyes and reclined, a glow coming over her.

Lily stayed in the tub, eyes closed, taking a deep breath from time to time and letting it out slowly. *Take this moment, memorize it, keep it with you always.*

The piece finished, and the spell was broken when Ben began chording the piano the way one does a guitar, and singing along:

> Come and sit by my side if you love me.
> Do not hasten to bid me adieu. . . .

Lily Frost smiled and shook her head as she reached and pulled the plug on the drain, noticing again that his voice had a slight patina of rust, yet was always, always on-key. She stood up and reached for the towel as his voice bounced down the hall and into her heart.

> But remember the Red River Valley
> And the cowboy that loved you so true.

It was cold in her bedroom, so she hurried to get dressed. Besides, she couldn't wait to be in his company again—even after thirty minutes. She took out a black gored skirt. She rummaged through her drawer looking furiously for nylon stockings like a girl getting ready for her first date. She found two stockings that had runs. The other two didn't match. So she gave up. She put on some navy blue socks, went back to the closet and found her navy pleated wool slacks. She had started wearing dress slacks during the war after watching Katharine Hepburn in *The Philadelphia Story*—and had worn them ever since, finding them well-suited to both her figure and the Maine climate.

She went to her cedar chest and took out the soft pink sweater with a scalloped neckline and tiny white pearl buttons—a Christmas gift from years back she had never worn. It had somehow ended up with the many things the young women had put in cedar chests during the war. And left there.

In the cedar chest, too, she spotted the tortoiseshell comb her grandmother had left to her. She twisted her hair up and secured it with that comb. And then lipstick—a light touch of rose. One of the Christmas presents from her young pupils had been an atomizer of cologne with a flowery smell. She held it away from her and gave it just a quick squeeze in the general direction of her neck. Then she looked into the walnut-framed swivel mirror that had been her mother's and her mother's before her.

Lily, do you know what you are doing?

And the mirror answered back: *Yes*. And *No*.

———————

Ben McBride was going through the collection of records when he looked up and saw her in the doorway, caught in the saffron light coming from the kitchen. Light that seemed almost like moonlight.

"Food's ready," she said, and there was shyness in her smile.

He followed Lily into the kitchen, unaware that his standing in the certain light of the fireplace had almost taken her breath away. They both picked their way through the meal of squash, green beans, chicken potpie, and a dessert of baked apples. In later years, neither could remember a thing they talked about at the supper table, or as they were doing the dishes together. But the rest of the evening would forever be burned into their minds . . . and their hearts.

Ben had fed the parlor fireplace and turned off the overhead light, leaving on the lamp next to the sofa, when Lily, coming in from the kitchen, said, "Let me turn on some more light so you can see."

"I can see just fine," he said. By then she had her hand on the light switch, but she let it drop. She looked down at her socks and realized she had forgotten to put on shoes.

"Do you mind if I play this?" he asked, holding up a record.

She smiled and gestured toward the phonograph with her hand, a gesture that said *be my guest*.

Then Lily walked over to the wine-colored sofa, sat down, picked up a magazine, and began to flip through the pages. Out of the corner of her eye, she saw Ben McBride put on the record of his choice and drop the needle gently. Which had he picked?

Sinatra. At that first beat of the song, Ben knew he had to hold Lily Frost in his arms, if only for a dance, a real dance. He could not leave here without that memory, a memory he knew he would keep no matter how many miles or how many other women he put between them.

And she knew as much as she had known anything in her life that Ben McBride would walk up to her, hold out his hand, and say, *I'm taking you up on last night's offer.*

She was right, almost. He stood before her, held out his hand, but he said nothing. Not one word. Lily pretended to be engrossed in an ad for tires. "Our tires make use of the highest technology known to man," she read. He stood there for what seemed forever until she closed her magazine, put it on the side table, and without looking directly at him she put her hand in his.

He pulled slightly as she stood. Still holding her hand, he put his other hand on the side of her waist. Frank began to sing:

> This is the day I'll hold on to
> When all the blue skies turn to gray. . . .

Ben McBride and Lily Frost moved in the quick, smooth, rhythmic steps of those who are born to music. She knew now his eyes would be smiling, even if he was not, but she would not look at his face. She looked at his shoulders, square, wide. She looked at the way he had left the buttons open at the top of his shirt. The tufts of chest hair peeking through.

> This is the moment I'll cling to
> When all those dark clouds seem to stay.

One thing you could say for Frank—his voice could melt a glacier. Ben turned her out, held her at arm's length. She looked at the way he had rolled the sleeves of his red flannel shirt to just below the elbow. They moved in sync, as if they had danced together for a lifetime.

> This is the moment I'll treasure,
>
> Holding you close to my heart . . .

Ben drew her closer to him, his hand at the back of her waist. She smelled the spice of his neck, and she felt herself grow weak. She took a deep breath for strength. *Lilian Frost, look anywhere but in his eyes.* She looked out the window and she saw snow was falling harder now, in dense, tiny flakes.

Ben McBride tried to keep his eyes on Lily's face. Surely she would look at him with those eyes that he had first seen on a green and blue summer day. He looked at how the tortoiseshell comb holding her hair caught a gleam of light from the lamp.

> Knowing this feeling I'm feeling . . .

Had he prayed for her without even knowing it? He spun her out again, her stocking feet sliding easily on the wide chestnut floor in perfect time to the music as Frank finished the line.

> Will still warm me when we're apart. . . .

Lily looked at his cowboy boots. That's it. Look at his feet. Those boots. Watch them move. Lord, the man can dance.

Then Ben, his hands on the small of her back, pulled her toward him. Closer, closer. He could feel the heat of her body through the thin sweater. She drew in her breath.

She found herself moving nearer, leaning in to this man she had tried to dislike since that time he ran her off the road, since the time he laughed at her with that laugh of his as if he carried a secret, something she did not yet know.

> I know after searching a lifetime
> I'm finally finding my way
> To a love that will fill my tomorrows . . .

She leaned her head against his neck. By now they were standing in one spot, still keeping up the rhythm with small steps and the slight rhythmic movement of their bodies. Closer and closer still, until she felt her breasts touch his chest.

She felt his lips brush her hair, her temple. He smelled her shampoo. And the hint of gardenias on her neck. He brought her hand to his mouth and kissed it. Then his warm lips were on her neck. She closed her eyes.

> A love that's forever today.

His hand moved to her hair. He removed the comb, and Lily's hair cascaded down. Finally, Lily Frost opened her eyes and locked her gaze on Ben's. And the thought skittered across his mind that those eyes were, above all, the color of a bottle of Evening in Paris perfume.

His hand on her back slowly eased inside her pink cashmere sweater, where he could feel her smooth, warm, skin. The top button of his flannel shirt was unbuttoned, and he felt her lips moving on his neck. He lifted her chin, kissed her forehead, her cheeks, her neck.

His hand found the small white pearl buttons of her sweater. The quickness of her breath seemed to be in rhythm with the beating of his heart. He unbuttoned the top button as he kissed the hollow of her neck. Then his lips came back to hers. He had wanted women before, had *had* many

189

women before, but he had never, ever, felt the passion he was feeling now.

And not only passion. That, too, but something more. Love, love as powerful as the yearning they both were yielding to.

But Lily suddenly pulled herself away. "No," she said, and she quickly began buttoning her sweater, "this is where it has to stop."

She said it with such finality, with such certainty, he was sure she meant it. And he was sure she would not explain any more. Maybe it had made her think of the boy who was killed at Pearl Harbor . . . or did she still have that lovesick pen pal in Montana? Maybe she was simply afraid.

He wanted to tell her he was afraid, too. Because he was. He wanted to tell her he loved her. Because he did.

But this was not the time. It would seem like a ploy.

"Do you want me to leave?" he asked.

She looked outside at the falling snow. Her eyes brimmed with tears, but she would *not* let him see that. She would not let him see that she was afraid of the sheer power of what was happening to her. But it wasn't desire she was afraid of. She was afraid this man was going to leave this place with her heart in tow. And she simply could not let that happen.

"The weatherman said it would quit snowing and clear up during the night," she said. "You should be able to get an early start tomorrow."

She made sure she was in the dark of the hallway before she said a hurried good night and added, "Put the screens in front of the fireplaces before you go to sleep." Then she went up the stairs, leaving Ben McBride feeling as if the breath had been knocked right out of him.

Lily Frost lay in bed, using all her willpower not to go down to Ben McBride, to slide in beside him as he slept, to give herself to him with the wild abandon her soul and body urged her toward. To give herself to this man of the road who had driven here and gently invaded her heart.

She lay there for what seemed like hours, struggling with herself, searching for sleep.

Suddenly, she heard a sound she recognized hitting the tin roof: ice. Her first thought was *the trees. The damage this will do to the trees.* Nothing to do about most of them, of course. Just wait and pray. Then she knew there was one she *must* save.

Downstairs, Ben, also unable to sleep, had risen, put on his jeans and shirt, and gone into the parlor. He moved the screen and fed the embers with pine kindling and a large piece of hardwood. He sat there looking out the window at the snow and rain and ice falling, and tried to make sense of all that was churning inside of him.

Then he heard Lily's steps, bounding down the stairs, into the kitchen, and out the kitchen door that led to the barn.

He found her in one of the rooms between the house and the barn. She was gathering two-by-fours—to further prop up the limbs of the old Ribston Pippin, she told him.

"I'll go with you," he said. "Let me go get my boots on."

"No need," she said.

"I'm going," he said with determination. He headed back to dress and grab his coat and put the screens on the fireplaces.

Ben carried the two-by-fours as Lily flashlighted the way to the orchard through the dark and the rain. They tried to see and at the same time shield their faces from the sleet and ice, sharp as glass.

Once there, Lily insisted that Ben hold the flashlight while she propped the limbs that were not already supported. The Southern gentleman in him wanted to say *let me do that—it's a heavy job.* But somehow Ben McBride understood that this was something she wanted to do herself. And he knew it had to do with her link to this place, this land.

That done, she took the flashlight from him, and as she did so, the light spanned across the field and the pond.

"What's that?" Ben asked, startled.

"Where?"

"I thought I saw something on the pond."

She pointed the light in the direction of the pond, and this time she saw it too. Lily took off, and Ben followed in her path and in the path of light, both of them tramping over snow that was quickly being covered with a layer of ice.

They could not see what it was until they were at the pond's edge. Lying sprawled in the center of the pond was a small deer, a yearling by the size of it. The creature had obviously ventured out on the pond, slipped, and not been able to get enough purchase on the ice to stand again. It lay almost motionless, clearly spent. It must have been there for some time.

"Poor thing, it's exhausted and distressed," Lily said, trying furiously to think what to do.

"Lily, go get some rope."

She hesitated, about to say the ice was too thin to go out there.

"Hurry," Ben said, "I'll keep an eye on the little fellow."

Lily rushed through the freezing rain to the barn, slipping twice on the newly iced snow. When she returned, almost gasping for breath, Ben wasn't where she'd left him.

"Ben," she hollered, flashing the light wildly across the pond. And then she found him, out on the pond, lying spread-eagled next to the animal, his gloved hand resting on the deer's back.

Lily, frightened that Ben and the deer would go through the ice any second, was about to yell, *are you crazy, crawling out there? You should have at least waited until we got the rope around you,* when Ben yelled, "Stay put and throw the rope out to me."

The rope reached him on the second try. He'd have time to be astonished at her throwing arm later. Now he had the deer to see to.

When Lily saw that he was using the rope for the deer and not himself, she yelled, "Ben, tie it around yourself and hold onto him."

"No, he might squirm, and then we'd both break through."

She kept the flashlight on them as Ben—still lying flat as possible to distribute his weight—tied the deer's feet together the way a cowboy ties a calf. So he had learned some country ways after all, probably from watching the same movies she had.

"Okay, Lily, pull. Slow and easy."

Lily positioned the flashlight in the snow and began pulling the small deer to the bank. Ben, still lying face down, using his elbow and the toes of his boots for leverage, scooted behind, a few inches at a time, the same way he had crawled to the deer. It was something he had learned from listening to an army buddy. A buddy named Tad Frost.

The flashlight fell from its perch, and the mix of ice and rain and spits of snow was so thick that Lily could not see Ben or the deer. All the while she pulled the rope toward shore, she found herself listening, in fear and dread, for the cracking of ice. But it did not come. And soon there they were, in the short scope of her sight.

She wanted to laugh and cry and shout. But she did none of those things. Instead she began untying the deer as Ben stood and steadied himself. Once untied, the yearling made several attempts at standing, but it was too spent. So Ben took off his coat, wrapped it around the tiny creature, and lifted the deer into his strong arms. And without a word between them, Lily pointed the way with the flashlight as they moved across the icy ground and through the dark and freezing rain toward the barn.

They took the deer to the three-sided shed attached to the back of the barn. It would, Lily said, give him shelter but leave him free to return to the woods when his strength returned.

They put him in a thick bed of hay, set some water out, then hurried through the barn, stopping in the kitchen only long enough for Lily to take off her coat and for both of them to take off their boots before rushing to the warmth of the still-burning fire in the parlor fireplace.

They were both flushed, breathless from the effort and from the wet and cold. Ben grabbed a piece of maple from the wood box and added it to the fire that he, in his restlessness, had fed just before Lily rushed down the stairs and into the night.

He stood up, and then, for the first time since the episode of the ice and tree and deer began, they looked at each other. They began laughing at their accomplishments, almost as if to say, *we did it.* And then the laughter faded, replaced by smiles that faded too as Ben and Lily fell deeper into each other's eyes, both of them trying to slow their hurried breaths.

"You've got to get out of those wet clothes," she said, looking at the shirt plastered against his body.

"You're not exactly dry yourself," he answered. But he was thinking, I've got to get out of this room, out of this spell this woman has put me under. I've got to leave her alone—just as she wants.

"I'll change in the hallway," he said. He started by her, only to feel her hand on his forearm.

"No," she said.

What he saw in her eyes only fueled his breathlessness. And her voice almost gasped for breath as she added, "Don't go."

Soon he was holding her face between his hands. Soon his lips, warm as fire, were kissing her cheeks and finding their way to her mouth. Soon his fingers were threaded through her wet hair.

Soon her hands had found the buttons of his cold wet shirt. Soon her lips were moving across his chest, which seemed to grow warm at her touch.

Her lips found their way back to his mouth and her body leaned into him. The yearning of the last days, the yearning that had hidden in their hearts for a lifetime was being fed.

As Ben McBride and Lilian Frost gave themselves to each other on the wine-colored sofa in a parlor on Eden's Ridge, the tortoiseshell comb Ben had removed from Lily's hair earlier in the evening still lay on the floor, catching the yellow and orange and red and even the blue of the blazing fireplace, turning it all to golden flames.

Fifteen

ily woke to soft yellow sunlight sifting through the bedroom window.
She lay there in the cradle of Ben's arm, his chest against her back,
his legs entwined with hers, thinking she might be dreaming.

Then she sat up with a start, grabbed a nearby throw to wrap around
her, and hurried to the window. There was a coat of ice on everything, but
not as thick as she had feared. And the temperature was already warm
enough to begin the melting. The ice would no doubt damage some of
their trees, especially the brittle birches. But apple trees are strong, even old
ones—so Lily felt sure the orchard would come through with only minor
damage if dry weather and above-freezing temperatures held long enough.

She crawled back into bed. She looked at this man beside her, listened
to the steady calm of his breathing. *A contented sleep,* she thought. She had
never known such contentment as what she felt waking up in his arms. She
had never known such bliss as last night. She drew in the sight of him, the
spicy smell of his body.

After they made love last night, they had put on jeans and sweaters and
thick socks and boots, wrapped Hudson Bay blankets around them, and
gone outside to check on the deer. He was already on his feet, eating hay.

They were almost upon him before he turned in their direction. His dark eyes locked on theirs, and he froze. They stood completely still. In a few seconds, almost as if he understood, the deer turned back to nibbling on hay.

"I do believe," Ben said, "that with some encouragement, you could domesticate that fella."

"It's been known to happen," Lily said. "Once a little doe joined the cows at the Lamentovs'. Victor and Katrina finally got her tame enough that she slept in their barn. That deer eventually became so tame that she'd ride into town on the back of their truck and would stay there while Victor and Katrina did their errands. She'd even let the kids pet her."

"Then why don't you try to tame this one? Think how Tad and Sarah's little one would love it," Ben said.

"Because," Lily said, "the same thing would happen to it that happened to Victor's deer. One day, it would stand there and let some hunter walk right up to it, get close enough to slit its throat. Besides, a deer is born to the woods." *Like you are born to the road,* she added to herself. But she didn't say it out loud because she really didn't want to think about it.

"And besides," she had said, "if he can't make it out there, he knows the way back."

But that had been last night. And now, even as she lay in bed beside Ben McBride, last night already seemed a distant memory, something to be held and cherished because she knew even in the gentle, clear light of this day that it was true—that Ben McBride *was* born for the road. That Eden's Ridge could never be his life, but only a detour.

And what was he to her? How would he change her life? Here she was, the most practical of women, though what she had done was anything but practical. But she had known this was something that would not come twice in her lifetime.

She listened to his steady breathing beside her. She smiled in pure joy and leaned down and brushed her hair over his face, tickling him awake. They made love again as the pale yellow sun added to the warmth in the cold room. Then they dressed in warm clothes to go see about the deer.

"Oh Lord, what a glorious sight," Ben said as they stepped out into a world transformed by ice, a crystal kingdom.

"Yes, nature has a way of bringing destruction and beauty at the same time," Lily said, leading the way to the shed where they had put the deer. He was gone, his small, sturdy tracks visible in the ice-crusted snow.

"Good luck, little fellow," Ben said, looking toward the woods. He expected Lily to check the old tree right then, but she said they could do it after breakfast, that it would take thicker ice than what they had got to bring down that tree.

"Things have to be sturdy to survive up here," she said. And he expected she was talking about much more than trees.

Ben helped her do the chores. Then, over a breakfast of pancakes and syrup from the sugar maples on the Frost farm, they told each other stories from their lives with the comfort of old friends.

"I'll refill our cups," Lily said, rising. Ben watched her as she walked back to the stove. Watched her caught in the squares of sunlight coming through the kitchen window as she walked toward him. He was awestruck by the beauty of it all, awestruck that this strong, spirited woman had made herself vulnerable to him, and awestruck, too, that he was equally vulnerable to her.

"I love you, Lilian Frost," he said. He had already told her that as he made love to her last night. "I love you. Dear God, Lily, I love you," he had said. And she had answered, but not with words.

This morning, she tried to turn his words into something light. "I bet you say that to all the women you make love to," she said, sitting back down across from him.

"No," he said, and then somehow he couldn't resist a tease. "I don't call them Lilian." Always one step forward and one step back when it came to matters of the heart. She smiled, but it seemed wistful.

"Seriously, Lily. You must know . . . that this, that I, that what we have . . ." He couldn't believe it. He, Ben McBride, was at a loss for words. What could he say?

What he said was that he wished it would start snowing, that blinding snow would fall for weeks so no one could get out or in and they'd have nothing to do for the whole winter but take care of the animals, load the stove, and make love. And he might write a song or two if the blizzard was long enough.

"You could even try your hand at writing some good ol' country songs," Ben said, only half-kidding, she suspected. Then he added, "Seriously Lily, if you ever wrote a song, what would it be about?"

"You're the songwriter," she said, getting up to clear their plates.

"But you are the song," he said, coming up behind her at the sink, putting his arms around her and burying his face in her hair.

She breathed in deeply, holding on to the feel of him, to the smell of him. She would never remember who let go first so that they could finish clearing the table. "You forgot we'd have to eat. What should we lay by for this fantasy snowbound winter?" she said, telling herself she was indulging *his* fantasy.

"Oh no, I didn't forget. Just hadn't gotten to that part yet." He reached his hand to the radio. "Do you mind if we turn this on just long enough to get the forecast for tomorrow? If the fates are with us," he said, "the good weather will hold until tomorrow at least. I could stay one more night, leave in the morning, and get there in time to get ready for the show. Or you could go with me," he added casually.

Lily didn't answer, couldn't answer. She turned on the water for the dishes and watched Ben tinker with the dial. That would be the story of his life. Watching the weather. The condition of the roads. Reading road maps. Always on the move. She had accepted that from the start. Had known that even as she gave herself to him, even as she took all that he had to give. That was part and parcel of who this man was.

So on December 30, 1949, Lily Frost moved Ben McBride's hand from the radio dial and found the station that would give the most accurate weather report—which would be the deciding factor in his staying yet another day.

The forecast was for clear weather the next day. "Lady luck is on our side," Ben said, picking Lily up and turning her around. "If you don't put me down, I'll never get these dishes done," she said, as if it were an ordinary day, never showing that she was elated he would be there one more day or that she was already thinking of the parting that lay ahead.

Their boots broke through the melting crust of ice as they made their way, late morning, to check the old Ribston Pippin tree. As Lily had been sure it would, it had weathered yet another assault, with just a few minor branches broken and hanging down.

Lily took Ben to the stand of sugar maples. She explained how they harvested the sap in March when day temperatures rose to near fifty and night temperatures dipped below freezing—the perfect condition for the sap to congeal and flow. She told him about boiling down the sap, bottling it, and then storing it on shelves in the cellar.

"Isn't that a lot of work when you could just buy some from your neighbor?" Ben asked.

"You are a city boy at heart," she said and laughed, even though the weight of the statement made its way to her heart. "We could do that. But then we'd miss out on . . ."

"A lot of work," Ben said, grinning and putting his arm around her.

"But we'd also miss out on . . . I don't know how to explain it. It's part of being . . . connected. Connected to . . . the land. To the ages. *Connected.*"

What I know is how connected I feel to you. Ben was about to say it aloud when she stopped at a particularly large tree.

"This is a rock maple," she explained. "Tad and I once got into big trouble for climbing it." She told Ben how she and Tad had once scaled that tree to the top, even though their protective mother had forbidden such things. "It's a wonder we didn't kill ourselves," she said, shaking her head.

Before she knew it, Ben had reached for the first limb and thrown a strong, lanky leg over it. He pulled himself up to a sitting position and grinned down at Lily. Then he looked up to decide which limb to stretch for next. Stretch, swing, sit, stand—until he was halfway up.

"Ben McBride, get down from that tree before you break every bone in your body," Lily yelled. But she wasn't serious. She laughed that rippling laugh that he loved to evoke from her.

Then suddenly, she wasn't laughing anymore as Ben McBride, hanging midway up the tree, slipped on an icy limb or let go somehow and plummeted through the air, slicing through the top coating of ice, and landing with a thud in a thick bank of snow. He lay there on his belly. Motionless.

"Oh dear God, no," Lily hollered, running to him. "Ben! Ben!"

She turned him over on his back. "Ben, Ben!" She yanked off her stocking cap and put her ear to his mouth to listen for breath. Ben McBride kissed her on the ear and started laughing.

In one of those moments of supreme thanksgiving followed quickly by fierce anger, Lily Frost screamed at Ben McBride the way she had never screamed at anyone in her life. "How dare you do that to me, Ben McBride!" she said. "How dare you!" She stood up quickly and made her way from him through the thick snow.

Ben caught her not twenty bootprints away. "Lily. Lily, I'm sorry. I thought you'd think it was funny."

"Then you don't know me, Ben McBride. You don't know me at all. How could you make me think you were hurt, or worse. How could you think that was funny? Lord!" Tears streamed down her face as she tried to break the grip he had on her arm and pull away from him. But Ben wouldn't let go.

"Lily, please, I didn't mean to scare you. Well, yes I did, but only for a second."

"A second is too much when it's someone you . . ."

She slung his arm away from her. This time he turned loose. She tromped away toward the orchard. He followed close behind. "Someone you what? Lily . . ."

Go ahead, Lily, he said to himself. *I've told you I love you, told you when we were making love. Told you at breakfast. Go ahead and say it. Please.* But to Lily he just repeated the question as he caught up with her, "Someone you what?"

She didn't answer. By then they had reached the edge of the orchard and headed through it. Ben had to fall behind to follow her in the narrow path between rows.

"Lily Frost," Ben hollered as she kept tromping ahead of him. He noticed it was still cold enough for fog to roll from his voice. "I love you. I want every one of these trees to know it. Hey trees," he shouted, "I love Lily Frost." And even louder, "Hey sky, I *love* Lily Frost. I will always love Lily Frost."

Ben stopped suddenly. Somehow the words scared him even as he said them. Yet in all of his long life, Ben McBride would look back and know that was the moment when he knew, with more clarity and sureness than any other time, that he had spoken a truth that would last far beyond that moment, that day, those few days. That truth would last a lifetime.

"And," he shouted to the trees and the sky, "Lily Frost loves me and will love me forever and ever, even if she won't say it."

Lily, who had continued marching away, stopped in her tracks and let the words sink in. She wanted to turn around and yell, *I love you too, Ben McBride.* But the reserve of New England was bred in her bones.

She did turn, though. "Exactly what is it, Ben McBride—king of the cowboys—that makes you think just because we spend one night together that you can run away with my heart?"

Ben McBride's heart leaped with joy at the bite of her words—having come to understand the feelings they covered. He couldn't help but resort to his playful ways. "Well, ma'am," he said, "I'm not rightly *king* of the cowboys—that title belongs to Mr. Roy Rogers. But to get to your question," he said as he took slow, heavy steps to break through the ice and onto snow. He couldn't believe how breathless he was when he finally reached her. "First of all, I don't care if this sounds like one of those honky-tonk songs you so disdain—you *do* love me, even though you don't *want* to love me. You love me even if you don't *know* you love me. And it doesn't matter if we fight over music, or over who gets the center of the road, or anything else. We are *bound* to love each other, Lily Frost, and you know it. I think we've both known it since that day you took to the ditch as a ploy to get me to stop."

Lily opened her mouth in astonishment, ready to protest such a charge, when Ben stepped even closer and put his fingers to her lips to shush her. "What it is *exactly* that makes me think you love me now and will love me forever is that we are linked in a way I'll never be able to explain, no matter how many songs I write."

His breath looked like puffs of smoke in the air. "What it is *exactly* is this." Ben put his arms around Lily, and moved his body up against hers, looked into her eyes with pure joy, and waited for her to bring her lips to meet his.

When she did, Ben McBride knew that sometimes just kissing a woman is making love.

———

They made love that day in the loft of the barn—having laughingly confessed to each other it had always been a fantasy to "roll in the hay."

But they cheated and lay between two thick Hudson Bay blankets, the flaxen light of high noon streaming in through the gaps between the weathered boards of the old barn. Lying there afterward, they told more stories. Lily told him how she had fallen in love with Mozart when she was four years old.

"And when did you fall in love with Jack Tate?" Ben asked.

Lily sat up, pulled the blanket to cover her chest, picked up a piece of straw, and gave thought to what she said. "I grew up with Jackie. He was the sweetest boy I've even known. I'll always miss him and wonder what kind of life he would have had. He wanted to come back here to Hadley's Curve and farm and raise a family. But then they bombed Pearl Harbor, and . . ."

They were silent for a while, reliving their separate memories of that day that had destroyed or damaged or forever changed the lives of everyone.

"Would you have married him?" Ben asked, finally breaking the quiet, running the flat of his hand up and down Lily's back.

Lily pulled the blanket higher on her chest. "I honestly don't know." She began breaking the straw into small pieces. "All of Hadley's Curve think they know," she said with a slight hint of irritation in her voice, but mostly with a sense of gentle understanding of the world she lived in. "Even today, eight years later, everyone thinks Jackie was my one true love, and to correct that impression would somehow seem . . . unfair to his memory. Hadley's Curve needs to hang on to what few romantic ideas they were able to salvage from that awful war."

But you were not a virgin he started to say, but didn't. Whatever she had done with Jack or with anyone else belonged to her. They were her memories, and he would not invade them. They were hers to keep until she shared them of her own choice.

Then she lay back down, her head on his shoulder as he told her about growing up in Memphis, in an area teeming with warehouses and jazz joints. He told her about Tater, whose mama and daddy had been slaves, and who along with Ben's mother had been Ben's anchor in childhood, told how Tater had sung blues songs under a magnolia tree and how he had taught Ben to play the guitar. And he told about his mama, the woman who had held her life—and his—together when her world fell apart.

"I wish you could have known my mama," he said. "But you two would have ganged up on me about my music." He chuckled at the thought of it. "Mama used to shake her head every time I was late for my piano lesson. But believe it or not, she never lectured me. And Lord, I feel guilty now, knowing how hard she worked to pay for those lessons. Actually, I loved my piano lessons. But I passed that old magnolia tree every day on the way to my lesson, and the lure of those songs ol' Tater sang was like the songs the sirens sang to what's-his-name."

Lily smiled, knowing Ben knew full well what his name was. Ben paused and ran his long fingers through Lily's flyaway hair as if to let time pass, years he did not want to talk about. And then he said, "Lied about my age and enlisted in the army. After the war, I decided to give my all to my music. By then Mama was gone. Tater was gone. But they both left me my music, and that's not only in my blood—it *is* my blood. My life."

"And you never married," she said, sitting back up again, pulling the blanket around her again. It was both a statement and a question.

"Came close a couple of times."

"So what happened?" She tried to sound much more casual than she felt.

"The road happened, mostly. By the time I got very far down the road I'd always changed my mind."

Lily threw down the last bit of straw and picked up another, hoping to sound nonchalant. "Did you love them?"

"I thought I did. I guess I thought I did. But not," he said, "like I *know* I love you." He wanted to pull her to him. But he didn't. He felt like the boy who cried wolf. He was telling the truth, but how could she believe him? *I told them I loved them,* he wanted to say, *but even as I said it I knew it wasn't a feeling or a word that would last.* But if he said that, would she understand? How could she understand it when even he didn't understand what had suddenly happened to him?

Once again, Lily didn't say anything. But she lay back down and put her head on his chest. The thought came to Ben that after searching all his life—even if he didn't know he *was* searching—he had finally found his way *home*.

———

After feeding and watering the animals and mucking out the stalls, after bathing and feasting on leftover ham, potatoes, and candied carrots, after kindling memories of their childhoods by roasting marshmallows in the open fireplace, Lily played the piano for Ben while he lay on the sofa, eyes closed, journeying to some long-ago and faraway place. She watched him as she played, praying for time to stand still just a little longer.

Later, as they held each other under the thick covers of Lily's bed, Ben asked her once more to go with him to the New Year's Eve concert. And once more, she explained she had to play at the service at the church.

"Lord, you'll probably be dragging me to church just like Mama used to," he said.

Lily just smiled, a smile that seemed sad to him. Later he would understand why.

"Guess you'll be all decked out tomorrow night in that black sequined shirt," she said. "Sure hate to miss that sight." And then her rare impish smile, which elated him.

"No, ma'am," he said in his phony hick accent, "it's gonna be New Year's Eve, so Ben McBride's not a-fixin' to wear black. Got me a red shirt with white fringe that'll just knock your eyes out." Then Ben McBride quit feigning. "Lily, I can't bear to think of the time separating us. If for some reason I can't squeeze in some days before we leave New England, why don't you join me and the boys on our tour through the Midwest—got about six weeks lined up there."

"Now you *are* dreaming," she said. Then she turned toward the fire so he would not see the tears welling in her eyes.

————————

Lily woke Ben at seven just as the sharp sound of sleet started to mix with the rain outside. "The weatherman was wrong yet again," she told him. And of course, if she were truly honest with herself, she hoped he'd say *damn the concert, I'm staying here.* Instead he looked out the window, sat up suddenly, and said, "Damn. I'd better get on the road before it gets worse than it is, don't you think?"

And of course she said, "Of course."

Ben washed up and threw on his sweater and jeans while Lily fixed him a breakfast of toast and jam and coffee. "I took your car out of the shed and got it running so it'll be warm," she said.

"I'll be warm just thinking of you all the way there," he said, gulping down the last of his coffee.

Lily walked him to the car. Since she would do chores as soon as he left, she had on her baggy jeans and a long-tailed, faded blue flannel shirt—she hadn't bothered to put on a raincoat or cover her head.

"Lord, you look so seductive in your barn clothes that I can barely bring myself to leave."

"And I'm especially seductive with my hair plastered down by the rain," she said, reaching up to wipe tendrils from her face.

"That you are," he said, "that you are." And in the cold rain of a New Year's Eve morning, Ben McBride tilted his hat, put his hands through her wet hair, and brought her face to his for a sweet, warm kiss.

"I'm taking you with me here, inside my heart," he said. "You know that, don't you, Lily?"

"Yes," she said, "I do know that."

"I'll see you soon, then—soon as I can. I'll call too. And write." Lily turned as if to start toward the house. But just as he stepped toward the car, she reached and took his hand, looked into his eyes, drew him to her, and kissed him. He felt her lips melting into his. Then she gave him a friendly push and said, "Now go. You've got the world waiting to hear you."

Later he would know that what he felt in their last kiss was deeper than just a yearning to make love again. But it was that, too. "Drive with care, Ben McBride," she said, "and on your side of the road."

"I'll call Butters' store and tell them to let you know I got there," he said.

"No need," she answered. "I'll listen to the beginning of your concert on the way to church—my car radio picks up WBZ at night." He kissed her once more, a short one this time, then another, and another, and another.

She pushed him toward the car door. "Now be off with you," she said, forcing yet another smile.

Then he saw. "Why, Lily Frost, I do believe you are crying."

"Of course I'm not crying," she said. "It's the rain."

Sixteen

By the time Ben arrived at the auditorium for a run-through early that afternoon, the sun had appeared again. It would dry the roads for the New Year's revelers. The show was sold out.

Ben's changed state of mind did not escape his band, and they teased him to tell them what had happened during those two days he'd disappeared. But this was not yet the time to share his supreme good fortune with them. He would do that later.

That time, of course, never came. When Ben McBride, back at the motel, set about to dress for the concert, he found the letter, written on onionskin paper, tucked into the neck of the red shirt fringed in white.

He almost didn't open it . . . because he knew, somehow, what Lily Frost would have to say to him.

Dearest Ben,

I ask you, first, to forgive me that I do not look you in the eyes as I say these things to you. But I so cherished each minute, each second I had with you that I could not bear to fill them with the sadness and pain we would both feel at the moment of ultimate truth.

There is, of course, more than one truth afoot here. I know, as surely as I know that spring will eventually melt this winter snow and ice, that what we have shared is a precious treasure—something most people don't find in a lifetime.

But I also know another truth: you were born to sing in a thousand smoke-filled taverns . . . and auditoriums . . . and concert halls, born to climb to heights you could not reach here on the ridge above Hadley's Curve.

You will find your place in the world, but it is not on Eden's Ridge. And it is here on this ridge, where I was born, that I belong. I know that as surely as I know my name.

You may sing of country life, but we both know it is not within you to live on a farm in Maine. And it would be a disservice to our love to pretend I can be the girl patiently waiting for your call, waiting for you to come driving up this road, waiting for your journey to end. Always waiting.

I am writing this in the dark of night by the light of the golden moon on fresh snow—as you sleep contentedly in my bed. I will tuck it into the shirt you will wear tonight, knowing that having to go out on stage and sing will help heal what heartache this letter brings.

And how will my own heart heal? I have a rich life here. I have Tad and Sarah and little Max and my students. I have good friends. And I have my music, which is at the core of who I am in much the way yours is.

Still, I know there will be times when none of that will seem enough. And it is at those times that I will journey deep into my heart and you will be there walking toward me in the field of wild flowers, in the glorious pink of that last light of day. You will be there on the porch as fireflies dot the lawn and fields and orchard. You will be there climbing that rock maple, or flailing about on ice skates on a small Maine pond, or cradling a yearling gently in your arms.

You will be there sitting in the kitchen sipping coffee while squares of sun find their way into the room and find your eyes, making them shine like chestnuts.

You will be there standing on our porch in the icy rain of a December night, as out of place as the rain itself in a Maine winter. But still, there you'll be, smiling at a woman with a broom in her hand who is, shall we say, a bit under the weather. There you'll be as if that woman had willed you to suddenly materialize. I must be more careful what I wish for when I've got a broom in my hand.

At this point, Ben McBride couldn't help but smile, even though he was already fighting back the tears. *Damn, Lily, what are you saying?* He read on.

You, Ben McBride, will go on to be more famous than even you could have dreamed—that is something I know. And I confess I still don't understand this bond you have with such music. At least I understand that I don't understand—that the limitation is mine.

And I understand you have been given the gift of song. Now you will give that gift to the world—and those who hear you will return that gift in a thousand ways you can only begin to imagine now.

You will be nurtured by their love, just as you have given me the greatest love, the greatest passion, a woman can know. This knowledge will warm my heart in the coldest of nights ahead, will lift my spirit in its deepest moments of despair, will nourish my soul, helping me to be whole.

Lord Byron, another of my favorite poets, once wrote, "All farewells should be sudden." In our case, at least, I believe he is right. So I ask you—if not for your sake, for mine—in all the roads you travel, do not travel this road to Eden's Ridge again. Do not put me through the pain of yet another goodbye. One goodbye to you in a lifetime is, I'm afraid, all that I can bear.

I look at you now, watch your chest rise and fall to your slow, steady breathing—and my heart almost splinters at the thought of never seeing you again, never again waking to find you looking at me with that certain look of love, never again hearing that slow, Southern drawl of yours calling my name, or calling me ma'am. Still, we both know this is a decision I must make, and you must honor.

This will never happen again for me, and maybe not for you. I do know you will have other women in your life, but I hope you will tuck me somewhere within that vast and playful and kind heart of yours for safekeeping.

And now I will crawl back into bed and feel you awaken next to me. Then you and I will make love one last time in the light of the early morning moon.

> Be well, be safe, be content,
> and be free,
> Lily

Ben McBride, who had sunk heavily onto the sagging motel bed after reading the first sentence, lay down, put the letter on his chest, and closed his eyes. Of course she was right. Wasn't she? The road was his home, always would be. If he stayed with her, he would come to feel like a hummingbird who had somehow been caged. And Lily's place in life, she knew and he knew, was on that ridge, on that farm at Eden's Ridge.

She was like that apple tree—strong, beautiful, enduring, and firmly *placed*. The things he loved about her were the things he would take from her, even if he could convince her to go with him from town to town, from motel to motel, from gas station to gas station, from tavern to tavern and tent to tent and all the roadside cafés in between.

And he had somehow known she wasn't the type to sit at home and wait for her man. No, if she took a man into her life, she'd want him *there*, on that farm with her. She'd want him totally or not at all. There was no halfway for Lily Frost.

The very reasons he loved her were the reasons he had lost her—even as he found her. Hell yes, she was right. But Lord, Lord, Lord it hurt.

Ben McBride lay there on the sagging bed, tears sliding from the sides of his closed eyes—until Curly James knocked on the door and said, "You ready, Ben? We got a show to do."

The crowd was much bigger than the organizers had dreamed possible, and Ben McBride and his Crooked River Boys did not disappoint. This was, however, one of the few times Ben didn't begin with his trademark opener, "Just Outside of Little Rock." Nor did he, as is the custom in a concert, save his best song for last. Instead, it was Ben McBride's first song that evening that stayed with the audience.

They noticed the song had not been planned. Ben had walked out on the stage as the band played the lead-in to his usual opener. He had faced the audience for a few minutes looking confused, like a deer caught in headlights. Then he had stepped away from the mike, turned to the band, and motioned for them to stop playing the lead-in.

He said something to the band. A few heard the guitar player say, "We've never even done that one, Ben." And Ben said, "Well, we're doing it now."

Then Ben stepped up to the mike and sang a song the great Fred Rose had written, a song that many would record in the years to come, including the Willis Brothers and Roy Acuff. In 1975, Willie Nelson, his friend, would give it great fame. But on this night, Ben McBride sang it for the first and only time in his life.

> In the twilight glow I see her,
> Blue eyes crying in the rain.

When we kissed goodbye and parted,
I knew we'd never meet again. . . .

Those there in the audience, and those listening on the radio that New Year's Eve, never forgot Ben McBride's rendition of the song, no matter who sang it over the years. Many of them swore he must have written it, that those were surely Ben McBride's own words coming from the depths of his being.

They would never understand the strength it took for him to sing it, all the time telling himself that if he could make it all the way through this song, he at least would have taken the first step of the rest of his life.

Love is like a dying ember.
Only memories remain.
And through the ages I'll remember
Blue eyes crying in the rain.

And on a farm, on a ridge in Maine, Lily Frost had finished dressing for the evening church service. She had busied herself with every major and minor chore she could think of that day. She had even undressed the Christmas tree, carefully packing the decorations that she would pass down to Max and any other children Tad and Sarah would have. But time had slowed so that a minute became forever, and the weight of each minute pressed on her heart.

She couldn't get warm no matter how much wood she put in the stove, no matter how much she stoked the fire—even though it was not a particularly cold day. She had wrapped herself in a Hudson Bay blanket, bits of hay still clinging to it, sat at the piano, and played Chopin as she looked at the cobalt vase she had found on the piano when she returned to the house that morning after walking Ben to the car, having kissed him one last time. Her tears had mixed with the rain as she smiled and waved until his car was out of sight.

When she came back into the house, she had broken into hard sobs upon seeing the vase. Tucked under the vase was a note:

Dear Blue-Eyed Lady,

Found this vase for you in Tennessee a lifetime ago, when I returned there from the first time on your farm—you know, when we had such a friendly encounter on that rocky, dusty road.

I had meant to give this little thing to you that first night, but seeing as you were under the weather, I thought it best to wait. Little gifts for Sarah and Tad and little Max are under the Christmas tree.

Your gift, small as it is, was intended—or so I told myself—as a peace offering, considering our first meeting. But even then I think I knew it was a love offering. And so now I offer to you, Lilian Frost, all that I have, all that I am, all that I can be.

Yours,
Ben

As evening came to Eden's Ridge, Lily Frost left the amber glow of the parlor. She looked one more time at the cobalt vase, designed for one long-stemmed rose, and looked at what Ben had left in it—the birch twig that he must have put in his deep coat pocket that day in the woods. After that first dance in crisp air and the white of new snow. That first kiss.

Lily Frost walked out of the house and to her car, her heart breaking, yet knowing what she had done was right. *Right as rain,* came to mind, and it made her think of Ben and his many expressions. She smiled through the tears—something she would do many times in her life.

By the time Ben's show began, Lily was driving toward Hadley's Curve and the service at church. The rain had moved on, and the stars had come out. Later, the bright moon would chase them away.

She drove the crest of Eden's Ridge, listening to Ben McBride on the radio of the Chevrolet, the reception, miraculously, as clear as the night itself. Drove down into the valley, listening to Ben sing the first song of the evening, his voice thick and laced with pain.

Sending her his message, sending her his goodbye, as best he could.

Part Three

The hours will hurry,
The flowers will fade,
The memories will linger
And go their own way.
But when it's all over
And the dancin' is through,
This old song will
Still be for you.

—MARK DIX, "THIS OLD SONG"

Seventeen

June 20, 2000

S arah Frost's voice quivered and broke as she finished telling the story. Tears fell down Lindsey's face, tears of sadness for her Aunt Lily and for Ben McBride. But tears of a certain joy, too. Some lines from Tennyson came to mind:

> 'Tis better to have loved and lost
> Than never to have loved at all.

Lindsey wiped her tears with the tail of her shirt. "Aunt Lily and Ben McBride," she said in amazement, still trying to take it all in.

Now, so many things in her life began to make more sense. The look on her Aunt Lily's face when she'd find Lindsey playing Ben's records. And even the times Lindsey had caught Lily going through his records, claiming to be straightening them. The looks Lily and Sarah had exchanged at times over remarks that Lindsey couldn't even recall now. But she *could* recall the look that passes between two women who share a secret.

Now Lindsey began to understand the look on Ben's face when he first saw her and knew who she was. The look on his face when he asked how things were on the farm—and the drop of his face when she had said that Lily had died.

In fact, the night that Ben McBride first met Lindsey, there had been expressions of shock and surprise and gladness and deep sadness on his face, looks that Lindsey had taken to be related to his friendship with her grandfather. Now she knew the expressions were layered with meaning.

"Well," Lindsey said to her grandmother, "I for one think it's great that Aunt Lily"—she searched for words—"followed her heart those two days."

"That's not the way Lily would have put it," her grandmother said rather sternly. Sarah Frost had never been impressed by some of the modern expressions.

"So do you think *Aunt Lily* is the mystery woman of the magazine interview?" Lindsey asked, knowing somehow what the answer would be.

"There's not one iota of doubt in my mind that she is," Sarah Frost answered, staring off into the darkening sky. Lindsey remembered how quickly Ben had offered to come to Maine. "For an old friend," he had said. But hadn't there been a pause, a sputter? "For . . . an old friend." She had assumed the friend was Tad. "And they never saw each other again?" she asked.

"Never."

"But if she is the one he talked about in the interview, why didn't he come back when he decided to give settling down a try?" Lindsey asked, suddenly irritated. "Instead of marrying someone else?"

"That's something I have wondered many times over the years. And I still wonder," her grandmother answered. Sarah's voice took on more firmness when she added, "And I might just ask Ben McBride that question myself when I see him. Might just tell him he did a fool thing by not coming back. But," and she paused to give the word *but* its full weight, "I know it wasn't because he didn't love her. Lily could spot fake from real in anyone, and what she felt from Ben McBride was real.

"I *know* that, even though she—none of us—ever heard from Ben again. I *did* try to call him when Tad died, even though Lily was adamant that I not do so. At the time I didn't understand why she'd feel that way. So I snuck down to Butters' and put in a call. Thought he'd want to know. But the operator in Memphis couldn't find a Ben McBride, and I think I was in too much shock to figure out how to go about looking any further for him. I sometimes wonder how things might have changed if I had reached Ben and if Ben had come up for Tad's funeral . . ." Sarah's thoughts seemed to wander off again.

Lindsey tried to imagine how her Aunt Lily must have felt, having missed out all those years, and yet not having missed out. She tried to imagine how she would feel, years later, without Michael. He, too, had become part of her life so quickly—and was gone just as quickly.

Her grandmother rose suddenly and said, "Ayuh, there's no use wondering what you can't know."

Lindsey thought for a moment her grandmother had read her thoughts about Michael, but she was of course talking about Ben and Lily. Sarah, empty sherry glass in hand, headed for the front door in the slight waddle she had taken on with age. Lindsey expected her to say what she said every night about this time. *Time to turn in. Long day tomorrow.*

Instead Sarah said, "I'm going inside for a few minutes, and then I'll get some throws for us. Bit of chill in the air."

Lindsey sat on the porch and waited for her grandmother to return. It was dark now. The day birds had ceased their singing, the frogs at the pond had a loud chorus going, and the sad, haunting song of the whippoorwill floated up from the orchard. The world Lindsey had written about in the song "Eden's Ridge."

What would Ben say when she told him she knew about his affair with her great-aunt? Would he remember it as anything more than a pleasant interlude in his life?

Her grandma came back out, put a throw over Lindsey's shoulders, sat back down in her porch rocker, and spread the second throw over her lap and legs. She remarked that it had been a wet spring, which was why they had to have so many bug candles, as she called them, out.

Lindsey said that at least the blackflies disappeared at night, and Sarah reminded her for the thousandth time that the blackflies—except for a few stragglers—had left on the twelfth of June as always. Just as they arrived, Sarah maintained, on the first of May.

Lindsey laughed at Sarah's insistence that blackflies were so precise. She wondered if she could find a place for that in some lyrics she was working on.

"Your laugh sounds so much like Lily's I can't believe it," Sarah told her then, as she had done many times. Ben had said almost those same words to her that first night in Tennessee.

"Ben and Aunt Lily," Lindsey said once again in a tone of wonder, trying to let it sink in. "When did she tell you all this—about Ben's visit? Was it when you and Grandpa Tad got back from Pennsylvania?"

"No. Lily wasn't one to talk about herself—you know that. And we were not that close. Not then." Again there was a long, heavy pause. "She just told us that Ben had come by and gotten snowed in for a day. And when Tad asked her if they had managed not to insult each other too much without his being there to keep the peace, Lily hit him on the shoulder and said, 'Oh, you.'"

Sarah paused again. Then she said, "They loved each other so much, Lily and Tad did, that I have to admit I was a little jealous, even though Lily did everything in her power to make me feel like I was the lady of the house. I might have noticed that Lily was different after we got back . . . but I had little Max to tend to, and we both had so much to do around here. And Tad was in the woods at that time of year from daylight until dark . . ."

She let out a deep breath, as if she were dragging up an old, heavy memory. She reminded Lindsey that it had been that January, just weeks after Ben's visit, that Tad had been killed. A chain had broken on the logging truck, and he had been pinned underneath a fallen log. "That was the darkest journey I—and Lily—had to walk through in life. At that time," she added. And Lindsey knew the later loss her grandmother alluded to was the death of Lindsey's mom and dad.

Grandma Sarah rocked back and forth a few times in the chair. "Lily had always been the strong one, and that was true when Tad died, too. I couldn't take in what had happened. Couldn't function. Couldn't even take care of little Max, much less make the arrangements. Lily did it all. She even found the strength to play one of Tad's favorite pieces at the funeral. And she tended me for days—weeks, I guess it was. Never once told me to snap out of it, never once said what so many others said and what is true but what we don't need to be told at the time—that I had to find the strength to go on. Lily knew that I needed time to grieve, and she gave me that time. Trouble is, looking after me didn't allow Lily the space she needed for her own grieving. It was later that I understood that."

Sarah stopped talking and began rocking. Lindsey thought her grandmother had journeyed as deep into that particular memory as she cared to go.

Sarah Frost was silent the way people are silent when they are revisiting places they haven't seen for a long time. Lindsey sat on the porch steps, staring at the orchard. In the dark that had come upon them, the branches of the apple trees now looked like so many twisting arms. Then Sarah brought the rocker to a standstill.

Her grandmother took a long, slow breath, looked at the star-clad sky, and said almost in a whisper, "I pray to God I am doing the right thing." Her voice seemed thin but determined as she said, "Lindsey, just listen and don't say anything until I'm finished. Then I'll answer any questions you have."

Lindsey, who had put the throw aside, felt a shiver pass through her, knowing somehow that a curtain was about to be raised—or dropped.

"It's a wonder she didn't burn herself . . ." Sarah's voice trailed off as she traveled back to 1950 and she was no longer an old woman on the porch. Instead, she was young—a new mother. And newly widowed.

She sits trancelike at the kitchen window looking out over the orchard in the pale light of a late February morning.

It has been four weeks since her husband died. It seems like four years, like forty years, like four days, like four minutes since that terrible day. The man running into the house. Lily and Sarah screaming and running toward the woods, running through the snow. Sarah with little Max in her arms, trying to catch up. Then Lily, after seeing . . . running back toward Sarah and little Max, using all her strength to hold Sarah against her will, saying "Don't go there, don't look. Don't go there," and Sarah screaming, "No! No! No!"

But in the time and place Sarah has returned to it is four weeks and four days after that awful day, and she sits in her protective trance while Lily stands at the stove stirring the oatmeal and making small talk with little Max, something Sarah hardly has the energy to do anymore. Suddenly there is a clanging of pots and a thud, and Lily is lying on the floor—oatmeal spilled all over the stove and the counter.

"Yes," Sarah said, and once again she was an old woman, a woman who has just told that story to Lindsey. "Sure is a wonder she didn't burn herself bad. When Lily fainted was when I suddenly came awake, came out of my anger and despair enough to consider someone else.

"At first I marked it all up to Lily's having to do everything and having no time to mourn since I had taken up all the grieving room in the house. Then I began to remember I had heard Lily throwing up in the mornings, seen her sit down from dizziness.

"Suddenly I recalled that certain look on her face when she told us Ben had been here, and I remembered how vehemently determined she was that I *not* call him when Tad died. And to this day I don't know how I had the wherewithal to drive down to Butters' and try to call Ben behind her back when I could hardly function. But something told me Ben should have been here for Tad's funeral.

"Still I didn't say anything that Friday morning that Lily fainted. I remember it was a Friday. I just insisted she go lie down and let me clean things up. But that night at the supper table I asked her, 'Lily, are you expecting?'

"Of course the first thing she did was look at me with that how-dare-you look of hers, but I just kept looking back at her. Then I finally said, 'It's Ben's, isn't it?'

"Lily's face began to soften, then it just crumbled and she dissolved into tears—and I can count on one hand the times I've seen Lily cry. That's when Lily told me the story of Ben's visit.

"She made me swear on everything sacred that I would not tell Ben—although I thought he should know. Part of that was pride, of course. She didn't want to catch Ben by having his baby. Part of it was her certainty of who Ben McBride was—one of those men who would feel imprisoned by marriage and family. And part of it, too, was the shard of hope that he would decide he couldn't live without her and find his way back. Or at least I think it was.

"That night we stayed up until dawn talking. At first she had refused to believe she was pregnant because old Doc Simpson had said her uterus was tilted and she would need an operation if she wanted to have kids.

"Anyway," Sarah drew in yet another deep breath, "we talked endlessly about her options—which were not at all the same as what women have today. Back then an unwed mother might as well have had a scarlet letter branded on her chest. There was just no way Lily could raise the child on Eden's Ridge. It wasn't that she didn't have the courage to face down the talk and tattle—Lily would look the devil in the face. But Lily knew that a child born out of wedlock would be branded far beyond what you young folks today can imagine. It's not the same world now as then, Lindsey. You have to understand that before you can understand anything.

"Lily's option was to give the child up for adoption or to go away somewhere, pretend to be a widow, and raise it away from anyone who knew her. I knew she wanted that child. And wanted to raise it. I had told her she could go stay with my folks, whatever her decision.

"But I never knew what Lily would have decided because I was the one that made a decision—for all of us. Spring had come. Buds on the trees. Grass was greening. And finally the ground had thawed. It was time to bury those that had died that winter. Time to commit Tad's body to the earth."

Again, another long pause, filled only with the sounds of crickets and frogs and the sound of loss in Sarah Frost's voice.

Lindsey was about to break the silence when Sarah said, "Let me get through this before you say anything."

Sarah continued, "So after the interment, the whole town came to the house with food and kind words. Lily was now four months gone, but she managed to hide it with those long shirts she always wore. And besides, with Lily, no one would have suspected. On this day, she had a dress with a million gathers in the front.

"Anyway, somehow it just came to me. Lily and Tad had always been the decision makers, but this decision came to me almost as if Tad had whispered it in my ear. I called Lily into the kitchen and said, 'I've got the answer if you are willing.'

"Later, I gathered everyone in the parlor and thanked them and told them that I had an announcement to make. I said that in all of my grief, I took strength from the love Tad had given me. And from our young son, little Max. Then I said that Tad had given me one last gift. And I announced that I was expecting Tad's child. I said I hoped everyone would be as joyous as I was about it.

"Since I've always been on the plump side, to say the least, folks believed it; some even said they had suspected I might be. They also believed me when I told them that I was going back to Pennsylvania to live with my folks and that Lily had kindly agreed to go with me until the baby was born, and then she would be coming back to Eden's Ridge. We got rid of the few animals. Albert Tikander agreed to look after the haying and the harvest, and Victor and Katrina would see after the house. Well, Victor was growing senile by then, but Katrina and his son could be trusted to look after things.

"And," Sarah sighed as if to gather strength, "that's what we did. Went to my folks, where Lily gave birth in late September . . ."

Before she could finish that sentence, thoughts flickered through Lindsey's head like flash lightning. What had happened to the baby? Did she give it away? Did she go away to one of those homes for Little Wanderers, where a woman would disappear for a few months and then come back and resume her life? Was the baby a boy or a girl? Did she ever see it? Did she know who raised it?

Sarah looked both startled and relieved that she had finally told the story aloud. "And then we both returned to Maine—as I had promised Lily I would do before she agreed to the plan. I would have come back in any case, because I realized while I was gone that the farm had become part of me and that this was where I wanted to be.

"And we told everyone it was *my* baby." Sarah stopped to grab yet another deep breath.

Another flash . . . and time distorted. Uncle Max? Uncle Max is really Lily's. No, he was born before Grandpa Tad died. Oh my God, it must have been . . .

And then the lightning struck. Sarah said it softly: "It was *Lily* who gave birth to Jenny, not me."

"What are you saying? What? . . ."

"And we raised Jenny as ours, not as hers or as mine but as ours . . . raised Max that way too."

Sarah paused now, and somehow Lindsey knew this time that she would not continue, that she had finished the story and was giving Lindsey time to react.

Lindsey looked at the night sky, at the lighted houses dotting the valley, trying to take in what her grandmother—who was *not* her grandmother—had told her.

Lily was her grandmother. And Ben was her grandfather.

She was stunned into silence.

In the days that followed, Lindsey's emotions flew around like a flock of birds flushed from hiding. Sadness. Anger. Amazement. And some righteous indignation. How dare they not let Ben McBride know he was going to be a father? He had a right to know, didn't he?

Grandma Sarah sighed when Lindsey said it. Again she talked about how times had changed. And again she recalled Lily's independence, pride, her outright stubbornness, her determination not to try to mold Ben McBride into what he wasn't. Her determination to let him live the life he was meant to live.

"Still . . . ," Lindsey started to protest.

"I know . . ." Grandma Sarah held up both hands to indicate she understood. "But actually, Lily did try to get in touch with him."

"Then why? . . ."

"I'm about to tell you. You see, *after* Jenny was born, Lily learned what a joy it was to have a child. So one day as she was nursing Jenny and singing a lullaby, she looked over to me and said, 'Sarah, I've got to let Ben know.'

"All I could do was nod my head. Finally, finally.

"I was sure that if she could reach him, Ben McBride would be here by Christmas."

Eighteen

Lily Frost, having put Jenny Lind in her crib, sat in her robe at her bedroom desk where, a year ago, she had written Ben McBride a goodbye letter as he lay sleeping in her bed. That time she was sending him away. This time, she was beckoning him to come.

Lily wrote the date in the right-hand corner: December 16, 1950. Beethoven's birthday. But it was Brahms, playing softly on the phonograph, that lulled little Jenny Lind to sleep.

"Dear Ben . . ." Lily looked over at her daughter. At their daughter. "You will truly need to be sitting down when you read this letter."

She kept it brief. She told him that first and foremost she wanted him to know she wasn't expecting or asking anything from him. Then she told him that he had a beautiful daughter, Jenny Lind. That she had not intended to tell him, but she didn't feel it was right for him not to know. Jenny was so beautiful, she wrote. "I imagine she looks much like you did when you were a baby. She has your chin. And your mouth. And when she cries, I have to admit, I think I hear a country twang in her voice . . ." No doubt Ben would smile when he read that.

That night as Lily Frost lay in her bed, watching the moon fall on their sleeping daughter, she dared to let herself dream that Ben McBride would feel the joy she had come to feel about this wonderful young life. She dared to let herself believe that in a few days, Ben McBride would come driving back into her life, bringing with him more love than he could ever put in any song.

———

Sarah had finagled Ben's address from June, who was practically a Ben McBride fan club by herself. And Lily Frost would have mailed that letter, which she planned to send special delivery to his recording company.

As it was, Lily remembered she needed to pick up some Ivory Flakes for Jenny's diapers, so she pulled into Butters' Corner Store on the way to the post office. Best to do it then, she explained to Sarah, since they might drive back by way of King Hill Road and thus not pass the store again.

Lily went in by herself, leaving Sarah in the car holding Jenny. But Sarah remembered that they were low on a few more items. She bundled up Jenny, making sure the blanket protected her tiny face from the biting wind, and hurried into the store. Inside, she told Lily they needed brown sugar. And maybe some mustard.

While Lily fetched that, Sarah went over to show off Jenny to Walter and June, who were eating breakfast at the far table. "Ain't she cunnin'?" June said. "Doncha know Tad would be so proud of her." Sarah saw Walter nudge June with his snow boots as if to chasten her for having brought up the tragedy that was not yet a year old.

June quickly changed the subject. "Did you hear 'bout Ben McBride?" she asked.

Sarah glanced back to the counter, where Lily held out her hand as Forrest counted out her change. But Lily had heard his name. Sarah was sure of that from the frozen look on Lily's face.

"Did we hear what about Ben McBride?" Sarah asked as she held the blanketed Jenny closer to her.

"He went and got married off to some woman in Texas. Just last week. Heard it on the Louisiana Hayride. You should listen to that sometime. It comes in pretty good."

Sarah heard a chinging sound. She turned quickly toward Lily, who stood there openhanded, the dimes and nickels and pennies that had been in her hand rolling in every direction on the floor.

By the time Sarah reached her, Lily and Forrest were bent down picking up the change.

"You feelin' poorly, Lily?" Madge asked, but didn't wait for an answer. "Something's been going round. Hope you aren't catching it."

"No, I just . . . wasn't paying attention to what I was doing," Lily said. She stood up, put the change into her pocket, and reached out to take Jenny from Sarah's arms—reached as one reaches for refuge.

Sarah gave Jenny to Lily, then she picked up the groceries and said, "Come, Lily."

This time Lily held Jenny and Sarah drove. Not to the post office. Sarah knew without any words that the only place to drive was home.

Lily didn't take off her coat when they got back from Butters' store. She just handed Jenny to Sarah. And while Sarah unwrapped the baby and put her in the crib they kept in the warm hallway, Lily marched into the kitchen.

Sarah stood there next to the crib and heard the lifting of the eye on the wood stove in the kitchen. She heard the tearing of paper, and she knew that was not all that was being torn. She heard the heavy metal eye clank back in place. Then Lily came into the hallway, still in her coat.

Without a word, Lily took the baby blankets, bundled up Jenny again, and went with her out to the orchard. Sarah would never forget how the sun made the snow sparkle that day. All that pain inside, and yet the sun made the world look like a crystal palace.

"It seemed a cruel sun to me that day," Sarah Frost said when she told Lindsey that story. All those years later, she could still see Lily and baby Jenny out in that orchard.

Her grandmother took the tip of her apron and wiped the corner of her eye and waited for the stirred-up places in her heart to settle so she could go on.

"Lily never spoke of the letter again. And I knew not to suggest that she tell Ben. Ever.

"Still, I had always thought Jenny should be told when the time came, when she was old enough to understand. It was after you were born that Lily came to the same conclusion. She stood at the sink one day and said, 'It's time we told Jenny.'

"And though it hadn't been mentioned for years, Lily didn't need to say what it was she meant But before we could tell her . . . there was that awful car wreck, and Jenny and Kevin were gone . . ." Sarah Frost stopped as if she once again had to garner strength to travel back to that memory. "And once again," she said, her voice gaining strength with every word, "it was a child that brought us out of that long tunnel of darkness. You.

"After that, Lily threw herself into living as she had always done. You know, in spite of all the grief, all the tragedy, I think she would say she had a full life."

"Did she ever talk about Ben?" Lindsey asked.

"Not for years. Then, not long before she died, we sat here on this porch having our sherry, and she told me she was sure she had done the right thing for Ben. 'Birds don't belong in cages,' she said. But she wondered if she had done right by Jenny, and by you. I know she struggled with that her whole life. She believed so much in the truth, yet she knew that truth carries with it its own pain.

"And another night on the porch—soon after, I think it was the next night—I said there never was a day when I didn't look up and expect Tad to come walking out of that barn, coming for his supper, ambling along in that lopsided walk of his.

"Lily said that she missed Tad terribly too, and then I finally asked her, 'And Ben? Do you still think about Ben?'

"At first I thought she wasn't going to answer. Then she said, 'There is hardly a day when I don't look down that road and let myself imagine for a fleeting second that Ben McBride will drive up in a rusty old Hudson, coming back to Eden's Ridge.'

"It just about broke my heart to hear that," Sarah Frost said.

And hearing it tore at Lindsey's heart too.

In the coming days, Lindsey asked the same questions over and over again, even though Sarah had answered them as best she could. Why did they wait so long to decide to tell Jenny? Or to tell Lindsey?

"I broached the subject of telling you a few times over the years," Sarah said, "especially when you fell in love with Ben's singing and his music. But Lily said to let the past be in the past.

"Besides," Sarah added as she chopped onions for meatloaf, while Lindsey washed the beet greens, "after a while, in my mind, even though he was gone, Tad *became* Jenny's father, your grandfather. One thing is certain: if Tad had lived, he would have loved Jenny like his own, like our own, and would have loved you too. He would have been the one there for Jenny and for you."

Lindsey found herself being angry with Ben McBride. How could he have loved Lily as much as she thought he did and then go and get married to someone else just a few months down the road?

"I can't claim to know the workings of Ben's heart," Sarah Frost said a week before Ben was to arrive. "I only met him that once. But I do know, somehow, that it was Lily he was talking about in that interview."

"I don't know about that," Lindsey said sharply. "But I believe he has a right to know. And I'm going to tell him, and that's that."

Sarah shook her head as she crumbled crackers into the bowl. "Be careful how free you are with the truth," she warned. "I pray I was right in telling you. But not everyone is always best served by truth, especially when it comes so late."

"But if you tell a lie, you live a lie," Lindsey said, and she heard the judgment in her own voice.

"No," Sarah said, without any wavering, "we *told* a lie, but we sure didn't *live* a lie. Jenny was mine, just as Max was Lily's. We raised both of them as ours. And we raised you as ours too." Sarah wiped her hands on her apron and sat down on the deacon's bench. "You know that's true, Lindsey. You know that you were always as much Lily's as you were mine. You know . . ."

But Lindsey didn't give Sarah a chance to finish her sentence. She walked out the door and then broke into a run toward the barn. She would, Sarah knew, saddle up Fiddle and ride through their land, ending up walking with her horse through the orchard, where she had always taken solace.

Just like Lily.

In the following days, Lindsey spent long hours riding Fiddle or walking for miles on Eden's Ridge. She still had questions and moments of anger—at Lily for not telling Ben in time, for not telling her daughter. And at Lily and Sarah for not telling her. But as the days passed, Lindsey worked her way toward an understanding of sorts about Lily and Sarah, worked toward a kind of admiration for what they had accomplished. She had always known that she was loved deeply, even though neither of the women were much for speaking the words.

Then she'd think about what Sarah had said about the obstacles they had faced, about the times they had lived through, about choices, and about the timing. If only Ben had not married so quickly. Especially when he was supposed to be such a rambling man, and especially if he loved Lily so mightily. How could that be? She didn't know.

What she did know was that on the way back from Portland, after she picked Ben up at the airport, she would tell him he was her grandfather.

How he chose to handle that piece of truth would be up to him.

There was another piece of truth Lindsey had to handle as well. About Michael. And that chicken came to roost, as Gabby would say, that Tuesday before the concert, when Lindsey came back home from dropping Sarah off at Esther Miller's for her bridge club luncheon. There was a message from Gabby demanding that Lindsey call her immediately.

Lindsey called their apartment. No answer. She left a message and then fixed herself a peanut-butter-and-pickle sandwich the way Lily had taught her. Michael had shaken his head at her sandwiches. And yet he put mayonnaise on his chocolate cake, a concoction he had picked up as a boy from Ben and Curly.

Lindsey sat there at the old kitchen table, eating her sandwich and missing Michael. She missed the way he laughed at her. Missed the way he made her laugh. Missed making love to him, even though they had *not* made love.

Of all her friends, she realized, Michael was the one she needed to tell her story to. She needed his attentive ear. Needed him to hold her. Wanted him to hold her. Wanted him. Maybe it was because she was feeling so much loss after hearing the Ben and Lily story. Maybe because something about Ben and Lily reminded her of Lindsey and Michael . . . And then lyrics came to her. A song she would have to write someday:

This woman who's afraid to love
Is afraid that she's in love.

She wanted to hear his voice. That was really all she wanted just now. She felt her breath quickening as she walked to the phone on the kitchen wall.

She was reaching for the phone when it rang. It was Gabby. "I was washing my hair and didn't hear when you called," Gabby said. "And I didn't leave a message when I called you because I thought I should tell you in person—well not in person since we are so far apart, but on the phone, which is closer to in person than the answering machine. Did you know that my crazy Aunt Lettie left a message on my Aunt Ruby Jean's answering machine that their brother had died—can you believe that anyone would do that? Which just goes to show Aunt Lettie's crazy as a fly caught in a jar—especially since they don't even have a brother—so that's why I didn't leave the message—even though no one has died, or is even hurt or anything like that."

"Leave what message, Gabby?"

"Well, it's about Michael—don't panic, he's okay and everything. But he's dumb as dirt, that's for sure. He's gone and gotten himself engaged to Cynthia. Cynthia told her friend, who is the boss of my friend, that they would probably just marry in Italy when they go to Europe in August. Of course I didn't tell my friend that Michael had driven all the way to Maine to see you even though you are supposed to be just friends, because my friend might tell her boss, who would tell Cynthia, and I wonder if Michael even told her that he went, because she should know a man doesn't drive to the ends of the earth unless he's in love."

Gabby drew out the word *love* into two or maybe three syllables. Lindsey couldn't tell for sure because her ears had frozen on the word *marry* and the word *August*, and everything else Gabby said seemed like a record turning too slow, or too fast. Or not turning at all.

Somehow Lindsey got through a conversation about the concert—what songs they would sing, what they'd wear, what Gabby should pack for the ride up on the bus Ben had chartered for the two bands, where they'd be staying—at some cabins at Papoose Pond. "Put my boys and their families on a lake for a little vacation, and they'll do it for free," Ben had said.

Gabby had decided that instead of staying at the Frost place with Lindsey, she wanted to stay with the others at Papoose Pond. "I have to tell you something," she was saying now. "J. J. and I are not just best friends anymore. We think we might have loved each other all these years—except for fourth grade, of course, when we—"

"I know." Lindsey laughed. "You hated each other."

Somehow, Lindsey was able to be happy for her friends. And to laugh at Gabby's strung-out sentences and familiar phrases. But she felt her strength ebbing, so she told Gabby she had to hang up, that she had to go and pick up her grandmother. *Who is really my great-aunt.* But of course Lindsey did not say that. In fact, she still thought of Sarah as her grandmother. How else could she think of her?

"I think I'll hang up and call Michael James and tell him he's a bushel shy of a load," Gabby said.

"No, you absolutely will not!" Lindsey said. "You have to promise me you won't, and I mean it."

"Okay. I promise. But—"

"Besides, I'm happy for him."

"Sure you are," Gabby said. "Happy as a pig at a barbecue festival."

A short time later, Lindsey picked up her grandmother at Esther's and went into town to buy a trunk-load of groceries for the upcoming weekend. It was a bright sunny day—good thing too, since sunglasses were good for hiding tear-swollen eyes—even in the grocery store.

Nineteen

Ben McBride shook his head in astonishment. Here he was, these many years later, once again driving to Eden's Ridge—this time from the Portland airport. Lindsey had planned to pick him up, but he had insisted on driving.

"It sure is gonna be good to see the old place again, and Sarah, and meet her boy," Ben had said to Lindsey on the phone the day before, and he had heard her soft laugh as she said, "Uncle Max isn't exactly a boy. He's a music professor—teaches theory at Berklee School of Music in Boston. And he's a grandfather, too."

"Lord, I must have slipped back in time," Ben had said. And to keep Lindsey from hearing the melancholy strain in his voice, he had chuckled and changed the subject to Gabby and how excited she seemed to be that the two bands would be riding in a chartered bus, a luxury one at that.

This time Ben was negotiating the Maine back roads in a brand-new Bonneville—the rental company hadn't had a truck available. He wondered what had happened to that old Packard he bought to come up here the last time. And the old Hudson. What would they be worth now? And what about that old green truck Lily drove that first day?

He could still see that truck now as if it were yesterday. And with that thought, memories flickered through Ben's mind. The look on Lily's face as she spun the wheels. As she turned from her piano to see him there with Tad and Sarah. As she told him about the saw-whet owl and tangoed in the woods and struggled to save the apple tree in the storm. The look on her face when he took the tortoise shell from her hair . . . and when she stood in the icy winter rain saying, "Now go. You've got the world waiting to hear you."

Those eyes. Those brimming blue eyes whose message he should have read before he read the letter she tucked in his red shirt with white fringes.

Even these many years later, when Ben McBride pictured Lily's face, her eyes, he remembered those long empty days after that New Year's Eve.

After getting that letter, he'd told himself Lily had done the right thing, the smart thing, the best thing for both of them. But then days had turned into weeks, and weeks had turned into months, and the miles had piled up, and the road always seemed to be taking him *from* and not *to*. He'd even tried to fill his life with women. Some who dreamed they'd be the one who captured his heart, who wanted him to settle down in a little house with a picket fence. Some who were waiting for a man to fill their lonely days and nights. Some who were hoping to fill the days and nights of a lonely man.

And Ben McBride was a lonely man. Always had been—wherever he went, whatever he did, even when he was not alone. Except with Lily Frost. With her, for the first time in his life, he had been anything but lonely.

But afterward, after she told him goodbye, the solitary life that had once felt comfortable and familiar had just felt empty. And then it was July and he was in Hope, Arkansas, having sung at their watermelon festival. And a woman slept next to him, but he could not sleep. It was there in the middle of a night of honeysuckle and glittering stars, lying next to a woman he cared about, that he knew he had to go back to Eden's Ridge.

He had thought his life on the road was enough. And it had been enough before Lily, and it had been enough after Lily. Almost. But the *almost* was a big empty place in his heart next to where Lily Frost abided. So on that hot July night in 1950, Ben McBride suddenly realized he didn't have to settle for almost. He had a choice.

And he chose to go see Lily. No, not just see her—he had known that if he went back it had to be forever. He would talk her into marrying him if it meant the only roads he traveled would be the dusty roads of Maine. He would learn to call square dances. Learn to do what he needed to do on the farm. He and Tad could be partners. Anything it took.

He canceled his coming engagements—"pressing personal business"— and bought a train ticket to Portland. The train was due in at night, so he'd find a hotel, grab some winks, and then take an early morning Greyhound to Butters' Corner Store, which was also the bus stop at Hadley's Curve.

On the three-day train ride—which he would later write a song about— he imagined how it would be to see Lilian Frost again.

The Greyhound pulls up to Butters' store, and Ben McBride feels as stiff almost as he would fifty years later. He is suddenly as hungry as a bear. He decides to have breakfast there at the store—since he will have to walk the four miles to Eden's Ridge unless he's lucky enough to flag a ride. Not likely on such a lightly traveled road.

He walks in, and a few heads turn to the door. He is accustomed now to being recognized in many places. But Mainers, he has learned in his two trips there, do not fawn. And are not overly talkative. Forrest, who would recognize him, is not there—probably out in the garage. And Madge is not there, either. If the others recognize him, they do not acknowledge it. Instead they turn their attention to their plates, or their cigarettes, and what talk there is concerns the blueberry crop—"a good'un, ayuh"—or the chance that this thing in Korea could brew up to something serious. "Gotta hope not, ayuh."

Ben takes a seat in a booth, puts his Stetson down beside him, and when the waitress comes with coffee and to take his order, he realizes he is almost completely happy. "What can I get you?" she asks, and he says, "How 'bout some of them home fries and eggs and bacon?" And the waitress, a woman with a square face and a square body says, "If I was you, I'd take the pancakes. Blueberries just picked yesterday." And so he does.

He has just taken his first bite of blueberry pancake swimming in maple syrup when the front door opens. And Ben McBride doesn't have to look up to see who has stepped inside. He knows from the ripple that passes through him that it is Lily Frost, coming inside for coffee—or milk for the pancakes she's going to make at home. Whatever it is, she has come here as he somehow expected, appearing like a mirage but not a mirage, wearing overalls and a man's shirt under them. He doesn't have to look at her to know that her hair, no doubt neatly pinned up, has already found its way out. Wisps of it fly about her face and her long neck.

Ben McBride, even though his heart is beating double at least, decides to keep silent. Decides to see how long it will take her to notice him there in the corner.

Lily Frost walks to the counter with that determined stride that he would never forget and says, "Anybody seen Forrest? He's not out in the garage."

"Just went to pick up something at the hardware," someone answers.

"Well, I need to know if that distributor cap I ordered came in on this morning's bus," she says. "Did anyone see if they left anything off?"

Her back is still to him, at much the same angle as when he first watched her play the piano.

"Well," one of the men at the counter says, pointing his cigarette in the general direction of Ben, "they left this fellow here off, but that's all, I think. You might ask him."

And Lily turns now to see who they have pointed to. She almost gasps as she puts her hands to her mouth. "Oh my Lord." And Lily Frost, forgetting there is anyone else in the store, tears brimming in her blue eyes, almost runs toward Ben McBride, who stands.

Just as she gets to him, he kneels down, takes her hand, and takes her breath *away as he says, in front of all those who took breakfast that morning at Butters' Corner Store, "Marry me, Lily Frost."*

———————

A nice imagining, but of course Ben had not taken an early morning bus to the stop at Butters' Corner Store. As it was, the train was much delayed and had not arrived in Portland until midmorning—and there were no buses until evening. He would have hired a taxi, but a disc jockey at a Portland radio station recognized him as he stepped off the train. After coffee and doughnuts, the man insisted Ben take his car for a journey he had sensed, from Ben's manner, was important.

So Ben drove to the Frost place on Eden's Ridge in the early afternoon of a hot July day in 1950—two years from the time he had first met Lily, the time he had driven those ridges lost as could be.

But this time, he wasn't lost. This time he knew exactly what he wanted. He wanted a life with Lilian Frost.

He knew immediately no one was home, even though the truck was in the shed. Maybe it was because the windows were all shut even in this heat. And then there were the weeds in the flowerbeds. What on earth was going on?

He told himself they had gone on vacation. But farmers don't take vacations. Not them anyway. Not in July.

Ben McBride's hope became fear, and fear became panic as he looked around, hoping that his eyes were deceiving him.

He saw an old man in coveralls, plodding up the lane. Ben almost broke into a run to meet him.

"Morning," Ben said, forgetting what time of day it was.

"Aft'noon," the old man said in an accent that sounded both Maine and not Maine. Maybe it was the old Russian neighbor who had built that wonderful stove.

"Wonder if you know where the Frosts are," Ben said. "I expected them to be home."

"What's that you say?" The old man cupped his hand toward Ben's mouth, and Ben realized he had a near-deaf man as his only source of information.

So Ben said again, loudly and slowly, "Do you know where the Frosts are?"

The old man dropped his cupped hand and said, "Not here."

That's obvious, Ben wanted to say. He was thinking how to pose the next sentence when the old man said, "The wife went back to Pennsylvania—right after they buried Tad."

Ben McBride would carry the shock and grief of that statement with him forever, carried it with him now as he drove to Eden's Ridge all these years later. At the time, back in 1950, what he had felt first was the numbness of protective shock. Then it turned to anger. He wanted to yell at the man and say, you don't know what you are talking about. Tad can't be dead. He survived some of the worst fighting of the war.

But words froze in his throat and all he could say was, "Oh dear God, no." Then finally he found the strength to yell into the man's cupped hand, "What happened? When?"

The old man dropped his hand again and pointed his shaky hands toward the timber as he told Tad about the logging accident. "Not his fault," he said. "Young man knew the woods. Not his fault. The chain, she broke."

Oh God, hearing that was painful. Trying to talk with a man who couldn't hear was painful. He needed Lily there. She would tell him it was all a mistake.

And if it *were* true—which it just could not be—then he needed to comfort her. To take comfort from her. Sarah might be in Pennsylvania, but Lily would be here. Lily would be on the farm. Must be in town. Must be . . .

"Where is Lily?" Ben finally managed to ask.

"Married and gone," the old man said, "to Wyoming. Married some fellow she met in the mail."

"Montana." Ben remembered Lily's correcting Tad at the supper table that first visit to Eden's Ridge. He remembered Tad's teasing grin as he looked at his sister.

"Do you mean Montana?" Ben asked the old man, not knowing why it mattered.

"Montana? Yes, I'm thinking now it's Montana," the man said. "But they're coming back soon's he sells his ranch. Coming back here. Sometime this fall, most likely. No way Lily could stay from this farm for long."

Ben never did remember the drive back to Portland. From there, he took his first plane ride—to Memphis. Had to get far away as quickly as he could from the shock, the sorrow. Tad dead. Lily married. He barely remembered the next few months—a haze of honky-tonks and highways and heartache. He did remember proposing to the woman in Blossom, Texas, a good woman who loved him and wanted him to be happy. Married her right before Christmas, 1950, and signed up for Korea the same month.

But that had been nearly fifty years ago. And it was only when he met Lindsey that he'd learned Lily had never been married at all. It had been all he could do not to register his shock on hearing it. Or maybe he had registered it all on his face, but Lindsey just hadn't picked up on it. It had been all he could do, too, not to tell Lindsey he had loved the woman who helped raised her. And not to ask Lindsey how it could be that Lily never married when he had been told she had.

He had grown to care for Lindsey, partly because she reminded him of the Lily he knew, not just in her looks but in the dogged determination that was her strength—and maybe her weakness. Anyway, Lindsey obviously knew nothing of him and Lily. And if Lily had chosen not to tell her anything about them, had probably chosen not to tell anyone, who was he to do so?

And now, these many years later, Ben McBride was passing by Butters' Corner Store. Lindsey had told him the place was still there, run now by a daughter and son-in-law. Still had a jukebox there, too. Too few jukeboxes left in this world. He was surprised to see that from the outside, except for the fact that the garage had closed and an expanded general store had been added, it looked much the same. More so than he had hoped anyway.

He turned at the Y—had no trouble finding it this time. And the road, too, was remarkably the same except for the blacktop. And a few new houses. And a mobile home or two.

He crossed the bridge, which had been widened and paved. He looked at the clock. About the time he said he'd arrive. He liked to be on time. Lindsey would be waiting. And Sarah. It would be so good to see Sarah. He found his hands trembling as he came upon the ridge, and he knew it wasn't just from old age.

Lindsey and Sarah were on the front porch waiting for Ben McBride's arrival. Sarah had fidgeted all morning—with her hair, with the house, with the food—and now she fidgeted with the geraniums in the flower box on the porch railing. "Are you sure he still knows how to get here?" Sarah asked Lindsey, and not for the first time.

"He said he could find this road with his eyes closed."

"Well," Sarah said, plucking off a brown geranium petal, "sure hope he don't run anyone off the road this time."

In spite of the tension Lindsey and Sarah had been through, they found themselves smiling, even chuckling a bit at a memory they now shared. Then they grew quiet as they saw a late-model car turn into their driveway. "Oh dear, he's really here," Sarah said, removing her apron. "Lindsey . . . think carefully before you . . ."

Sarah didn't even bother with the last words, but Lindsey knew what they were. Lindsey wouldn't have heard her anyway because she had already started toward the driveway to greet Ben. And she *was* going to tell him the first chance she got.

"Well look what the cat dragged up," Sarah Frost said, standing to greet him as he walked behind Lindsey to the porch. Ben put his suitcase down. Then he and Sarah hugged each other as if they had been old friends.

After both of them had told the other they hadn't changed and then laughed at themselves for saying something so ridiculous, they went inside and sat down to a lunch of shepherd's pie. Afterward, Lindsey promised herself, she would take Ben for a walk—and a talk.

But they had hardly finished eating when a car turned off the road and drove up the lane. And then another. At least a dozen that afternoon. And even though Sarah acted surprised to see each one—"wonder who that could be," she had said each time—Lindsey suspected Sarah Frost had been rather generous with invitations to neighbors and friends. *Drop by and meet Ben in person, why don't you?*

By the time the last neighbor left, it was midafternoon, and Sarah insisted they go to Papoose Pond before the bus arrived later that afternoon—she wanted to leave what she called hospitality baskets in each cabin.

They were putting baskets—boxes really—of bread, jam, peanut butter, Marshmallow Fluff, nuts, cookies, soda, and shampoo—in the cabins when the bus arrived and everyone piled out to greet Ben and Lindsey and to meet Sarah. Gabby, of course, had Grandma Sarah charmed in no time, and in no time had put on her bathing suit and headed for the water, and in no time had come out teeth chattering, asking how water could be so cold in July.

Then, still shivering, she pulled Lindsey aside. "I saw Michael James the other day. I just happened to be in his office building."

And even though she had not been in the cold lake water, Lindsey was suddenly chilled.

"And I had to bite my tongue to keep from saying anything to him," Gabby continued, "but I didn't. Didn't even bother to ignore him. Just kept walking right past him, and then he said, 'Gabby?' And I turned and said, 'Oh hi,' like I simply hadn't noticed him instead of having *chosen* to ignore him. And he said, 'Have you heard from Lindsey?' I said, 'Of course.' And he said, 'How is she?' And I wanted to say, what concern is that of yours? but instead I said, 'She's never been better . . . or happier.' And then I walked away. But just as he got in the elevator, and just as the door was closing, I turned and said, 'Michael James, you are a fool.'

"Oh my God, Gabby, I told you not to . . ."

"Well, he may not have heard me. But I couldn't help myself. He is a fool—and you're a fool, too, because he loves you and you love him."

"I do not love him, Gabby. We are just—*were* just friends."

"Yeah, well, as we say in Arkansas, you can say that all you want to, but that old dog just ain't gonna hunt," Gabby said, shivering again. "And speaking of Arkansas, at least the water's warm down there. I'm surprised you don't have icebergs floating on that lake."

Twenty

It was late Thursday afternoon on Eden's Ridge. The bands and crew were at the football field with their sound engineer. Everyone would rise early on Friday morning to get things set up. After a light supper, Sarah had finally gone to her bedroom to rest up for the square dance at the Legion Hall, which she had talked them all into attending. It would be a benefit put on by the local group, the Dancing Bears, as their contribution to the Opera House renovations.

Roland, a champion square dance caller, would be there. Roland, Sarah had explained to Ben, still talked about the time when, as a child, he had gone with his parents, Walter and June, to see Ben in concert in Lewiston. Front row seats.

With Sarah resting, Lindsey and Ben finally had a chance to practice their duet. They took their guitars out on the porch so they wouldn't disturb her. Lindsey had to shake her head to remind herself the whole thing was real. There, on Eden's Ridge, she was actually about to sing with the man whose voice had drawn her to country music.

She had to go inside for a minute to answer the phone. And when she returned, she found Ben standing in the parlor, looking at the pictures on the old upright. Tad and Sarah and Max, shortly after Max was born. Lily and Sarah and two-year-old Max holding baby Jenny. Lily and Jenny at Jenny's high school graduation. (Lindsey could see Jenny's resemblance to Ben now. The dark brown eyes. Does he notice they are his?) Baby Lindsey with her obviously proud mom and dad. Lindsey on her horse. In her prom dress.

In the center of all those sat a portrait of Lily, taken the year she retired after nearly forty years of teaching music in the public schools—a job she had taken when it became harder and harder to make it by farming alone. In the picture, Lilian Frost is surrounded by flowers and her last class of the kindergarten choir and band, the kids holding bells, triangles, and sticks.

Lindsey saw Ben staring at that picture. Looking at Lily with her silver hair, her face softly wrinkled. Lindsey wished desperately she had taken that picture down. Wished Ben could have always remembered Lily as the young woman he had known.

Lindsey walked up beside Ben. "She touched so many lives," she said. "Students will fly in from all over the country and even Europe for the dedication. Some of them went on to stellar careers in music—not just Uncle Max . . . Many went on to become band or choir directors. One sings opera in Germany. Another has been in off-Broadway plays. One is with the Boston Pops, another with the Dallas Symphony. And the kids here always won big at music festivals. You wouldn't believe the musicals this little town puts on. Both of the music teachers at the schools now were her students. She was such a wonderful teacher."

"And she's as beautiful here as the day I first saw her," Ben said, his eyes still glued to the picture.

This was the time to ask him questions. This was the time to tell him. She was just about to open her mouth to suggest they take a walk when Ben said, "Now, I know we still have to learn that duet I want us to sing. But before that, I'm wondering . . . is she buried here on the farm?"

The last sliver of sun was behind the line of tall pines and scattered birches as Ben and Lindsey walked silently down the worn path to the small fenced-in cemetery. The old iron gate groaned as they stepped inside and made their way through the uneven lines of slate and granite headstones to Lily's, the chunk of pink quartz.

Ben took his hat off. He was such an easy man to be with. They stood there several long minutes before Lindsey broke the quietness. "I know about you and Aunt Lily."

He did not answer for a long time. He just stood there looking at Lily's tombstone, which at her insistence showed only her name, date of birth, and date of death.

"Lord, I loved that gal," he finally said.

Lindsey did not answer. She could tell he did not expect her to.

"I came back to marry her, you know."

No, she did not know. She certainly did *not* know. But Ben did not give her time to say that. And it was then that Ben told her the story of his loneliness after he left on that New Year's Eve, the story of his return—the time on the train, the drive up the lane to find the place deserted. And then the old man who appeared almost like a ghost and delivered the news.

"My heart just froze up on me right there," he said, gesturing toward the lane where he had stood that day. "Froze up partly from your grandfather's death. Lord knows, Tad Frost and I were as different as sand and silver. But we had gone through fire together, and we had helped each other hold onto the good in life in the middle of all that death. So even though we weren't buddies in every sense of the word, we were buddies in the best sense of the word."

Ben shook his head as if this many years later he was still in disbelief.

"Hearing Tad was dead and hearing Lily was married was like going through two deaths, in a manner of speaking. I thought my legs weren't going to get me back to my car."

Again Ben was silent, and Lindsey knew to be silent too, knew he was finding his way through the pain yet again.

"That's why, even though you might not have noticed, I was so shocked when you said Lily had never married. And that Sarah had also lived her life on Eden's Ridge. I had thought it was Lily and her husband." Then Ben McBride again looked out over the valley. Out over the years.

He shook his head in confusion. "How could that happen? How could that old man have told me she was married and moved to Wyoming—or Montana or wherever. How?" Ben looked mystified and pained.

Ben had filled in one missing piece of the puzzle. He had come back after all. And suddenly, Lindsey realized she could fill in another piece. The story had been passed down to her for amusement. But this time there was no amusement in telling it.

"It wasn't Lily who married the pen pal in Montana. He *had* asked Aunt Lily to marry him time and time again. So finally, Aunt Lily gave his address to Maudie Tripp, the beautician in Hadley's Curve. Maudie was desperate for a husband, so the story goes, and agreed to marry him sight unseen. She got on a train and headed out and didn't come back until her husband died thirty-eight years and eight kids later."

Ben looked puzzled but said nothing.

Lindsey continued, "Victor Lamentov, the old Russian neighbor whose grandson now manages our orchard, was getting senile, and he got it into his head that it was Aunt Lily who married and moved to Montana. Every time she went by to check on him and Katrina, he asked Aunt Lily if her husband had sold his place in Montana yet and when he would be joining her. Or sometimes he said Wyoming, or California.

"Aunt Lily, after trying to explain over and over, finally joined his reality and took to saying, 'He'll be here any day now, Mr. Vic.'

"It must have been Victor who told you that she had married and gone west. But she was in Pennsylvania . . ."

"At Sarah's folks, with Sarah," Ben finished the sentence for her. Lindsey nodded, but she wasn't sure he saw her. He did not need to. He knew there was nowhere else she would have been.

Ben McBride closed his eyes and shook his head. Then he looked out over the orchard, at the trees bursting with tiny green apples. A promise of another harvest.

"The old apple tree finally gave up the ghost?" Ben asked, nodding toward the young, strong tree that stood in its place.

"Aunt Lily and my mom planted that one together when my mom was expecting me. It's a Ben Davis tree, an old variety you don't see much of anymore."

Ben stepped back to look at the double tombstone of Lindsey's parents: *Kevin Dean Briggs and Jenny Lind Briggs.* "Jenny Lind," Ben said, and he smiled slightly as he said, "I bet it was Lily who gave that niece of hers a name like that."

Tell him now, Lindsey. Tell him that it was Lily's daughter not her niece, tell him it was his daughter who planted that tree with Lily. But the words stuck in her throat.

Ben McBride once again fixed his eyes on Lily's pink granite marker. Finally, he looked at Lindsey, and his eyes seemed to well up. "If that old man had not told me she was married, I'd have tracked her down to the ends of the earth."

"But you got married yourself right after that, didn't you?" Lindsey said, her words more like a statement than a question. She detected the hint of accusation in her own voice, because what she had wanted to say was, *if you loved her so much, how could you marry so quickly after?*

"The next Christmas. On the rebound. I was grieving—heartbroken, probably a bit angry with Lily. With myself. Married a good woman and took off for Korea—the war was starting up about then. Came back and tried to make a go of it, too. Wanted to prove Lily was wrong about me, I think. At any rate, it was unfair to my wife, who always thought I didn't love her the way I should because she couldn't have children. But that had nothing to do with it. I *couldn't* love her the way I should—because Lily Frost had my heart, always would."

He smiled ruefully at the tragedy of it all before he continued, "After ten years, my wife and I finally agreed it was hopeless. We divorced. And she married a man who loved her the way she deserved to be loved and who had some kids she could help raise."

Ben looked out over the valley again, and then his eyes lighted upon the pond. His eyes stayed there, and Lindsey thought perhaps he was going to tell her about the time he and Lily rescued the deer, a story Lily had told Sarah and Sarah had told Lindsey on the porch. But he said nothing. Just stared trance-like at the pond.

Lindsey took him gently by the arm to lead him away from the cemetery, but he did not budge.

"And I came back again," he said. Before Lindsey had a chance to register her surprise, he added, "The day the divorce was final." His eyes left the pond and went back to Lily's marker. "In the fall. I told myself if I could talk to her, see her in her role as wife—maybe I could be more at peace. So I drove here one day, drove all the way from Tennessee, stopped to sleep by the side of the road when I couldn't go any longer.

"But when I got here—I remember it was on a Saturday morning—somehow I couldn't drive up that lane to the house." Ben nodded toward the main road. "So I sat down there for what seemed an eternity, and then I left the car by the mailbox and walked up to the house. And again, no one was home, but there were signs of life this time. Flowers tended, you know. The apples were yellow and red. And the leaves were, too.

"I knocked. No answer. Knocked again. No answer. Then I heard voices. I stepped to the side of the house and there . . ." Ben pointed toward the riding ring in the field behind the house. He did not finish the sentence, but his face lit up from the memory, "The girl was about ten I guess, a pretty thing sitting on that horse. She was putting the horse through some kind of pacing they do with those saddles without any horns."

Lindsey smiled slightly. She had done a lot of that kind of riding back before she switched to Western.

"There was a man there too, leaning against the fence. I thought that was Lily's husband."

Probably Albert Tikander, Lindsey thought. He had helped out around the farm when Lindsey was little.

"I thought the girl was Lily's daughter," Ben said. "I know now that it was your mom."

And you are right on both counts. But still she could not bring herself to say it. She knew she could not bear to add to his pain by telling him what he had missed. Her grandmother had been right.

Ben looked away and took a deep breath as if to draw in the courage to relive the story. "And when I saw Lily, even from that distance, I knew that I loved her as much or more than ever. Thing is," Ben said, "maybe I loved her at first sight because of her spit and vinegar and independence—no way she was out to trap anyone. And then I loved her because she set me free. But I also loved her for enough reasons beyond that to want to stay. She was the other part of me. The part that for a brief time in my life made me whole."

Lindsey was mute as Ben took a step closer, bent down, and with trembling hands put something he had taken out of his pocket onto Lily's grave. A birch twig, newly budded leaves clinging to it. He placed it there gently, as if it were a long-stemmed rose.

Lindsey knew the story of the birch twig still in a cobalt vase on the top of the chiffonier, where Lily had always kept it out of reach of any harm. But for now, it was *his* memory.

"You were so right, Lily. And so wrong," Ben said, seeming to have forgotten that Lindsey was there with him. "Mostly, I wish I could have heard you tell me you loved me just once, even though I know you did. And I wish I knew if you knew that I carry your love with me as my greatest treasure." He shook his head slightly. "Lord, I'm starting to talk like the lyrics of a country song."

Lindsey smiled back at him, a sad, understanding smile, all the while trying to think of something to say. But what was there to say?

Just then, a gentle breeze stirred the nearby lilacs. And just as suddenly a brilliant scarlet tanager swooped across the field and landed—purposely it seemed—on the gate. He heard Lily saying, *My father always said he sounded like a robin with a sore throat.*

It was only a matter of seconds before a female tanager lighted beside her colorful mate.

Ben and Lindsey stood there transfixed by the two birds, who seemed content to sit there looking back. And then that famous smile spread across Ben's face. "We can go back now," he said.

They headed back to the house, Ben McBride walking with a lighter air—a bit more square of shoulder, a bit more relaxed, as if some burden had been lifted. Or as if he had once again come in contact with Lilian Frost.

They walked back through the field where they had just mowed the second cutting. At this time of year, Lily had always said, "Don't you just love the smell of fresh-cut orchard grass?" But Lindsey didn't tell him that. Nor did she know when, or if, she would tell him the rest of what Sarah had told her. The real truth of a story, she was learning, is not easy to know, "what's best" not easy to determine. For now, they had to get back to get ready for the benefit square dance that night.

Ben stopped, picked up a piece of hay, and chewed on it as they ambled on toward the house. Then, almost as if he read Lindsey's mind, he took it out of his mouth and said, "Now, Lindsey-gal, what about you and Michael?"

"What about us?" Lindsey said, looking over the field so she didn't have to look Ben in the eye.

"Are you in love with him or not?"

"I've only known him a few months," she said. "It takes time to fall in love."

"Sometimes it does," Ben said, "but sometimes all you have to do is take off your hat and look her in the eye . . ." And for a minute, he was obviously back in another time with Lily. Then he returned to the present. "I think you know already if you love him or not."

Lindsey shrugged. "Even if I thought so now, it's too late. He's getting married—to the beautiful Miss Cyn-thi-a." She knew she sounded childish, drawing out Cynthia's name like that, but she couldn't help it.

Ben didn't seem to notice. "Where'd you hear that?"

"Gabby heard it. They are planning to elope—if that's what you call it nowadays—when they take their vacation in Italy."

"Well, that's the first I've heard of it. But I haven't seen that boy since the first week he got back from Maine, and I can tell you he was sure looking hangdog back then. So I'd say yep, he's in love—with you. And my guess is it's vice versa. I'm betting the whole thing is just too scary for you to handle, which sounds pretty damn familiar to me. See, you may have the mettle of your great-aunt, but you and I are kindred spirits somehow. I guess country music does that to you. You're like I was—you want to stay free of anything that might tap too deep into that heart of yours. But love is its own kind of freedom . . . and they never tell you that."

Ben stopped again, threw the piece of hay away, and put his strong, broad hands on Lindsey's shoulders so he could look her square on. "I'm telling you now, honey," he said. "Don't let it slip away the way I did. The way Lily and I both did."

That was when Lindsey grabbed Ben and gave him a fierce hug. "I've got to run on ahead," she told him. "I've got a call to make."

And then she was running to the house faster than she had ever run in her life. Running, this time, not away from love, but toward it.

The phone rang three times as Lindsey's heart raced, anticipating the sound of Michael's voice. Then the pickup of the answering machine. "Hi, this is Michael, and I'm out of town—a long way out of town—for a while. Leave a message."

No. He can't be gone. Feeling panic, she dialed the private number at his office. It rang and rang. Finally, his voice. On voice mail. "This is Michael James. I'll be out of my office the next several weeks. If it's urgent, please call my secretary at the main number. Otherwise, leave a message and I'll get back to you."

This is Lindsey and my message is I love you. But she couldn't say that on his office phone. Almost without thinking, she dialed her own apartment number and pressed the code to check messages. Maybe, just maybe, Michael had left her a message. Told her where he was going. Told her he was coming up to Maine. Told her anything.

But there were no messages.

Her panicked thoughts were interrupted by Ben opening the screen door. "Well?" he asked, his voice hopeful. And then he saw the look on her face.

"He's not there," Lindsey said.

"Try the office. The boy works ungodly hours."

"No, Ben, his answering machine and his voice mail at the office say he'll be gone for several weeks. He didn't leave a message on my phone. Don't you understand?" she said. "He's in Italy with Cynthia. He's gone." *Don't you understand I've lost him. I was too late . . . just like you.*

Ben reached out with open arms, and she walked into them. "You just go ahead and cry all you need to, little girl. Sometimes writing and singing just won't do the trick. Sometimes you just have to cry. Besides, we got all night to learn our duet if we have to."

Lindsey sobbed until Ben's shirt was wet with her tears. Sobbed until there were no more tears. Then she wiped her face and smiled bravely. "I need to get myself together, and you need to get out of that wet shirt before we go to the square dance."

Twenty-One

The turnout at the benefit concert that weekend was even bigger than Lindsey or the R&R committee had dreamed of. Thousands jammed onto the high school football field. And the weather could not have been more perfect. Sugar Creek kept their time on stage short since they knew that Ben was who the crowd really came to hear, and they saved "Eden's Ridge," sure to be their most pleasing to the local crowd, for the encore they knew the audience would politely request.

The response to "Eden's Ridge," though, was much more than polite, and after coming up for a bow, J. J., Gabby, and Billy Earl left the stage.

"I've got one more song I want to sing," Lindsey said. "But first, I've got to get rid of this guitar."

On her signal, her Uncle Max's six-year-old grandson marched on stage and took the guitar. The first rows laughed at how cute the boy was and how seriously he was taking his responsibility. Lindsey turned to the audience. "Those of you who knew my Aunt Lily will remember that country wasn't exactly her favorite music." A ripple of knowing laughter moved through the audience. "Still," Lindsey said, "she put up with it in her house all those years."

She paused for a second and then continued, "I suspect some of you in this audience remember the many admonishments I got as a little girl for writing lyrics on the back of the church bulletins and such. And I apologize to all the regulars at Butters' store who put up with all the songs I inflicted upon you as a four-, five-, six-, seven-year-old . . . and even now." Again, the audience laughed, and then Lindsey continued. "But this song I'm going to sing is not one that I wrote. Late last night I found the music and lyrics in a box of Aunt Lily's music. With this note."

Lindsey's hands trembled as she opened the note. Her voice broke slightly as she began reading it to the audience. "Lindsey, this is the closest I can come to a country song—maybe you will sing it someday. Fondly, Aunt Lily." Lindsey folded the note, put it back in her pocket, then walked over and sat at the grand piano that now belonged to the high school but had once graced the old opera house. The sheet music was there, waiting.

"This is that someday," Lindsey said. "And this is that song. And I think it's only fitting to dedicate it to Mr. Ben McBride, my . . . my grandfather's good friend, who has made Lilian Frost's dream of restoring the opera house a soon-to-be reality. It's called 'If I Ever Write a Song.'"

Lindsey put her hands on the piano keys and looked off the temporary staging to where Ben McBride stood, guitar strapped on, waiting for his time on the stage. His face had the look of someone hearing something—a saying, a sentence, a phrase—that he recognized but couldn't quite place.

———

He stands there, quietly, as Lindsey plays a long lead-in. As she begins to sing:

If I ever write a song that song will be
A celebration of the love you gave to me. . . .

And suddenly it comes back to him. His own words come back to him. Lily, if you ever wrote a song, what would it be about?

> The tender way you touched my soul,
> Just walked right in and made me whole,
> The silly things you did to show your love for me. . . .

He puts the birch stem in her mouth and they dance a tango. He climbs a tree and pretends to fall . . . and she stalks away, furious.

> A gentle man is hard to find,
> A man who's passionate, yet kind. . . .

He puts his coat around a weakened deer. He puts out an arm to draw her close, and she comes to him. But she would never say I love you, never would say the words . . .

> And I found that man in you.
> You were my every dream come true
> And I'll tell you that—if I ever write a song.

———————

Lindsey could not look at Ben, but she knew he was listening. She knew he was hearing. She continued the song, looking out over the Maine hills. She looked at the audience. Some of the old-timers the committee had put in front row seats—mostly the regulars at Butters' Corner Store—no doubt they thought it was a song for young Jack Tate. *Let them think so. It is fitting that Ben and Sarah and I are the only ones who know that this song is for Ben McBride.*

If I ever write a song, that song will say . . .

At that moment, Lindsey looked away from the audience, and finally she looked directly into Ben McBride's eyes.

> That I love you and I will
> Till time itself has slipped away.
> Yes, I found my dream in you.
> You were my fantasy come true,
> And I'll tell you that—if I ever write a song.

With those words, Lilian Frost had traveled back over the years to tell Ben McBride, finally, what he wanted all his life to hear. Ben smiled. Lindsey was sure no one else noticed that under his brown Stetson hat, his eyes brimmed with tears. And Lindsey knew, more than ever, the healing power of a song. She knew, once again, that the gift of song would help sustain her now and in years ahead.

She finished and walked offstage, where Ben waited to give her a hug. She stood there with his arms around her waiting for the applause to stop so she could go back and introduce him. They kept clapping. "Looks like they want another song from you," he said.

"No, I think that ovation is for Aunt Lily . . . for her song," Lindsey said.

"Don't be such a Mainer," Ben said. He gave her a slight shove. "Now go back out there and sing one more song . . . and this time look around for what you've been missing."

Whatever does he mean? I've made eye contact with everyone I know. I've nodded to friends in between verses, winked as I sang some lines, noticed the backdrop of these Oxford Hills and the powder-blue July sky. What have I been missing?

She certainly hadn't planned an encore. She looked over at Gabby and J. J. and Billy Earl with *help* written on her face.

"Let's do that one we just learned," Gabby said with a knowing look, her fiddle in one hand and Lindsey's guitar in the other. Then she pulled Lindsey on stage, seemingly pulling the others behind her. As Sugar Creek settled back in, Lindsey slipped her guitar strap back over her shoulder.

"Now we're going to sing a song by a favorite singer and songwriter of mine—Heather Myles." She nodded to Billy Earl and J. J. to begin the lead-in, then began to sing.

How was I supposed to know I'd miss you . . .

Lindsey smiled down at her grandmother, who motioned for her to look over to her right, into the sun. She did. And finally Lindsey saw what her grandmother had been craning her neck for all through the concert. Standing next to Lindsey's cousins, Kristina and Whitney, was Katy—home a month early from Japan and holding Lindsey's chubby little namesake.

That's what all the hush-hush has been the last two days. Lindsey could barely continue singing.

When I couldn't kiss you anymore? . . .

Her grandmother motioned to the right again. *I see them, Grandma Sarah.* Lindsey almost said that out loud in between the lines, figuring the audience would get a kick out of that. But somehow that song was not a song to interrupt.

How was I supposed to know I'd need you
When I couldn't reach you on the phone? . . .

She looked offstage at Ben, who also pointed to the sun. *He doesn't know Katy, so why is he pointing in that direction?* She turned and looked at Katy again and smiled, still singing,

I never knew how much I loved you
Until I couldn't have you. . . .

Then she saw him. *Michael? Get a grip,* she told herself. *It's like in those movies where someone sees someone she loves and runs up to him and it's not him at all. You'll be having these hallucinations for years. Get used to it.*

She tried to focus on the song. And then the man stepped out of the glare. It was Michael. He was not in Italy. Not in Tennessee.

She only realized she had stopped singing when she felt Gabby step up to fill in with her fiddle. And then somehow, Lindsey found the words again:

Here's to all the words I should have told you—
Like I wanna hold you
One more time. . . .

And then there it was—that smile on his face.

Here's to all the songs I should have sung you
Instead of run from you.

And she was smiling back at Michael, her eyes filling with tears, as she found her way to the end of the song. The second she finished, Ben—not waiting to be introduced—walked, or rather strode, on stage, looking at Lindsey and clapping. He squeezed her shoulder. "Now *go,*" he said, nodding toward Michael.

Few in the audience noticed Lindsey run off the stage and straight into the arms of a tall young man, who swung her around and around in the sunlight. Their eyes instead were on Ben McBride, looking dapper, all the ladies would say later, as he began his show with the song he had used to open all his shows for fifty years—except for that one New Year's Eve in 1949:

Well it's three in the morning,
And I'm almost where I want to be—
Just outside of Little Rock
And headin' for Tennessee.

The audience erupted in the loudest applause of the afternoon.

For the next few days, all the talk in Hadley's Curve was about the benefit concert, which raised enough money to actually break ground on the renovation. The regulars at Butters' Corner Store had a field day rehashing who had been there and what had gone on—although they didn't use any more words doing it than they absolutely had to. In addition, the next edition of the weekly *Hadley's Curve Gazette* carried a guest editorial and review by publisher and retired editor Jim Ellingwood. Sarah Frost tucked it in the family Bible for safekeeping:

Hadley's Curve enjoyed a rare treat last Saturday afternoon when country singer Ben McBride gave a fund-raising concert as a favor to our own Lindsey Briggs. We were blessed with perfect weather, and the concert raised enough money to make the Lilian Frost Opera House something for the ages.

First, we were treated to a warmup by Lindsey, who is Lily's own greatniece, and her band, Sugar Creek, who sang a medley of country hits and some of her own songs, which we have no doubt will make her the next rising star. Sugar Creek ended their set with Lindsey Briggs's own "Eden's Ridge." Then, to our delight, Lindsey played and sang a song that Lily Frost herself had written.

Ben McBride, who was a friend of Lindsey's grandfather (my classmate Tad Frost), sang his all-time greats and proved his talent and style have simply mellowed, not diminished with age. Then he and Lindsey brought the audience to their feet with their duet "No One Is Gonna Love You Better."

Still, I have to say the highlight of the afternoon was Mr. McBride's third encore. We expected him to sing yet another of his well-known hits. Instead, he came back on stage without his band and without his guitar. He bowed to the audience's sustained applause. Then he walked over and sat down at the grand piano.

He took off his trademark brown Stetson and placed it on the bench beside him. He put his long fingers on the keys and sat there with his eyes closed. And he sat there. And sat there. Finally, it was obvious he was not going to hit one single note until we came to an absolute hush. When we got quiet enough to hear the birds in the nearby maples, Ben McBride began playing—are you listening folks? Are you ready for this? Ben McBride began playing Schumann.

The sounds of that piano floated out over the football field and over the schoolhouse where Lily Frost for more than forty years passed down her knowledge and love of music to our youngsters. And there were those of us there this past Saturday afternoon—the old-timers, as you younger folks call us—who closed our eyes as we listened.

We closed our eyes, and for a fleeting moment we were once again in the bloom of our youth. We had not yet lost our classmates to war—or to time. And all of us young men were half in love with our classmate Lily Frost. We closed our eyes and breathed in the soft, sweet air of a perfect Maine summer day as we listened to Ben McBride playing the "Reverie" from *Scenes from Childhood*.

And there were those of us who were no longer in folding chairs in the middle of our football field, but were once again in the old opera house listening to Lilian Frost, just returned from college, playing—with an angel's touch—that very same song.

Twenty-Two

Dusk on Eden's Ridge. The R&R committee and other neighbors and friends gathered at the Frost place for brown bread and franks and beans after the concert—and were treated to Ben McBride's storytelling and pies baked by Sarah Frost and her bridge club. Just as J. J., Gabby, Billy Earl, and Ben's band and roadies were heading back to Papoose Pond for the night, Lindsey and Michael walked out to the driveway to see her Uncle Max and the cousins and their families off. They waved until cars and vans were out of sight, then Michael put out his hand and said, "Now can we have that talk?"

They walked through the orchard in silence, the sweet twittering calls of the barn swallows breaking the quiet. "This is my favorite time of day," Lindsey said in a near whisper, and then she told him the story of *edentide*. Hand in hand, they made their way across the field and stopped under an old maple tree. Michael reached out and brushed a strand of hair from her face.

"This time, Lady Lindsey, you must let me have my say. And I'll begin first by saying I never gave Cynthia that ring. Well I did *give* it to her."

"What? Then—"

"No, don't interrupt," he said, putting his fingers softly to her lips.

"It's true that the night I saw you and Gabby outside 12th & Porter was the night I was supposed to be giving Cynthia a ring. Everyone had assumed for so long that we would get married that I'd come to assume it myself. Anyway, we'd found the perfect ring, found the perfect fit, and headed out for dinner. I was just thinking that I should be much happier than I was when I saw you and Gabby across the street, wearing those crazy T-shirts, carrying on with that hog call . . ."

"That was Gabby, not me," Lindsey protested.

Michael put his fingers to Lindsey's lips again to shush her. "And I was suddenly happy, but not because I was with Cynthia. It was because I had seen you. At dinner all I could think of was you—in your T-shirt and jeans, pulling Gabby toward the Pub of Love. Or riding that dad-blamed horse, or writing down lyrics on napkins like you do every time we're at Brown's. Or coming up with words that do not exist, hoping to beat me in Scrabble."

"I do *not* come up with words that don't exist—"

"Anyway, I got out the ring, opened the box, and then suddenly I knew," Michael said, ignoring her interjection, "just as if I'd been hit on the head with a hammer or in the face with a pie—it really did hit me *that* suddenly—that I was in love with you.

"So I closed the box and told Cynthia that I could not marry her—that I was in love with someone else. I handed the box to her, told her the ring was hers to do with as she wanted. And she left, but not before making a scene right out of a movie. But mad as she was, she didn't neglect to take the ring." Michael smiled a bit at that.

"Actually," he added, "I'm surprised Gabby didn't hear about the scene. I think the rest of Nashville did. And to tell you the truth, I don't blame Cynthia. But to continue the story, I waited for folks to go back to eating, then I paid the bill, went and found me a guitar, got into my getup, and set about to begin our courtship by coming over in the rain. But then you up and ran off on me."

"Michael, why didn't you tell me all this?"

"Because you wouldn't give me a chance."

"You could have *made* me listen."

"Yes, I guess I could have. But to tell the truth, I was afraid my being in love with you might scare you away even more—if you hadn't yet realized you loved me, which I was pretty sure you had not. I was pretty sure you did—love me, that is. You are pretty high-minded about your independence, you know. I mean, all that business about not taking my calls and all. So when I got to Maine and didn't get the reception I'd dreamed of, to say the least, I decided I'd just go back to Tennessee and wait you out—even if you were an old lady before you came to your senses. And I knew your life now was in Nashville, Tennessee, even though your roots are here," he said, looking back at the house with reverence. "I knew you'd be back there before long."

"But Cynthia told Gabby's friends—well, anyway, she said you were getting married in Italy."

"Cynthia may be getting married in Italy, but not to me. She's always wanted us to elope to Italy—a dream of hers way before she met me. Used to tell her coworkers that if she didn't show up to work the next week, she was in Italy on her honeymoon."

"But your phone message said you were out of the country for a while, so I thought . . ."

"No, it said I was out of town—a long way out, or something clever like that. You know me—clever. Truth is, I found out I wasn't as patient as I thought. In fact, I gave restless a whole new definition. So I took off to just drive around the country thinking about you. And after getting to the center of Texas—did you know Willie Nelson is from this little town down there called Abbott?—anyway, I suddenly found my car turning in this direction. And when I called last night—"

"You called? When?"

"Your grandmother answered and put Ben on. They said you were on

271

your way back from the square dance with Gabby and the gang. And Ben told me to get off my behind and get myself up here if I had to hire my own plane. Fortunately, I didn't have to, since I was already in the Berkshires.

"So now," Michael said, pulling Lindsey behind the old maple tree, "what were you going to say to me when you called?" He brought his face to within inches of hers, those laughing eyes just waiting for her reply.

"I . . . was going to tell you not to marry Cynthia . . . until I had a chance to tell you how I feel."

"And how *do* you feel?" he asked, running a finger up and down her neck.

"I feel like I'm going to faint."

"Then let's sit down." Michael sat down and tugged her hand to sit beside him.

"Now you won't fall," he said. "So tell me, Lindsey Briggs, how do you feel?" His smile faded, and he was asking her to be truthful.

And finally Lindsey was not afraid of her feelings. "I love you, Michael James."

He brought her face to his and her lips to his. She wanted to melt into him. Into that moment. Into that place.

They walked back toward the porch in the fading light. Ben McBride was in the swing entertaining Grandma Sarah with tall Tennessee tales. From the distance, Lindsey could almost wipe away the years and see a young Sarah, filled with the happiness of someone who has, at least for a time, all that she ever wanted. That was no small thing—her grandmother had always known that. And Lindsey could see Ben as he must have looked the first time he stepped upon that porch and into Lily's life. For a brief time. And forever.

Lindsey had once told Gabby that she had been raised on the Boston Red Sox, Saturday night Scrabble, Emily Dickinson, and Chopin. And that she had learned at an early age how one play can decide a baseball game, one letter can win a game of Scrabble, one word can transform a poem, and a single chord can transform a piece of music. Now she had learned how one story can forever change a life. Or many lives.

She knew she still had to work through this story that her grand-mother—who was not her grandmother but would forever be her grand-mother—had given her. And it was, she knew, time to tell Ben.

He, too, would have many things to work through once he learned that he had lost a daughter he never knew he had. And that his daughter and the mother Lindsey did not remember—except for the whisperings of her voice that sometimes seemed spun like gossamer in the corners of her memory—were one and the same. But Lindsey *knew* Jenny Lind Frost from a thousand stories, and she would help Ben to know her, too. They would walk through this together.

"You seem lost in thought, Lindsey," Michael said, his arm still around her as they neared the porch steps.

"I am deep in thought," she answered him, "but I am not *lost*."

Sarah Frost was having her evening sherry while Ben had a beer. Over the past few days they had become friends, even though in a sense they always had been.

"Would you mind keeping Grandma Sarah company for a while?" Lindsey asked Michael.

He looked puzzled.

"I have a long story to tell you. But first, I have something I must tell Ben."

Michael was even more puzzled, but he also sensed he should not ask any questions as he and Lindsey walked up the porch steps. Lindsey kissed Sarah Frost on the top of her head and said, "I'm going to steal Ben for a minute. We need to take a walk."

Sarah Frost looked at Lindsey and knew what she had decided. Sarah hesitated for a moment and then gave Lindsey an almost imperceptible nod of approval. "Besides," Lindsey said to her, "you and Michael probably have some more getting acquainted to do. Even if you did spend all that time on the phone."

And then, Ben McBride and Lindsey Briggs began their walk down the lane he had first driven on all those years ago. They walked into the past, but they walked toward the future.

In the last light of day, the moon hung thin and pale above the apple trees. Darkness would have fallen by the time Ben and Lindsey finished the walk. But in the darkness, the moon would turn golden, shining there above them, above this place on Eden's Ridge, like a lantern—lighting their way.

No One Is Gonna Love You Better*

Words and music by Heather Myles

LINDSEY: *I don't like to think about tomorrow*
When you're right here beside me today.
We never speak of future plans—
I know you're a rambling man,
But no one is gonna love you better.

TOGETHER: *We might not share those golden years together.*
LINDSEY: *Is there really something called forever?*
If we don't brave through the storm,
I know someone will keep you warm,
But no one is gonna love you better.

BEN: *We can't change what's meant to be,*
Where the wind will blow the seeds,
But your love is growing like a weed.
I don't care what people say,
If we go our separate ways,
No one is gonna love you better.

TOGETHER: *We might not share those golden years together.*
BEN: *Yes, there really is something called forever.*
TOGETHER: *If we don't brave through the storm,*
BEN: *I know someone will keep you warm,*
But no one is gonna love you better.
LINDSEY: *Oh, but no one,*
BEN: *No one,*
TOGETHER: *Is gonna love you better.*

* Duet sung by Lindsey Briggs and Ben McBride at the July 8, 2000, concert at Hadley's Curve, Maine.

Acknowledgments

Friendship and a love of language, storytelling, music, and laughter brought this book to life, but it would not have taken form without encouragement and support from

- Our husbands, Bob and Steve, and our daughters, Kristina, Whitney, and Sarah.
- Our agent, Jane Chelius.
- Producer Lindsay Doran and screenwriter Garry Williams.
- All the folks at Rutledge Hill Press and our editor, Anne Christian Buchanan, who made revision fun.
- Our readers, Cindy Anderson, Patsy Crihfield, Shannon Cunningham, Marge Eliscu, Rita Goldberg, Sarah Griner, Liza Hoyt, Marilyn Huber, Debbie McGrory, Sue McKinney, Emily Miller, Dr. Peter Rosenblatt, and Betsy Tosczko.
- The people who gave helpful advice about Nashville music, especially Ralph Murphy, Bart Herbison, Jennifer Carrington, Bob DiPiero, and Peter Guralnick.

- Three nice guys who answered our never-ending questions— Robert Jack, computer whiz; David Morin, physicist; and Alex Tait, cartographer.

- A string of friends who helped along the way: Larry and the Bardistas (writers all), Dennis Anderson, Victor Belanger, Jim Blair, Dorothy Jean Bridges, Brenda Fincher, Judy Hendrix, Carolyn Simpson, and Stephen Woolverton.

- Those songwriters who were so generous with their lyrics and melodies, especially those who consented to put their lyrics in Lindsey's heart and voice. They are Mark Dix, David Kelly, Taylor Kitchings, Ike LaRue, Brady Peterson, Bruce Peterson, and, last but not least, Heather Myles. We wish them all fame and fortune and the audience they richly deserve.

- Bill Nowlin and the people at Rounder Records, who were behind us from the start, and to whom we give a special thanks.

—Myra McLarey and Linda Weeks